Print ISBN: **978-1-971405-01-8**
www.zorastone.com

For the ones who hide sharp things in soft hearts.
You always belonged in the dark with me.

Content Warnings

This book contains mature themes, emotional intensity, and explicit content. Please read with care.

Violence & Combat

- Fantasy battle sequences involving weapons and magic

- Death of secondary characters

- Descriptions of blood and injury

- Magical corruption affecting characters physically

Mental Health & Trauma

- Panic attacks and anxiety episodes

- Emotional breakdowns and psychological distress

- Themes of self-doubt, identity crisis, and survivor's guilt

- Characters struggling with a loss of control

Sexual Content

- Explicit sexual scenes between consenting adults

- Multiple romantic/sexual relationships (reverse harem)

- Detailed intimate encounters

- Persistent sexual tension and arousal

Magical Coercion & Consent Issues

- Forced magical bonds without full consent

- Soul-level connections imposed without choice

- Magical manipulation and violations of agency

- Characters grappling with feelings of magical violation

Emotional Manipulation & Betrayal

- Trusted characters revealed as traitors

- Gaslighting and psychological manipulation

- Undermining of personal agency

- Betrayal by mentors and authority figures

Imprisonment & Captivity (limited)

- Brief instances of magical confinement

- Descriptions of restraint and powerlessness

- Interrogation-like questioning

Family Trauma

- Absent or deceased parents

- Painful family revelations and generational trauma

- Themes of legacy, secrecy, and inherited burden

Loss & Grief

- On-page mourning and emotional processing

- Characters coping with loss (emotional and physical)

Power Dynamics

- Conflicts with authority figures and institutional control

- Student/teacher imbalance (no on-page romance until after)

- Magical hierarchies and consent-adjacent gray areas

Note: While *Shadows Rising* explores mature and intense themes, all romantic relationships occur between consenting adults. The story centers agency, identity, and reclaiming power in the face of manipulation.

Note 2: The next page contains spoilers from Book One—a quick recap to get you caught up.

A Quick Recap from Your Friendly Neighborhood Author

Because let's be honest—it's been a while. Even *I* had to reread my own notes to remember who Carl was...

So! When we last left our delightfully chaotic found family, things were... well, let's call it "complicated."

Kaia went from slinging questionable diner eggs to discovering she's actually a time-traveling Valkyrie princess (because of course she is). Her "pet cat" Mouse? Yeah, he talks now. Sometimes. Her shadows—Bob, Patricia, Finnick, and the gang? Turns out they're the souls of ancient warrior women who died protecting little Kaia centuries ago. No big deal.

And speaking of complications... remember when Kaia thought her biggest issue was wrangling her sassy shadows? Simpler times. Now she's got glowing wings, a necklace called the Heart of Eternity that might be the key to everything, and four gorgeous, infuriating men who've basically decided she's worth dying for.

There's Finn—chaos incarnate with a punchable grin.

Malrik—the brooding shadow prince with a past full of secrets.

And Aspen and Torric—the elemental twins who could probably bench press a dragon and still have time to emotionally scar you before lunch.

Professor Thorne? Totally evil.

Plot twist: he's actually Mikhael Aldrich, right-hand creep to Alekir the Soulbinder—the ancient psycho who murdered Kaia's parents (and, ya know, all the other Valkyries) way back when. Thorne's been playing the long game, waiting to use Kaia to shatter the seals between realms and unleash whatever fresh hell lies beyond.

As for Darian—the morally gray transfer student with suspicious timing? He got caught in the middle. Manipulated by Thorne. Maybe not fully evil. Jury's still out.

The good news? Kaia unlocked her full Valkyrie power, sprouted those majestic wings, and vaporized some Nightwraiths.

The bad news? Lady Virath (yep, *Alenya's* mother) is also Team Evil, the academy board is useless, and Alekir is starting to bleed through the cracks between worlds.

So basically, we're exactly where every good fantasy series ends Book One:

– Powerful heroine.

– Devoted found family.

– Ancient evil ready to unmake reality.

No pressure, Kaia.

Ready for Book Two?

Because things are about to get even more complicated...

CONTENTS

PROLOGUE

Alekir, The Soulbinder

Shadows ripple against my skin, alive with whispers no one else can hear. They curl and twist at the edges of my vision, not obeying but... waiting. Listening. I press my palm against the cold stone wall, feeling the vibration beneath—faint now, barely there, but unmistakable.

The God stirs.

Not a full awakening. Just the barest flutter of consciousness long buried, but it's enough to make the air in Absentia feel thick, wrong. The corrupted magic scrapes against my senses like rust on silk.

"She's begun," I murmur, more to myself than the darkness.

My voice doesn't echo. Nothing does here. The darkness drinks sound like it drinks hope; greedily, leaving nothing behind.

The Heart's pulse reaches even this far, each beat an unwanted caress across my senses. Distant yet insistent. With each flare of its power, I feel the mate bonds shifting, straining against the barriers I crafted centuries ago. The spellwork isn't breaking, but it's... remembering. And memory is a dangerous thing.

I don't turn at the sound of approaching footsteps. Don't need to. Thorne's energy announces him long before his shadow detaches from the greater darkness.

He kneels, head bowed. "Master."

His deference doesn't mask the hunger beneath. The boy's gotten ambitious lately. It would be concerning if it weren't so predictable.

"Rise, Thorne." I gesture him forward with fingers that gleam too pale against the shadows. "Tell me."

He straightens, trying not to look eager. Failing. "The girl grows stronger. The Heart of Eternity awakens in her, but she hasn't mastered it." A pause. His brow furrows. "And her chaos mage... there's something about him. The way magic responds, it's not—"

"Of course there is." I cut him off, suddenly irritable.

The God's presence flares briefly, drawn to the mention of the boy like a snake to warmth. My skin prickles with it, the ancient awareness brushing against mine. Interesting. The connection runs deeper than I'd thought.

"And the academy?"

Thorne's lips curl. "Frightened. Divided." Pride slips into his voice, he thinks this is his accomplishment. "They can't decide whether to shape her into a weapon or cast her out as a threat. I've ensured they consider both options."

Good. Fear is a blade that cuts deeper than steel, particularly in the hands of the powerful. The academy masters will either crush her or sharpen her. Either outcome serves.

The air shifts, thickens, and Lady Virath materializes from the gloom. Unlike Thorne's cautious approach, she moves like she owns the shadows, like the darkness is merely an inconvenience to be brushed aside. Light magic glows at her fingertips, a deliberate rebellion. She knows I allow it only because it serves me.

"You summoned me, Alekir." Her voice is honey over gravel. Her gaze flicks dismissively to Thorne. "And yet, I find your pet already here. How quaint."

Thorne bristles like an offended cat. I silence him with a glance.

"Play nicely, Virath."

She arches a brow, unconcerned. The light at her fingertips pulses. "The God of Chaos stirs?"

It's not really a question. She knows. She feels it too, the weight in the air, the pressure behind reality. The way Absentia itself seems to hold its breath.

I incline my head. "Kaia has accelerated the timeline. Every time she touches the Heart's power, the God feels her." I let the truth slip between us, dangerous and seductive. "She is not just a vessel. She is a beacon."

Virath's fingers twitch, her light magic flaring before she reins it in. Something like fear slides across her face, quickly masked. "Then we should act now. Send her into Absentia. Let the corruption take her."

"And if she succeeds?" Thorne counters, stepping closer, forgetting his place in his eagerness to challenge Virath. "If she masters the shadows, the Heart will only make her stronger."

Virath smirks, all elegant contempt. "A weapon for the academy. Or for you, Alekir."

"Precisely."

They think in such small terms; power and control, strength and war. They plot and scheme while standing in the shadow of a god, and they don't see. They don't hear what Absentia whispers in the dead of night, when even my dreams aren't my own.

The God's presence intensifies whenever the chaos mage draws near her, as if recognizing something long lost, something stolen.

The God does not want her dead.

The God wants her whole.

The Absentia challenge will push her to her limits, force her to break or rise. But it's not just a test of her will. The shadows will not merely watch her.

They will mark her.

They will claim her.

And when the time comes... so will he.

I close my eyes against the certainty of it, against the vision of what comes next. The shadows press closer, almost eager, sensing my weakness. I push them back with a thought.

Not yet. But Soon.

Chapter 1
KAIA

I wake to a tangle of limbs and shadows, my bed a battlefield of masculine bodies and writhing darkness. For a moment, I'm convinced I'm still dreaming, or trapped in some bizarre shadow realm where personal space doesn't exist and everyone is unnervingly attractive.

But no. This is real. This is my life now.

I, Kaia Draven, formerly unremarkable shadow student, am now the talk of Arcanum Academy. And apparently a living, breathing teddy bear for four impossibly hot guys who decided my bed was communal property.

I blink, vision adjusting to the dim light filtering through heavy curtains. Aspen's icy blue gaze meets mine, a gentle smile curving his lips. He's perched on the edge of the bed, rigid-backed and alert, like he's been keeping watch all night.

"Morning, little star," he murmurs, reaching out to brush a strand of tousled blonde hair from my face.

His fingers ghost against my cheek, and my skin prickles with awareness. I try to sit up, but there's a heavy arm draped across my waist. Torric, golden eyes still clouded with sleep, tightens his grip. "Five more minutes," he grumbles into my shoulder, his breath hot against my skin.

On my other side, Malrik stirs, silver-gray eyes flickering open. Even first thing in the morning, he looks like he just stepped out of a dark fairy tale—all pale elegance and seductive danger. "Good morning, nightshade," he purrs, his voice like silk against skin that shouldn't be this sensitive.

And at the foot of the bed, sprawled out like an oversized cat, Finn lifts his head. His auburn hair is a disaster, but his green eyes sparkle with mischief. "Well, well, sleeping beauty awakens. And here I thought we'd need true love's kiss to rouse you."

I snort, even as my heart flips in my chest. "You guys do realize this isn't actually a slumber party, right? What happened to your own beds?"

They exchange glances, a silent conversation passing between them that makes my chest tighten. It's Aspen who finally speaks, his voice soft but edged. "We couldn't leave you alone. Not after everything that happened."

Right. Everything that happened.

The battle. The revelations. The terrifying surge of power that had coursed through me, electric and ancient and so much bigger than I could handle. The wings. Always the wings.

I feel it, sharp and low, like dread, as the memories flood back: the arena floor cracking beneath my feet, shadows exploding outward, my body rising into the air, lifted by something ancient and wild pulsing just beneath my skin. The wings. The silence that followed. The fear in their eyes.

I force a grin, because if I don't joke about this, I might start screaming. Or crying. Or both, which would really ruin the whole badass Valkyrie image I'm apparently supposed to maintain. "Well, I guess I really messed up this time? Nothing says 'new girl' quite like unleashing ancient Valkyrie powers and nearly bringing down the academy."

My attempt at humor falls flat. Concern flashes across their faces—even Finn's—and I feel the weight of their gazes like physical pressure against my skin. Finn's usual grin fades, replaced by something serious that doesn't belong on his face.

"Kaia... it's okay if you're not okay, you know?"

For a moment, I freeze. Just a breath. Then—"Who says I'm not okay?" I snap, sharper than I mean to.

I need to look anywhere but at them, at the concern in their eyes that makes me want to crawl out of my skin or maybe just crawl into their arms. So I glance toward the far corner of the room and spot Mouse perched on the edge of a chair, his small form somehow managing to exude both curiosity and authority. He's watching the other shadows like a king overseeing his court, his delicate tail twitching in time with their movements.

"Mouse has been busy," I murmur, sitting up despite Torric's grumbled protest.

Finn stretches, then hops off the bed and strolls over to Malrik, throwing an arm over his shoulder with a cheeky grin. "Busy? He's single-handedly organizing a revolution. Look at those little guys. Bob's practically giving a TED Talk over there."

It's not just a joke. Every single shadow is visible now, from the smallest wisp curling near the baseboard to the broad, imposing form of Bob. I watch as Steve and Linda coax a newly arrived shadow into the fold. Their movements are fluid but deliberate, too purposeful to be random. It's mesmerizing, and also... unsettling.

"I think they're staring at me," I whisper, something cold slipping down my spine.

"They are," Aspen says, his tone matter-of-fact. "They always are."

I don't have a chance to respond before Mouse chirps, snapping his tail like a general issuing orders. Finn wiggles his eyebrows. "See? TED Talk. Bob's got slides and everything."

Malrik sighs, running a hand down his face. "This isn't funny, Finn."

"That's comforting," I deadpan, though I can't help the small smile tugging at my lips. Seems like my mouth has a mind of its own around Finn.

"Hey, don't knock it. The new shadows are thriving already," Finn says with a wink, nodding toward the newest shadow, which is now circling Mouse like a nervous intern on the first day.

A soft knock on the door interrupts whatever witty reply I might have managed. Aspen rises smoothly, his hand already on the hilt of the dagger at his hip. I tense, my shadows flickering in response, darkness rippling across the floor like disturbed water. But when the door creaks open, it's Seren who steps inside.

Her lavender hair is even more chaotic than usual, sticking up in all directions like she's been struck by lightning. Her mismatched outfit, a neon green crop top paired with plaid pajama pants and fuzzy unicorn slippers, is a visual assault that somehow works for her.

Her eyes widen comically as she takes in the scene before her. "Well, well, well," she drawls, a wicked grin spreading across her face. "If it isn't Kaia and her merry band of hunks. Should I come back later? Maybe after you've finished your... morning calisthenics?"

My face burns hot enough to melt steel, and my shadows ripple in response, darkening the corners of the room. "It's not what it looks like," I stammer, trying to extricate myself from the tangle of limbs and failing miserably.

"Oh honey," Seren cackles, "it looks like you've won the magical boy lottery. And here I thought I was lucky to find a matching pair of socks this morning."

Seren's grin turns absolutely wicked as she takes in the full scene—four gorgeous men tangled around one very flustered girl. "Survival Tip #7 in action, I see." She pauses for dramatic effect. "If you can't pick one, pick them all. Just hydrate first." Her eyes sparkle with mischief. "Though I don't see any water bottles, so maybe pace yourselves?"

Finn, never one to miss an opportunity for mischief, winks at Seren. "Care to join us? There's always room for one more."

Seren pretends to fan herself. "Tempting, but I'll pass. I prefer my men like I prefer my coffee—one at a time and not in my bed."

As I finally manage to sit up properly, Seren's gaze shifts, her eyes widening further. "Holy shadow puppets, Batman!" she exclaims, her jaw dropping as she takes in the writhing mass of darkness filling every corner of the room. "Kaia, darling, when did you start running a shadow daycare?"

I follow her gaze, suddenly hyper-aware of just how many shadows are crowded into the space. They're everywhere, curling around bedposts, sliding along walls, even hanging from the ceiling like inky stalactites. Bob, ever the overachiever, seems to be demonstrating some sort of complex maneuver to a group of smaller shadows. It looks suspiciously like a dance routine.

"I, uh... I'm not entirely sure," I admit, watching as Mouse scampers across the floor, herding a group of wispy shadows like a sheepdog. "They just sort of... showed up?"

The shadows ripple as if in acknowledgment, their movements almost synchronized. I don't miss the way Seren's hand tightens on the doorframe, her mask of calm slipping. Her smile doesn't quite reach her eyes anymore. And her fingers? Still white-knuckled on the wood.

I shift uncomfortably under her stare, unsure how to respond. Even the shadows seem to freeze, their writhing forms suddenly quiet and sharp-edged, like they're listening. Seren's always been the calm, sarcastic voice of reason, but something about her now makes my stomach knot.

"They're loyal," Aspen says quietly, his voice cutting through the silence. "To her. That's what matters."

"Loyal or not, this is more than we've ever dealt with," Seren replies. Her tone isn't harsh, but the weight of her words lingers between us, heavy with things unsaid. "And if I'm overwhelmed by this, imagine what the rest of the Academy is going to think."

She steps in, closing the door behind her and leans against it, her dark gaze flicking to each of us in turn. "We have a problem," she says finally. "Thorne isn't just gone. He's recruiting."

The room falls silent. Even the shadows seem to still, their movements less chaotic and more focused, as if they understand the weight of her words.

My spine stiffens, heart pounding against my ribs like it's trying to escape. "Recruiting for what?"

"For Alekir," Seren says, her voice low and steady. "He's building an army."

Torric growls low in his throat, the sound more animal than human. "Let him try. I'll rip his head off before he touches her."

"Easy, big guy," Seren says, raising a hand. "This isn't just about Kaia anymore. Alekir's moving fast, and Lira wants answers. She's asked for all of you to meet her first thing."

Malrik frowns, his silver-gray eyes narrowing. "First thing?"

"As in now," Seren replies, already turning toward the door. "So get dressed, get yourselves together, and meet me downstairs. And maybe try to look like you didn't just roll out of bed with the Academy's most-wanted."

"What are we supposed to do against an army?" I ask, the words tasting bitter on my tongue.

Finn snickers.

I turn to snap at him but freeze at the sight before me. Every single shadow in the room—from Bob's imposing form to the tiniest wisp—has arranged itself in perfect military formation. Even Finnick, who was doing aerial somersaults moments ago, stands at rigid attention.

Mouse, perched on his chair like a tiny general, looks entirely too pleased with himself.

"Oh," I say faintly. "Right."

I should feel relieved. Powerful. Instead, a cold weight settles behind my ribs.

Because I don't know how to command an army. I don't know how to be what they need. I don't know if I want to be.

But the shadows wait, patient and expectant, and four pairs of eyes watch me like I hold answers instead of questions.

And Mouse just stares at me with those violet eyes that see too much, like he's waiting for me to catch up to what he already knows.

Chapter 2
KIERAN

The ripple hits before I see it—a pulse of chaos splitting the stillness like thunder through a starless night. My shadows recoil, curling closer, their instinctive reaction making my scales itch beneath my human skin. The Heart of Eternity stirs, its power reaching even here, in the depths of my sanctuary.

"Stay back," I warn as a young griffin shifter stumbles through my wards, corruption eating at his wings. The others who've found refuge here press against the crystalline walls, their magic flaring in response to the newcomer's tainted power.

I move forward, shadows coiling around my hands. The griffin's eyes are wild with pain and fear, the same look I've seen too many times since Absentia fell. As I reach for him, another call from the Heart hits, stronger this time, and the memory crashes over me like a wave.

I was young, barely able to hold my dragon form for more than a few hours, when my father brought me to the Valkyrie sanctuary. We flew together, two shadows against the twilight sky, my smaller wings struggling to match his powerful beats. Dragon shifters offering protection to the Valkyries in exchange for their aid against the growing corruption.

The griffin's wing bleeds corruption under my touch—acrid, like burning metal and blood. I catch him before he falls, channeling my power through our contact. The magic buzzes with rot and heat beneath my hands while my mind races back through centuries.

She couldn't have been more than six, a tiny figure darting between the Valkyries' legs, wisps of shadow and light playing around her feet like mischievous pets. When she saw me, her eyes lit up with curiosity that mirrored my own. While the adults traded alliances, we slipped away—two children chasing wonder into the meadow.

"Hold still," I mutter, dragging myself out of memory as I focus on the griffin. The scent of meadow grass lingers in the back of my mind.

"Can you really turn into a dragon?" she'd asked, bouncing on her toes. Her excitement had been contagious, my own magic stirring in response. My little star, that's what I called her. The words just slipping out.

The corruption fights back, black veins spreading across the griffin's feathers. I push harder, letting my power flow through him. Behind me, I sense Revna moving closer, her phoenix fire ready if I need it.

I shifted for her that day, scales rippling across my skin until I stood before her in my dragon form, smaller than my father's, my obsidian scales still carrying hints of purple in the light. Where others might have feared me, Kaia laughed in delight. Her tiny hands reached out to touch my snout, fearless and gentle.

The moment her fingers brushed my scales, something sparked between us. The connection left a mark I still feel in my bones. The shadow magic inside her surged forward, wrapping around my wings like it found a piece of itself it didn't know was missing.

The griffin screams as my power burns through the corruption. I hold him steady, remembering another touch, another connection.

We spent hours in that meadow—me showing off aerial acrobatics while she clapped and created shadow shapes to chase me through the air. Her shadow magic never once shied away from my form, instead seeming to dance with my own magic in perfect harmony.

"Commander." Revna's voice slices through the memory fog like fire through smoke. The corruption finally breaks. The griffin collapses against me, his wings whole but scarred. Another survivor. Another soul saved too late.

When the diplomatic talks ended and my father called for me, Kaia hugged my scaled neck fiercely. "Promise you'll come back," she demanded, with all the authority a child could muster. I nudged her gently with my snout, a promise I wouldn't get to keep.

"Get him to the healing chambers," I tell Revna, my voice tight with memory. She nods, understanding more than I say. She's seen me like this before, when the past settles in my chest like a stone.

Within months, everything changed. Alekir's forces descended on the sanctuary. My father and I led the other dragons to their aid. But we were too late. I searched for her in the chaos, my wings beating against smoke-filled skies, but found nothing. When the Valkyries fell, I mourned her along with all the rest, carrying the memory of that spark between us like an open wound.

The Heart calls again, stronger now. Each beat carries her essence, that same bright magic that once danced with mine. For centuries, I believed her lost, until seventeen years ago when I felt it. That same spark, that same magical resonance, suddenly blazing to life across the realms.

I don't move. I can't. "She's coming," Revna says softly, her phoenix eyes seeing more than just the present. "The Heart calls her here."

I move to the edge of the sanctuary, where crystal walls hold back the corruption. Out there, chaos reigns. But in here, I've built something even Alekir couldn't destroy. A foundation for her return. My shadows coil tighter, eager for what's to come.

"She will be mine," I whisper, the words carrying centuries of promise. The sanctuary hums in response, the wards thrumming with my determination. Somewhere out there, Kaia fights her own battles, unaware of what awaits her in Absentia. Unaware of me.

But she'll remember. I'll make sure of it.

The Heart pulses once more, and I know it's time. I've waited centuries for this moment—and gods, it hasn't dulled. Not one damn second. No more watching from afar. No more protective distance. She's coming to Absentia, and this time, I won't fail her.

This time, I'll keep my promise.

Chapter 3
FINN

"An army, huh?" I say, trying to keep my tone light as we hurry down the corridor toward Lira's office. "Does that mean Thorne gets a cool evil general outfit? Please tell me there are shoulder spikes involved."

No one laughs. Not even a smile. Tough crowd this morning.

After Seren's bombshell about Thorne building an army for Alekir, we'd scrambled to get ready. Kaia had yanked on fresh clothes behind a screen of shadows (Bob apparently taking his privacy-protection duties very seriously), while the rest of us tried to look less like we'd spent the night crammed into her room like overprotective bodyguards.

Now we're rushing through the Academy halls, every shadow in military formation behind us. Mouse rides on Kaia's shoulder like a tiny general, his tail occasionally flicking commands that the other shadows instantly obey. It would be impressive if it wasn't so terrifying to watch Carl suddenly snap to attention like he's been possessed.

"Are we really not going to talk about the fact that Mouse has apparently organized an entire shadow militia in the span of, what, twelve hours?" I ask, jogging to keep up with Torric's long strides. "Because I feel like that deserves some discussion."

"Not now, Finn," Aspen says tersely, his eyes scanning the hall ahead of us. His hand hasn't left the hilt of his dagger since we left Kaia's room.

"Fine, but I'm just saying—Bob is wearing what looks suspiciously like shadow epaulets. That's commitment to the aesthetic."

Malrik shoots me a look that could freeze fire. "The academy is in danger. Thorne is recruiting. Alekir is planning something, and you're focused on shadow fashion?"

"I'm focused on not losing my mind with worry," I snap back, the humor dropping from my voice before I can catch it. "Some of us cope with impending doom through commentary."

The tension in the room shifts, heavier now, like someone's cranked up the gravity. Malrik's expression softens slightly, his silver-gray eyes glinting with something like understanding. Kaia brushes her fingers against Mouse as if drawing strength from him, her face too pale in the early light.

The walk through the Academy is... exactly what I expected and still somehow worse. The whispers start the moment we step into the hallway, growing louder with every step. Students press against the walls, their eyes wide. I catch snippets of conversation, each one more dramatic than the last.

"That's her."

"The Valkyrie."

"Look! She has an army of shadows."

"Did you see what happened to the arena?"

I grin, throwing an arm around Malrik's shoulder as we pass a particularly slack-jawed group of first-years. Their expressions are priceless, a mix of terror and awe that makes me want to start taking notes. Or maybe selling tickets. *Step right up, folks! See the amazing shadow girl and her entourage of hot, broody men!*

But then I catch the way some of them track her shadows' movements, like they're waiting for the darkness to turn on them. They don't understand that Kaia's shadows are more likely to offer you a PowerPoint presentation than actually hurt you. Unless you deserve it, of course.

"Fame suits you, Kaia," I say, watching as a cluster of Light Faction students literally stumble over themselves to get out of our way. Their pristine white uniforms are a stark contrast to the shadows that curl protectively around Kaia's feet.

"Finn," Kaia hisses, shoving me off. "Stop it."

"What? Just trying to lighten the mood. You've got to admit, they're impressed." I gesture to where Bob, ever the showman, is doing what I can only describe as a victory lap around our group. The newer shadows trail after him like eager pupils, and I swear I catch Patricia taking notes.

"They're scared," Malrik says flatly. His silver-gray eyes sweep over the corridor, catching the uneasy glances and hurried steps. A group of Elemental students whisper furiously behind their hands, their eyes locked on Kaia. "And they should be. Alekir's already got his claws in this place."

He's right, of course. Beneath the obvious fear and fascination, there's something darker in the way some students watch us. The way their hands hover near concealed weapons, the way their magical auras pulse with barely contained hostility. Thorne's influence runs deeper than we thought.

Mouse seems to sense it too from his spot on Kaia's shoulder. His tail twitches irritably, and the shadows around us respond, their movements becoming sharper, more purposeful. Even Bob drops the theatrics, falling into what I've started calling his "guard dog" formation.

"Well," I say, because someone has to break this tension before we all snap, "at least no one's throwing things this time. Remember when that Sorcery kid tried to hex you and ended up turning his own hair blue?"

Aspen's lips twitch, the barest hint of a smile. "That was your chaos magic and you know it."

"Prove it," I reply with a wink, and for just a moment, the heavy atmosphere lifts.

But as we round the corner toward Lira's office, the weight settles back in. The shadows tighten their formation, and even Kaia stands straighter, her violet eyes sharp and focused.

We're students in name only. The war's already claimed us.

But hey, at least we look good doing it.

As we approach Lira's office, hushed voices drift through the partially open door. I recognize Lira's calm, measured tone immediately, but it's the deeper voice that makes us all pause.

"They're targeting the students now, Orlin," Lira says, tension bleeding through her usual composure. "This isn't just about the Heart of Eternity anymore."

"I'm well aware," Headmaster Orlin replies, his voice grave. "The board is pressing for answers about Thorne's disappearance. They're not satisfied with our explanation."

"The board can go—" Lira starts, but she cuts off abruptly as Mouse chirps a greeting. The shadows around Kaia ripple in response, and I swear Bob looks embarrassed about blowing our cover.

"Come in," Lira calls, not missing a beat. "All of you."

I shoot Kaia a grin. "Caught like first-years at a midnight feast. Some things never change."

She rolls her eyes, but there's the ghost of a smile there. "Kind of hard to hide a small army of shadows, Finn, especially when most of them don't listen."

Malrik elbows me sharply as we file into the office. Lira stands behind her desk, her silver-streaked black hair pulled back in its usual severe braid. Beside her, Headmaster Orlin cuts an imposing figure in his formal robes, but there's something tired in the set of his shoulders, like he's been fighting too long without rest.

"Miss Draven," Orlin says, inclining his head toward Kaia. His eyes linger on the shadows swirling around her feet, but there's no fear in his gaze, only careful consideration. "I believe we're overdue for a proper conversation."

Kaia straightens, and I notice the way the shadows press closer to her, like they're trying to lend her strength. Bob actually moves to stand at her side, like a tiny shadow bodyguard. "About what happened in the arena?"

"About everything," Lira interjects. She gestures to the chairs arranged before her desk. "Sit. We have much to discuss, and very little time."

"The board," Malrik says, his voice sharp. "They're moving against us?"

Orlin paces behind Lira's desk, his robes swishing with each deliberate step. "The board is traditionally meant to oversee the academy's more... political matters. They represent the interests of each faction, balancing power between them. Under normal circumstances, they have little involvement in day-to-day operations."

"But these aren't normal circumstances," Lira adds dryly.

"No," Orlin agrees, his expression grim. "Thorne's monthly reports were concerning enough, but after the incident in the arena... the board saw everything—Darian's attack, your wings, your restraint. They're shaken."

"Why weren't we told about this board before?" Kaia asks, her voice sharp. The shadows around her feet curl tighter, reflecting her tension. Patricia starts frantically taking notes, while Carl looks like he's attempting to hide behind Steve.

"Because until now, they were content to observe from a distance," Orlin explains. "The board meets only quarterly, in the Celestial Chamber beneath the academy. They're meant to be... impartial observers. But Thorne's disappearance has forced their hand."

"And divided them," Lira interjects. "The Light Faction representative, Lady Virath—yes, Alenya's mother—is calling for immediate action. She wants you expelled, your powers bound."

Torric growls low in his throat. "Let them try."

"The Elemental and Sorcery representatives are more cautious," Orlin continues, holding up a hand to quiet Torric. "The academy's recording crystals captured everything that happened in the arena. They've seen how Darian attacked you, how Thorne orchestrated the whole thing."

"And how you only unleashed your power when backed into a corner," Lira adds, her tone sharp. "I've submitted my own testimony about your character, your progress in my classes."

"And I've given mine," Seren pipes up from her perch on Lira's windowsill, where she's been uncharacteristically quiet until now. Her lavender hair catches the morning light as she turns to face us. "Though I believe my exact words were 'academic idiots who wouldn't know a hero if one saved their pompous—'" She catches Orlin's eye and clears her throat. "Well, you get the idea."

"The recording crystals and character testimonies are the only reason the board remains divided," Orlin explains. "They can't deny the evidence of

Thorne's betrayal, of Darian's attack. But they also can't ignore the raw power you displayed. The manifestation of your wings, the way the arena shattered..."

"They're terrified," Malrik concludes, his silver eyes narrowing. "Not of what Kaia did, but of what she could do."

"Precisely," Orlin nods. "The physical evidence of your power, combined with Thorne's disappearance and your growing connection to the shadows, has them scrambling for control of the situation."

"But they're not united on how to handle it," Lira interjects. "Professor Voss from Sorcery has argued quite persuasively that your actions were purely defensive. And the recording crystals support this—they show clearly that you didn't attack until Darian forced your hand."

"The crystals captured everything?" Kaia asks, and I don't miss the way her shadows curl tighter around her feet, the way her fingers worry at the Heart of Eternity hanging at her throat.

"Everything," Orlin confirms. "The betrayal, the emergence of your wings, the way your shadows manifested and responded to protect you. It's irrefutable evidence of both your power and the threat you were facing."

"Which is exactly why Lady Virath is pushing so hard for immediate action," Lira says grimly. "She's seen what you're capable of, and she's choosing to see only the threat, not the circumstances that forced your hand."

"And the Shadow Faction representative?" Malrik asks, his silver eyes narrowed. Something in his tone makes me think he already knows the answer, and I don't like the tension suddenly radiating from him.

Orlin's expression darkens. "That's part of our problem. The Shadow Faction's seat has been empty since your father's disappearance, Malrik. Thorne was meant to be a temporary replacement, but now..."

"Now we have no voice on the board at all," Malrik finishes, his jaw tight.

"Exactly," Lira says. "Which is why we needed to wait until the right moment to bring all of you into this. The board meets again in three days. They'll want to question you, Kaia. All of you, actually. And they'll be looking for any excuse to prove Thorne's accusations."

"What exactly did Thorne tell them?" I ask, because someone has to. The temperature in the room seems to drop several degrees.

"That Kaia is a threat to the academy's very foundations," Orlin says quietly. "That her connection to the Heart of Eternity is corrupting the leylines beneath the school. That her growing army of shadows is the first sign of an impending catastrophe."

"That's ridiculous," Aspen says, but his usual calm seems forced. "The leylines are stronger than ever. Anyone with basic magical sense can feel it."

"Yes," Lira agrees, "but fear is a powerful motivator. And Thorne has had months to plant seeds of doubt. The question now is: what are we going to do about it?"

Kaia stands suddenly, her violet eyes blazing. The shadows rise with her, and even Bob looks serious. "We show them the truth," she says firmly. "All of it. The Heart of Eternity, the shadows, everything. Let them see what we're really fighting for."

"It's not that simple," Orlin warns. "The board operates on ancient laws and traditions. One wrong move, and they could strip me of my position, replace me with someone more... amenable to their fears."

"Then we play by their rules," Malrik says, and there's something dangerous in his smile. "After all, I believe I have a claim to that empty Shadow Faction seat. Maybe it's time I took my father's place."

Lira and Orlin exchange a look that speaks volumes. "That," Lira says slowly, "could actually work. But it would mean publicly acknowledging your heritage, Malrik. Are you ready for those consequences?"

"I'm ready to stop hiding," Malrik replies. His hand finds mine under the table, and I squeeze it gently, trying not to show how much his words hit me.

I've watched him carry the weight of his heritage like armor—protection and prison all at once. Now he's choosing to shed it, and I'm not sure if I should be proud or terrified. Probably both.

"We all are," he adds, his gaze finding Kaia's across the table.

The shadows whisper their agreement, and Mouse chirps what sounds suspiciously like approval. But it's Kaia's expression that catches my attention, a mix of determination and fierce pride that makes my heart skip. She looks at Malrik with something I can't quite name, but it's warm and fierce and makes my stomach twist with something between jealousy and pride.

"Three days," she says, looking around at all of us. "We have three days to prepare our case. To prove that we're not the threat Thorne claims we are."

"And if we fail?" Torric asks, though his tone suggests he already knows what she'll say.

Kaia's smile is sharp. "We won't. Because this time, we're not just fighting for ourselves. We're fighting for every student who needs protection. For every shadow that's found a home here. For the academy itself."

"Well," I say, grinning despite the gravity of the moment, "when you put it that way, how can we lose? Plus, have you seen our shadow army? Bob's got them doing synchronized dancing. If that doesn't impress the board, nothing will."

The tension breaks just enough for a ripple of laughter. Even Orlin's lips twitch. But beneath the moment of levity, we all feel it. The weight of what's coming, the battles ahead. Kaia's shadows press close, feeding off her fear—and her fire.

Three days to change everything. No pressure.

"You know what's weird?" I say as we file out, because I can't help myself. "A week ago most of these people couldn't even see your shadows, and now they're critiquing Bob's organizational skills."

"Really helping, Finn," Aspen says dryly, but Kaia's shadows flutter nervously at the reminder.

"Hey, I'm just saying—if they're going to stare, they could at least appreciate the showmanship. I mean, have you seen Carl's backflips?"

Kaia manages a small smile, though her shadows curl closer. "Because acrobatic shadow performances are definitely going to convince the board we're not a threat."

"Exactly! Who could be afraid of a shadow doing jazz hands?"

Behind us, as if on cue, Bob starts demonstrating what appears to be proper courtroom etiquette to the newer shadows.

Complete with jazz hands.

I laugh, but catch the way Kaia's hands tremble slightly as she adjusts the Heart of Eternity at her throat. Malrik watches her with quiet resolve. The way Aspen and Torric automatically position themselves on either side of her, a protective formation we've all fallen into without discussion.

We're joking, but we all know what's coming. Three days before we face the consequences of everything that's happened.

And somewhere out there, Thorne is gathering his forces. Alekir is waiting.

But hey—we've got jazz hands on our side. That's got to count for something.

Right?

Chapter 4
KAIA

I've seen my shadows do a lot of ridiculous things, but watching Bob try to teach Steve how to bow properly might be a new highlight. Or it would be, if we weren't hours away from a meeting that could destroy everything we've built.

"Bob, I swear by all that's holy, if you let Finnick and Carl near those papers again—" I don't finish my threat because the shadows in question are already zooming past my head, trailing what appears to be Malrik's carefully prepared speech. Perfect. Just perfect.

Finnick swoops up toward the ceiling, Carl tumbling after him in what might be an attempt at aerial acrobatics or possibly just pure chaos. Bob, somehow managing to radiate disappointment despite being made of literal darkness, forms into a tall column and snatches the papers back. At least someone's taking this seriously.

"The shadows are just nervous," Lira remarks from her seat by the fire, not looking up from the thick tome of academy regulations in her lap. Her lips twitch slightly as Linda attempts to corral the more enthusiastic shadows into something resembling order. "We all are."

I watch Malrik pace near the window, his silver eyes reflecting the early morning light. The sight of him this unsettled makes my stomach twist. In the three days since our meeting in Lira's office, I've barely seen him sit down. "The board will be looking for any excuse," he says, not for the first time. "Any sign that we're not in control."

"Yes, because nothing says 'in control' like wearing a path in the carpet," Finn quips from his sprawl across a nearby armchair. He's been tossing a glowing orb of chaos magic into the air for the past hour, much to Patricia's visible annoyance. My most meticulous shadow has been arranging and rearranging our notes, adding what appears to be her own commentary in swooping shadow-script along the margins.

"Finn," Malrik starts, his voice tight with tension, but whatever he's about to say is cut off by Steve's dramatic entrance through the wall, trailing what appears to be half the library's worth of scrolls.

"Please tell me those aren't more regulations," I groan, slumping further into my chair. Mouse, curled around my shoulders like a living scarf, chirps what sounds suspiciously like agreement. His weight is comforting, anchoring me as my anxiety threatens to spiral. The Heart of Eternity hums low against my collarbone, like distant thunder beneath my ribs.

"Worse," Seren announces, following Steve through the door like a normal person. Her lavender hair is wild, suggesting she's been up all night researching. "Historical precedent. The board loves that stuff. Also, Carl, if you eat that scroll, I will personally ensure you spend the next week as a very formal square."

Carl, caught in the act of attempting to consume what looks like a particularly ancient piece of parchment, deflates visibly. My shadows have definitely gotten more... personality since Finn started naming them. Finnick pats Carl consolingly with a shadowy tendril before immediately trying to steal the scroll himself, and I have to bite back a laugh despite my nerves.

I'm about to intervene in the scroll-stealing chaos when I feel a gentle touch on my arm. Aspen's icy blue eyes meet mine, concern etched in their depths. "Can we talk for a moment?" he asks softly, nodding towards the adjoining study.

Grateful for the excuse to escape the mounting tension, I nod and follow him. The study is quieter, lit only by the soft glow of enchanted orbs floating near the ceiling. My shadows trail after us, though Bob keeps most of them occupied in the other room with what appears to be military drills for scrolls.

"How are you holding up?" Aspen asks, leaning against the ornate desk. The faint shimmer of his water rune catches the light, reminding me of moonlight on a calm lake.

I open my mouth to say I'm fine, but the words catch in my throat. The lie tastes bitter before it even forms. "I'm terrified," I admit instead, my voice barely above a whisper. My fingers find the Heart of Eternity, tracing its familiar curves. "What if we can't convince them? What if they decide I'm too dangerous to keep at the academy?"

Aspen steps closer, his presence steady and reassuring. "They won't," he says with quiet conviction. "You've worked so hard, Kaia. We all have. The board would be fools not to see how much you've grown, how much control you've gained."

His faith in me is almost overwhelming. I wrap my arms around myself, the shadows Bob couldn't keep out pressing in tighter, agitated. They flicker in nervous patterns, reflecting the anxiety I'm trying to keep contained. "But what if it's not enough? What if—"

Before I can spiral further, Aspen closes the distance between us and pulls me into a hug. I stiffen for a moment, surprised by the sudden contact, before melting into his embrace. He smells like rain and pine, and for just a moment, I let myself feel safe. His heartbeat is steady against my cheek, his arms solid around me.

When we pull apart, there's something in his eyes that makes my heart race. Something warm and fierce that makes my shadows pulse with answering energy. But before either of us can say anything more, Torric's voice carries from the other room: "Five hours and forty-three minutes," he calls out, still aggressively sharpening his sword. "Not that I'm counting."

The moment breaks, reality rushing back in. Aspen's quiet "I'm here if you need me" follows me like a promise as we return to the chaos of the common room. My shadows curl tighter around my feet, their anxiety mirroring mine. Even Bob's etiquette drills seem half-hearted now, especially with Steve tumbling through the furniture.

"It'll be fine," Finn says, catching his glowing orb one final time before sitting up properly. "We've got this. We've got witnesses, evidence, and an army of surprisingly coordinated shadows. What could go wrong?"

As if in direct response to his question, Carl manages to tangle himself in the chandelier, sending tiny shards of crystal tinkling to the floor.

"You had to ask," Malrik sighs, pinching the bridge of his nose. But there's a fondness in his voice that wasn't there when I first came to the academy, and something in my chest loosens at the sight of his slight smile as Finnick launches a dramatic "rescue" mission that somehow involves more aerial acrobatics than should be physically possible for a being made of shadow.

Lira clears her throat, finally looking up from her book. "Perhaps we should review the testimony order one more time. Kaia, you'll speak first, then—"

She's interrupted by a knock at the door. We all freeze, even my shadows dropping into defensive formations that would be impressive if Steve hadn't tripped and caused a minor domino effect.

Professor Thaldris pokes his head in, his usually cheerful face unusually serious. "They're ready for you. The board has convened early."

The silence that follows is broken only by the soft thud of Carl finally freeing himself from the chandelier and landing directly on Finn's head.

"Well," I say, standing as shadows swirl protectively around my feet, "at least we don't have to wait any longer."

Mouse chirps encouragingly from my shoulder, his tiny form vibrating with determination. Bob straightens to his full height, somehow managing to look both regal and mildly concerned about Finnick's continued attempts to perfect his midair somersaults.

"Remember," Lira says quietly as we gather our materials, "they're looking for any reason to prove Thorne right. Don't give them one."

I touch the Heart of Eternity, drawing strength from its familiar warmth. Three days of preparation have to count for something. Three days of testimonies, evidence gathering, and yes, shadow etiquette training. It has to be enough.

As we file out of the common room, I catch Malrik's eye. The weight of what's coming sits heavy in my chest, but there's something else too, a fierce determination that makes my shadows pulse with energy.

Malrik meets my gaze, solid and unflinching. Behind him, Torric shifts his stance, Aspen adjusts his cuffs, and Finn spins his chaos orb one last time. It's not just my trial. It's ours.

"Together?" I ask softly.

Malrik's smile is sharp but genuine. "Together."

Behind us, Finn whispers something that makes Carl giggle-shadow all over the walls, and Patricia can be seen adding one final note to her extensive documentation.

We're as ready as we'll ever be. Which, given our track record, is either terrifying or oddly comforting. I haven't quite decided which.

My wings stir beneath my skin, an echo of power I'm still learning to control. The Heart responds with a gentle pulse, and for a brief moment, I swear I can feel something else. Something distant yet familiar, like a tug on my soul from somewhere beyond the academy walls.

But then Torric puts his hand on my shoulder, and the sensation fades. I square my shoulders. No more hiding. No more waiting to be judged. "Let's go show them what a Valkyrie can do," he says, his golden eyes fierce with pride.

And for just a moment, I almost believe we might pull this off.

Chapter 5
KAIA

I've never seen Bob look so stressed. My normally unflappable shadow commander is practically vibrating as he tries to maintain order among the others. He's formed what looks like a tiny shadow clipboard and is checking off some kind of military roster while shooting disapproving glances at Carl, who's currently doing somersaults across the ancient stone floor.

The Celestial Chamber lives up to its name—all soaring columns and hushed whispers, with enchanted constellations spiraling across the domed ceiling and whispers clinging to the stone like smoke. Recording crystals float near the ceiling like silent judges, their facets catching the ethereal light as they track our every movement.

Patricia, true to form, has manifested what appears to be a shadow notebook and is taking furious notes. Finnick and Carl, clearly bored with the proceedings already, have started what looks suspiciously like a game of shadow tag behind Lady Virath's chair. Mouse perches on my shoulder, his violet eyes tracking everything with ancient calm.

"The council will now review the evidence from the arena incident," Elder Thaddeus announces, his voice echoing through the chamber like thunder in a cavern. One of the recording crystals descends, projecting images that make my stomach twist.

There I am, suspended in midair as my wings unfurl for the first time—shadow and light intertwining as my power surged against Thorne's corruption. The memory slams into me: the searing pain of transformation, the sudden awareness of centuries of history flowing through my veins, the desperate need to protect my shadows. My sisters.

"As you can see," Lady Virath rises, her white robes seeming to glow against the darkness, "the display of power was... concerning." Her cold gaze fixes on me, clinical and calculating. "The question before us is simple: can we trust someone who commands an army of shadows?"

Mouse presses against my neck, a low growl building in his throat that only I can hear. Behind Lady Virath, Finnick pauses his game long enough to make a very specific gesture that has Bob practically dissolving in horror.

"If I may," Lira steps forward, her voice steady. "I've worked with Kaia extensively. Her control over her abilities—"

"Control?" Lady Virath interrupts, one perfect eyebrow arching. "Is that what we witnessed in the arena? When her shadows multiplied without warning, when her power shattered our wards?"

The Heart of Eternity pulses warm against my chest, responding to my rising anger. I force myself to breathe, to stay calm as my shadows coil tighter around my feet.

"Those wards," Malrik's voice cuts through the chamber like ice, "were already compromised by Thorne's corruption." He rises from his seat, silver eyes gleaming with dangerous light. "Or did the council miss that detail in their... thorough review?"

Lady Virath's perfect composure cracks slightly. "Prince Malrik, this matter concerns—"

"The Shadow Faction?" His smile is sharp enough to draw blood. "Precisely my point. We've allowed fear of shadow magic to blind us to its true potential. Kaia's power isn't a threat, it's proof that we've been mishandling our approach to shadow manipulation for generations."

Bob, apparently sensing an opportunity, creates what can only be described as a shadow presentation board. Patricia immediately starts filling it with evidence of my training progress, while Finnick adds what he probably thinks are helpful illustrations. I say probably because what he's currently drawing is... well... anatomically creative.

I bite the inside of my cheek to keep from laughing, even as my heart races. Malrik stands before the council like he was born for this moment, all royal bearing and barely contained power. My shadows ripple in response, drawn to his confidence like moths to flame.

"The Shadow Faction," Lady Virath recovers smoothly, straightening her already perfect robes, "currently lacks leadership to make such assessments. Unless you're offering to fill that role, Prince Malrik?"

"Actually," Malrik steps forward, and something in his stance makes my shadows ripple with interest, "I am. The faction needs leadership that understands both the politics of power and the nature of shadows themselves."

The chamber erupts in whispers. Even Elder Thaddeus looks taken aback, his bushy eyebrows disappearing into his hairline. "This is highly irregular—"

"What's irregular," Malrik cuts in, "is how long we've allowed fear to dictate our approach to shadow magic. The corruption in Absentia spreads while we debate semantics and protocol."

Lady Virath's eyes narrow. "You speak of corruption, yet propose no solution."

"Don't I?" Malrik glances at me, and something in his expression makes my heart skip. His silver eyes hold mine for a moment too long, something fierce and protective flashing in their depths. "We have a Valkyrie whose power bridges light and shadow. We have an ancient realm in need of cleansing. Perhaps instead of fearing what we don't understand, we should prove our worth to lead."

"A challenge then?" Lady Virath's smile turns predatory, all teeth and no warmth. "Enter Absentia. Face its corruption. Prove that your... unique abilities serve the academy's interests."

"Both of us," Malrik says before I can respond. "My claim to lead the Shadow Faction. Kaia's place at the academy. Let Absentia itself judge our worth."

The Heart of Eternity pulses warm against my chest, and for a moment I swear I hear my mother's voice—distant but clear: *Remember who you are.*

My shadows still, as if hearing it too. Even Finnick stops his inappropriate artwork to listen.

"The council accepts these terms," Elder Thaddeus declares, though his expression suggests he'd rather be anywhere else. "You will enter Absentia in two days' time. Face its corruption. Prove your right to remain among us."

As the council disperses, my shadows cluster close. Bob has given up trying to censor Finnick's increasingly detailed "art," while Patricia's notes have devolved into pure chaos.

"You didn't have to do that," I murmur to Malrik as we leave the chamber. "There's no sense in both of us dying for this."

His silver eyes meet mine, and something flickers in their depths that I can't quite read. "Yes," he says quietly, "I did."

The weight of those three words settles into my chest, making it hard to breathe. His eyes change to something softer, making my heart stutter in its rhythm. "No one is dying. I'm with you, Kaia. Always."

***

Tension coils in the air as we leave the chamber. I walk ahead, shoulders rigid, shadows curling around my feet like restless sentries. Finn stays close, hands shoved in his pockets, his usual grin subdued. Aspen moves beside me, his steady presence a quiet reassurance, though I catch the concern in his icy blue gaze.

Torric exhales sharply. "I still think we should've handled it differently."

"By handled, you mean punched someone in the face?" Finn arches a brow.

Torric glares at him. "If it worked, I wouldn't rule it out."

I don't speak. My mind still spins from the weight of the meeting, my shadows flickering with unease. I force myself to keep moving, to not let them see how shaken I am. The Heart of Eternity feels heavier against my skin, pulsing with what feels like urgency.

We reach the Shadow faction common room, the shadows along the walls shifting in response to our presence. I stop just inside the threshold, exhale slowly, then turn to face them.

"We have two days before we're sent into Absentia." My voice is steady, but my shadows twitch in agitation. "We don't have time to sit around debating what the council thinks of me. We need a plan."

Malrik watches me carefully, his silver eyes unreadable. "We'll prepare," Aspen assures me, his calm voice a balm to my fraying nerves. "We'll make sure you're ready."

I hesitate, my gaze dropping to where my shadows twist anxiously at my feet. Bob is already organizing them into what looks like a battle formation, but there's an edge of desperation to his movements that scares me more than I want to admit.

"I know Malrik is coming. But Aspen, Torric, Finn... I don't expect you to follow me into this." I force a small smile, trying to lessen the weight of the moment. "I wouldn't ask you to."

Torric stiffens. "Are you serious?"

Aspen frowns, stepping forward. "Kaia, do you really think we'd let you go into that place without us?"

Finn lets out a dramatic gasp, pressing a hand to his chest. "Wow. Just wow. The betrayal. I thought we had something special."

I groan, rubbing my temples. "That's not what I meant, Finn."

Torric lets out a sharp breath, shaking his head. "Gods, you really don't get it, do you?" His golden eyes blaze with frustration, but underneath, there's something else. Something softer. "You're not just some mission to us. You think we're standing here, training with you, pushing you, because we feel obligated?" He takes a step closer, the heat of him making my shadows stir. "I'm going because I choose to. Because I won't stand back while you put yourself in danger. Not when I can fight beside you."

Aspen nods, his gaze steady. "You don't have to ask us, Kaia. We're here because we want to be." His fingers brush my wrist, a quiet reassurance that sends electricity up my arm. "Because we care about you."

Finn makes a choked sound. "Well, that was disgustingly romantic." But the way his chaos magic sparks between his fingers betrays how affected he really is.

I huff out a breathless laugh, even as my chest tightens with emotions I don't have names for. "You guys are impossible."

Torric smirks. "And you're stuck with us."

Malrik folds his arms, watching me with an unreadable expression. "Then it's settled. We'll spend the next two days preparing. That means training, gathering supplies, and making sure we're ready for whatever Absentia throws at us."

My shoulders relax slightly, some of the tension easing. "Thank you." The words feel inadequate for the weight of what they're offering, but it's all I have.

Finn grins, throwing an arm over my shoulders. "What kind of romance would this be if we let you go off to certain doom by yourself?"

I groan, shoving him off, but the flicker of amusement in my eyes isn't lost on anyone. My shadows settle slightly, Bob actually relaxing his rigid posture enough to pat Finnick on what might be his head.

Two days of training. Planning. Pushing. My shadows whisper in corners I can't reach. Mouse never leaves my side.

By day three, I'm sparring at dawn. Aspen corrects my form. Finn goads my instincts. "You're thinking too much," he tells me, deflecting my latest strike with infuriating ease. "Shadow magic isn't just about control—it's about feeling. Let them guide you."

I growl in frustration, my shadows coiling tighter. "Easy for you to say. Your magic literally thrives on unpredictability."

His green eyes soften. "And yours thrives on connection. So connect."

Malrik watches from the edges more often than he participates, stepping in only when needed. When he does, it's unsettling how seamlessly we move together, like our shadows know something we don't. His silver eyes track my movements with an intensity that makes my skin prickle with awareness.

Torric pushes my endurance, running drills until my lungs burn, and then forces me through another round. "If you can't push past exhaustion," he grunts, tossing me a waterskin, "you won't survive in Absentia."

By the end of the second day, I collapse onto the couch in the common room, Mouse curling into my side. My muscles ache, and the Heart of Eternity pulses against my skin in rhythm with my heartbeat.

"You look dead," Finn observes from the opposite chair, spinning a dagger between his fingers with casual precision.

"Feel dead," I mumble, half-heartedly swatting at his foot when he nudges my leg.

Aspen chuckles, settling in beside me. "You'll thank us when you make it back in one piece."

I don't answer. I'm not sure what I'm expecting once we enter Absentia. I just know that nothing is going to be the same after this. The Heart seems to agree, its warmth pulsing with something that feels almost like anticipation.

My shadows coil around me protectively, sensing my unease. Bob attempts to organize the others into what appears to be a proper formation, but even he seems distracted. Patricia keeps taking notes, though I notice her usual methodical approach has been replaced by something more frantic.

Malrik steps in, shadows clinging to his silver eyes like prophecy. "We leave at dawn."

I nod, fingers curling into Mouse's fur. My shadows twist and stretch around me, already sensing the shift in fate awaiting us.

The next time I cross these walls, I might not come back. The thought should terrify me, but all I feel is a strange sense of inevitability. Like everything since I came to this academy has been leading to this moment.

The Heart warms against my skin, as if in agreement.

Absentia waits.

Chapter 6
ASPEN

I catch every wince Kaia tries to hide as she sprawls on the couch, each subtle shift of weight betraying what she refuses to admit. Her shadows move sluggishly around her ankles, even Bob's usually crisp formations wavering like disturbed water. She's been pushing herself beyond breaking, and something in my chest tightens watching her pretend she's fine.

One look at Torric confirms he sees it too. My brother's jaw ticks once, his golden eyes tracking her movements with the same concern twisting in my gut. We don't need words. When you've trained alongside someone for decades, a single glance carries paragraphs.

"Kaia." I keep my voice soft but steady. When she turns, the shadows under her eyes are deeper than the ones curling around her feet. "You need recovery time before tomorrow."

"I'm fine," she starts, but Torric cuts her off with a sharp laugh.

"Like hell you are. Your left side drops every time you breathe, your shoulders are locked, and even Bob looks ready to collapse." He crosses his arms, radiating the stubborn determination that's saved my life more times than I can count. "You're coming with us."

She bristles, violet eyes flashing, that familiar spark that makes my heart beat faster even when it's directed at me. "We don't have time for—"

"Actually," I interrupt, gentling my tone, "your body needs time to rebuild what magic has burned through. Going into Absentia like this would be—" I pause, knowing battle language will resonate more than concern "—tactically unsound."

Torric's lips twitch. He knows exactly what I'm doing, appealing to her practical side rather than trying to force her to rest. It's a strategy we've perfected over years of watching people push themselves to breaking.

"The healing rooms," I continue before she can protest, watching her shadows drift reluctantly toward me like they know what she needs better than she does, "have therapeutic pools specifically designed for magical exhaustion. An hour there would significantly increase your stamina to-morrow."

Her shadows shift restlessly, but I can see her resistance cracking. Patricia actually seems to be taking notes on my argument, her shadowy form bobbing with agreement.

"One hour," she says finally, the words dragging like they cost her.

"Two," Torric counters, his voice brooking no argument. "And that's non-negotiable."

I lead them through the winding corridors to the healing wing, noting how Kaia's steps falter, how she lists slightly to the left when she thinks we aren't watching. Now that she's admitted to needing rest, the full weight of her exhaustion seems to be settling into her bones. Her shadows trail behind like weary soldiers, barely maintaining their forms. Even Steve and Carl, usually bouncing with inappropriate energy, drag behind like sulking children.

The healing rooms are mercifully empty this late. Enchanted crystals cast soft, ambient light across the marble floors, their glow reflecting off the still water in pools set into the stone. Steam rises in gentle curls, carrying the scent of herbs and old magic.

"This one," I say, gesturing to a pool glowing with gentle violet light. "The minerals will help your muscles recover, and the enchantments work specifically with shadow magic."

Torric is already moving, gathering towels and healing salts in his efficient way. We've spent enough time patching each other up that this is familiar territory, caring for someone who'd sooner bleed out than ask for help.

"I can manage on my own," Kaia protests weakly, but her shadows betray her, drifting toward the pool like they're drawn to its healing properties. Bob actually dips what might be a toe in, then visibly relaxes.

"Of course you can," I say, keeping my voice neutral even as my fingers itch to help. "But you don't have to."

Kaia hesitates, her pride warring with exhaustion in the set of her shoulders. Finally, she nods, allowing us to help her toward the pool. Her shadows drift ahead, Bob and Carl testing the water's edge with ghostly tendrils.

"We'll be right outside," Torric says, his gruff tone belying the gentleness with which he hands her a stack of soft towels. "Call if you need anything."

I add a vial of concentrated healing salts to the pile. "A capful every fifteen minutes. They'll amplify the pool's restorative properties."

Kaia manages a tired smile, small but real. "Thank you. Both of you."

We step out, giving her privacy. The moment the door closes, Torric's shoulders drop, composure cracking like ice under pressure.

"She's pushing too hard," he mutters, running a hand through his hair. "At this rate, she'll burn out before we even reach Absentia."

I lean against the wall, letting out a slow breath that carries more worry than I want to admit. "I know. But we can't exactly tie her down and force her to rest."

"Want to bet?" Torric's golden eyes glint with a flash of his usual mischief, but it fades quickly, replaced by the weight I feel pressing against my own ribs. "She's not ready for this, Aspen. None of us are."

The reality of what we're facing settles over us like a physical thing. Absentia. The word alone brings cold sweat to my palms. A realm of nightmares and forgotten things, where reality bends and breaks. And we're willingly walking into it because the alternative is worse.

"We don't have a choice," I say softly. "If we don't stop the corruption from spreading..."

Torric nods grimly. "I know. Doesn't mean I have to like it."

We fall into tense silence, each lost in thoughts too heavy to voice. The gentle hum of healing magic seeps through the door, a counterpoint to the fears crowding my mind.

After what feels like hours but is likely only minutes, Torric speaks again. "Do you think her shadows will be enough? In Absentia, I mean."

I consider the question carefully. Kaia's shadow magic is powerful, but Absentia is... unpredictable. Especially for her shadows like Bob and the others who've been with her through everything. "I don't know," I admit. "But Bob and the others have been protecting Kaia since before she even knew who she was. That kind of loyalty doesn't just vanish, even in a place like Absentia."

As if summoned by our discussion, a tendril of shadow seeps beneath the door. The shadow Carl, I think, his energy is always a little more chaotic, gestures urgently then points back toward the door.

Torric and I exchange a glance before pushing through. The sight that greets us hollows me out.

Kaia is curled into herself in the violet-tinged water, her shoulders shaking with silent sobs. Her shadows swirl around her protectively, but even they seem diminished, flickering like candles in a draft. The healing salts float untouched on the surface, forgotten in whatever storm is breaking inside her.

My chest tightens, throat closing around words that won't come. I've seen Kaia face nightmare creatures without flinching. Watched her bend shadows to her will with fierce determination. But this vulnerability, this glimpse of the weight she carries, it breaks something in me I didn't know was whole.

We approach carefully, our footsteps echoing in the cavernous room. The steam carries the scent of lavender and something wilder—a hint of shadow magic, perhaps, or simply the essence of Kaia herself.

She lifts her head as we reach the pool's edge. Her violet eyes, usually so vibrant with life and stubbornness, are red-rimmed and swimming with unshed tears. For a moment, I don't see the formidable Valkyrie with an army of shadows, but a young woman drowning under too many expectations.

"I'm sorry," she whispers, her voice raw. "I didn't mean to... I just..." Her words scatter like leaves, lost in a fresh wave of tears.

Without hesitation, Torric and I step into the pool, clothes and all. The enchanted water swirls around us, warm and tingling with restorative magic that seeps into my own tired muscles—a quiet reminder of how much we've all been pushing ourselves.

Kaia watches us approach, walls of sarcasm and bravado stripped bare. There's a question in her eyes, a vulnerability that clutches at my heart with cold fingers. She's giving us permission, I realize. Letting us see her at her lowest. Trusting us with something she never shows.

I reach her first, gently pulling her into my arms. She stiffens for a moment, then melts against me, her tears soaking into my shirt. Torric settles beside her, his hand finding her back in slow, steady circles.

"It's okay," I murmur, running my fingers through her damp hair. "You don't have to be strong all the time. Not with us."

Her shadows drift closer, no longer sharp-edged formations but soft things seeking comfort. Bob, usually so dignified, wraps around my wrist like a child seeking reassurance. Carl nestles against Torric's shoulder, a dark patch against his golden skin.

"I'm scared," she admits, her voice muffled against my chest. "Absentia... what if I can't control my shadows there? What if I'm not strong enough?"

I hold her closer as Torric's hand stills on her back. "Listen to me," my brother says, his voice rough with emotion. "Your strength isn't just about controlling shadows. It's about bringing light to the darkest places, and you do that just by being you."

A small sound escapes her, somewhere between a laugh and a sob. Her shadows ripple in response, and I feel Bob pat my arm awkwardly, as if offering comfort for comforting her. The gesture is so perfectly Bob that I have to fight a smile despite the ache in my chest.

"Besides," I add softly, resting my chin atop her head, "you won't be alone in Absentia. Whatever's waiting there, we face it together."

"As a team," Torric agrees, his eyes meeting mine over her head. I see my own promise reflected there. We've trained for impossible odds. This one just matters more.

The healing pool's magic swirls around us, its violet glow intensifying where it meets Kaia's shadows. They seem to drink in the restorative energy, their movements becoming more fluid, more alive. Patricia has even started taking notes again, though her shadowy scribbles look more like comfort food recipes than her usual tactical observations.

"I don't deserve this," Kaia whispers, but her fingers curl tighter into my shirt. "Any of it. You both have already risked so much—"

The words hit like something sharp lodged behind my ribs. How can she not see what she means to us?

"Stop," I cut her off gently. "That's exhaustion talking. You're not just our leader or our friend, Kaia. You're family." The word settles between us, more true than I realized until I said it. "And family means no one fights alone."

Torric's hand squeezes her shoulder. "What he said. Though with less sappy phrasing."

That draws a watery laugh from her, and I feel some of the tension drain from her body. Her shadows settle into more natural patterns, though they stay close, as if reluctant to break this moment of connection.

"The salts," I remind her, reaching for the forgotten vial. "Let's get you properly healed. Then we can talk strategy, or not talk at all. Whatever you need."

She lets me add the healing salts to the water, their crystalline shimmer creating patterns that her shadows chase like fascinated kittens. Even Bob forgets his dignity, darting after the sparkling trails with childlike enthusiasm that makes my heart swell.

"Thank you," Kaia says after a while, her voice steadier. "For everything. For being here. For understanding."

"Always," Torric and I say together, and I feel her smile against my chest.

The healing room falls quiet except for the gentle lapping of the enchanted water. Outside these walls, destiny and danger wait. But here, in this moment, we're just three people holding each other up.

And sometimes, I think, the strongest magic is simply refusing to let someone fall alone.

Chapter 7
DARIAN

I've forgotten the color of her eyes.

The thought echoes through my cell in the academy's dungeons, bouncing off ancient stone walls that pulse with containment wards. They were violet—or were they? The memory shifts and blurs like the shadows that dance at the edges of my vision, taunting me with what I'm trying to forget.

Some nights I wake gasping, her name on my lips, the exact shade burning in my mind with perfect clarity. But by morning it fades, leaving only the ache of something precious lost. Like trying to hold water in cupped hands, watching it slip away no matter how tightly I clutch.

Light magic crackles beneath my skin, fighting against the corruption that seeps through my veins like oil through water. The torches outside my cell flare brighter in response, their flames reaching toward me like desperate fingers. Ever since her transformation, since those damned wings burst into existence, I can feel the Heart of Eternity's pull. Feel her.

The bond pulses, this new, maddening connection sending waves of her essence through me—warm and vital and absolutely destroying everything I thought I knew about power and control. I slam my fist into the wall, welcoming the sharp pain that blooms across my knuckles. Anything to distract from her presence suddenly threaded through my blood, my bones, my very soul.

"Get out," I snarl at the empty cell, but I'm not sure if I'm talking to her or the growing warmth in my chest that feels suspiciously like longing. Like destiny finally catching up to all of us. "Get out get out get out."

But she won't. She's there when I close my eyes, laughing in the library as she masters a new spell, eyes sparkling with triumph. She's there in my dreams, reaching for me with shadows that feel like silk against my skin, wanting to share rather than consume. She's there in every beat of my treacherous heart, making me question everything I thought I knew about power and corruption and the lines between light and dark.

"It wasn't supposed to be like this," I whisper to the darkness that won't answer. The bond surges again, and this time I catch fragments of her emotions—determination, fear, a fierce protectiveness that makes my chest ache with something I refuse to name. "You weren't supposed to matter."

Footsteps echo down the corridor, lighter than the guards', precise and purposeful. I don't bother looking up when Alenya appears outside my cell, her white uniform practically glowing in the dim light. But part of me, the part that still remembers the exact shade of violet in Kaia's eyes, wants to scream at her to leave before she offers what I know I'll be too weak to refuse.

"Poor fallen star," she says, her voice dripping false sympathy. "How the mighty Light Faction has dimmed."

I laugh, the sound harsh even to my own ears. "Come to gloat, Alenya? Or does your mother need another report on the academy's greatest failure?"

"I come with knowledge." She steps closer to the bars, and I catch a whiff of something ancient and wrong beneath her perfect light magic, something that makes the corruption inside me stir hungrily. "About why the corruption burns differently now. Why you can feel her."

The bond pulses at her words, and for a moment I'm drowning in Kaia's essence, her strength, her compassion, her absolute conviction that magic isn't about control but connection. The force of it nearly brings me to my knees.

"I see how you strain against it," Alenya continues carefully. "The corruption isn't sitting well anymore, not since she revealed what she is." Her voice drops lower. "He always knew you would be connected to her. That's why he chose you, prepared you. There are ways to ensure that connection serves our purpose rather than hers."

"You don't know what you're talking about," I snap, but my hand presses against my chest where Kaia's presence burns like an ember lodged beneath my ribs.

Her smile is sharp as a blade. "Don't I? He saw this moment centuries ago—the light bearer and the shadow walker, bound by power neither understands. But he wasn't the only one watching." Her lips curl with smug satisfaction. "The ancient ones thought they could contain the God by sealing the bloodlines away from each other. But he made sure you would find each other when the time was right. Made sure your magic would remember its true purpose."

"Alekir." The name tastes like metal on my tongue. "This was his plan all along."

"He offers freedom, Darian. From this bond, from her influence, from everything that would chain you to powers you were never meant to embrace." She leans closer to the bars. "He'll tear down the walls between realms, let power flow as it was meant to. And in that freedom, only the strongest magic will survive."

I press my hand harder against my chest, feeling Kaia's essence pulse beneath my palm. The corruption in my veins stirs hungrily at the thought of being free. But something else stirs too, something that remembers the way her power had reached for mine, almost like it saw past Thorne's corruption to something real beneath.

"And what does he want in return?"

"Only what we've been planning for centuries. The six bloodlines, aligned at last—but corrupted rather than pure. Breaking the seal instead of maintaining it." Her eyes gleam with zealous fire. "You're just the first piece. She's another. And when all six finally gather..."

No more her, I think, and suddenly I see her face with perfect clarity, violet eyes bright with betrayal as I attacked her in the arena. But beneath the betrayal had been something worse—understanding. Forgiveness. A willingness to still reach for me even as I tried to destroy everything we could have been.

"When?" I ask, and feel the corruption surge with victory even as something in my soul begins to scream.

"Soon." Alenya produces a key that shivers with power. "Very soon."

The bond flares one last time, and now I recognize what it's trying to tell me. This isn't about freedom, it's about fear. Fear of how deeply she's worked her way into my heart. Fear of how right it feels when our magic dances together. Fear of belonging to something larger than my own carefully constructed walls.

I'll forget the color of her eyes. I'll forget everything about her.

I have to.

Because if I don't, if I let myself remember exactly how her violet eyes sparkle when she laughs, how her shadows reach for my light like old friends coming home... I'll never be able to do what needs to be done.

Even if it means destroying the best part of myself in the process.

After Alenya leaves, I sink to the floor of my cell, pressing my forehead against the cool stone. The key she left, my promise of freedom, burns in my palm like a brand.

Something shifts in the shadows near the ceiling, a movement too deliberate to be natural. I look up, expecting another trick of the corruption, another phantom to torment me.

Instead, I find myself staring at the tiniest wisp of shadow I've ever seen, barely larger than my hand. It bobs peacefully near a crack in the ancient stonework, seemingly unbothered by the containment wards that should be keeping it out.

"What—" I start, but the word catches in my throat as the tiny shadow drifts closer. There's something different about this one, something pure and untainted. Starlight ripples through its form like captured moonbeams.

The little shadow does a lazy flip in the air before settling at eye level. If a shadow could look curious, this one definitely does.

"You shouldn't be here," I tell it, but I make no move to attack. My light magic stirs, but not aggressively. If anything, it seems... interested. "She'll be looking for you."

The shadow bobs in what might be agreement, then drifts even closer. My breath catches as it brushes against my hand. The touch feels like sunshine and laughter, nothing like the oily corruption trying to twist my power.

"Stop it," I whisper, but the shadow only repeats the gesture, more deliberately this time. Memories flash through my mind. Kaia's smile, her shadows dancing with my light, the way everything had felt right before fear poisoned it all.

The wisp expands slightly, showing me a glimpse of something—six points of light arranged in a perfect pattern, power flowing between them like rivers of starfire. At the center, a familiar violet glow pulses with possibility.

"I can't," I tell the shadow, closing my eyes against the vision that feels too much like hope. "I won't be bound. Not even for her. Not even if—"

But the shadow just bobs serenely, completely unfazed by my denial. It shows me another image. My light magic twining with her shadows, creating something neither dark nor bright but somehow both. Something beautiful.

Something free.

"Please," I breathe, not sure if I'm asking it to stop or show me more. "I can't... I have to..."

The tiny shadow settles on my shoulder, its starlit form pulsing gently. For just a moment, I let myself feel it. The echo of what could be, if I were brave enough to choose connection over fear.

Then I remember Alenya's key, Alekir's promise of freedom, and I force myself to stand. The tiny shadow drifts back, watching me with what feels like gentle understanding.

"Go back to her," I say roughly. "Tell her..." My voice breaks, shattering on the truth I can't escape. "Tell her I remember the color of her eyes."

The shadow does another lazy flip before floating back toward the crack in the wall. Just before it disappears, it shows me one last image—a future where light and shadow dance together, unbound yet perfectly aligned.

I clutch the key tighter, letting its cold metal ground me against the vision's warmth.

I have to forget that future. Have to forget her eyes.

Have to forget how much I want everything that tiny, impossible shadow just showed me.

Chapter 8
TORRIC

I reach Kaia's door before dawn, when the academy's shadows are deepest. My fire rune pulses with restless energy, making the corridor's torches flare in response. The power in my blood feels different lately, wilder, more demanding. Like it knows something's coming.

Through the gap beneath her door, I spot Bob patrolling in slow, purposeful arcs. The shadow pauses his rounds to investigate my boots, and I swear he gives me an approving nod before resuming his guard duty. Even now, their growing personalities throw me off—though Bob's stoic professionalism is easier to respect than Carl's ceiling antics.

"Kaia," I call softly, knocking. "We need to move."

No response, but her shadows shift beneath the door. Another one joins Bob—probably Patricia taking notes. A third shadow, smaller than the others, drifts through the gap like smoke. It bobs peacefully in the air before me, seeming to study my face with genuine curiosity.

"What in the void..." I start, but Finn's voice cuts me off.

"Walter!" he exclaims, appearing beside me with his usual terrible timing. "I was wondering where you'd gotten to, little guy."

I raise an eyebrow. "Walter?"

"Look at him," Finn gestures to the tiny shadow, which does a lazy flip in response. "He's clearly a Walter. Has that sophisticated explorer vibe, you know? Like an old cartographer who once mapped the stars and then retired to haunt a library."

"I don't know how you come up with these names," I mutter, but the shadow, Walter, seems pleased, drifting closer to investigate the glow of my fire rune.

The door opens before I can protest further. Kaia stands there, wings half-furled behind her, shadows coiling protectively at her feet. The sight still knocks the air from my lungs. Not just how beautiful she is, but the raw power she radiates. My fire rune burns hotter in response.

"Let me guess," she says, voice rough with sleep. "Time to go save the world?"

"Something like that." I try for gruff but probably fail. Hard to maintain distance when her violet eyes meet mine, when her wings shift like they're reaching for me too.

The small shadow floats between us, doing another pleased flip before settling near Kaia's shoulder. Her expression shifts to curiosity as she studies the unfamiliar shadow.

"Who's this little one?" she asks, watching as the shadow investigates her wings with delicate interest.

"Walter, apparently," I explain, gesturing toward Finn. "He's on a mission to name every shadow in existence."

"He's got that distinguished air about him," Finn defends. "Like a gentleman explorer who got lost in the library and decided to stay."

Kaia laughs, the sound hitting me square in the ribs. "Walter," she repeats, testing the name. "It suits him." Her other shadows seem to welcome the newcomer, even Bob pausing his patrol to acknowledge Walter's presence.

"We should go," I say, forcing myself to focus. "Malrik's waiting at the portal grounds."

She nods, sobering. Her wings draw closer, and her shadows shift into more defensive positions. Even Walter's peaceful bobbing takes on a purposeful quality.

"Ready to face certain doom?" Finn asks cheerfully.

Kaia's smile is fierce. "With you guys? I should be terrified."

The words settle something in my chest, even as my fire rune blazes with protective fury. Whatever we're walking into, whatever corruption Absentia holds, she won't face it alone.

I won't let her.

When we reach the portal grounds, Kaia pauses, her wings drawing close as she looks at our assembled group. Her shadows swirl anxiously around her feet as she turns to face us.

"Last chance to back out," she says, trying for lightness, but the shadows curling around her ankles betray the strain. "Except you, Malrik, I know this is your fight too. But the rest of you... you don't have to do this."

Finn, lounging against a pillar and tossing some glowing trinket in the air, snorts. "Nice try, Trouble. But we've been over this."

"More like organizing a revolution," I say, moving to stand beside my brother. "Did you really think we'd let you face certain doom without us?"

Bob, hovering near Kaia's shoulders, puffs up with what might be pride, while Mouse chirps his approval from her feet. Even her newer shadows seem to dance with excitement, feeding off her emotions.

"This isn't a game," Malrik starts from his position by the portal, but Aspen steps forward, cutting him off.

"No," my twin says quietly, his ice-blue eyes meeting Kaia's violet ones. "Which is exactly why you need us. All of us."

I move to stand beside my brother, feeling the familiar sync of our power. "We're stronger together." I hold her gaze, willing her to understand what we're really saying. "You're stronger with us."

The silence that follows feels heavy with meaning. Her shadows swirl around her in patterns that mirror the emotion I can see building in her eyes.

"You'd really walk into a corrupted shadow realm? Risk everything just to..." she trails off, like she can't quite believe we're all still here.

"Because you're family," Finn says simply, all traces of humor gone. "And family doesn't let family face ancient evil alone. It's like, rule number one."

Something in Kaia's expression softens then, making her shadows dance. The sight does something strange to my ribs, makes my fire rune pulse with a warmth that has nothing to do with power.

"I just want you all to be sure," she says quietly. "Once we cross over..."

"Save the noble sacrifice speech for after we survive," I cut her off, but I can't help smiling. "Now, can we get this apocalyptic field trip started before Malrik's frown becomes permanent?"

"Final equipment check," Malrik announces, all business despite the way his silver eyes keep darting to Kaia.

That's when we see it, Walter bobbing peacefully near the portal's edge. Unlike the other shadows that pulse with nervous energy, Bob maintaining a perimeter while the others dart between us - this one seems utterly unconcerned with the tension around it. Walter doesn't just observe—he studies. Like he already knows what we're walking into.

"Walter?" Kaia breathes. "How did you get here?"

The tiny shadow does a lazy flip in response, somehow managing to look both innocent and pleased with itself.

"He probably knew we'd need him," I say, watching as the little shadow drifts closer to investigate my boots.

Walter bobs in what might be agreement before floating up to eye level, regarding me with what I swear is curiosity. Despite myself, I feel my lips twitch into a smile. There's something endearing about the little guy.

"Two minutes," Malrik calls out. The portal's hum deepens, making my bones vibrate. "Remember, we stay together. No heroics."

That last bit seems directed at me, which is rich coming from the guy who basically volunteered us for this suicide mission. But before I can respond, power surges through the archway. The portal's surface ripples like black water, and something stirs in my blood.

I watch as Kaia takes a deep breath, her wings unfurling slightly as she turns to face the portal. The shadows at her feet swirl in anticipation, and I can feel my own power responding, fire coursing through my veins.

"Everyone ready?" Kaia asks, her voice steady despite the tension I can see in her shoulders.

"Always," I reply, stepping closer to her side. Our eyes meet, and for a moment, the world narrows to just us. The fire in my blood surges, not with the familiar heat of battle, but with something warmer, more protective. The moment stretches, charged with unspoken words, until Finn clears his throat.

"As touching as this pre-battle bonding is," he says, "we should probably get moving before the portal destabilizes or something equally dramatic happens."

Kaia nods, breaking our gaze. "Right. Let's do this."

The moment we step through the archway, Absentia slams into me like a physical force. The corruption in the air is thick, heavy, clinging to my skin like oil. An unfamiliar ache blooms in my chest—not pain exactly, but a hollow warmth that demands attention. I try to ignore it, focusing on the wrongness that permeates this place.

"Everyone alright?" Malrik calls, his voice tight. I notice him press a hand to his chest, just for a moment.

Before anyone can answer, my blood ignites. The fire rune on my chest blazes like it's trying to consume me from the inside—but beneath the burn is a new kind of ache, hollow and magnetic, like gravity bent around Kaia. Beside me, Aspen staggers, his water rune flaring bright enough to cast eerie blue shadows across the jagged landscape.

"What's happening?" he grits out, frost spreading from his feet in patterns like lightning. The burning spreads through my veins like molten metal, my muscles straining against my clothes. Everything sharpens—sounds, smells, the pulse of wrongness in the air.

I glance at Aspen and see the change taking him too. His lean frame expanding, shoulders broadening as ice crystals dance across his skin. My shirt tears as another wave hits, power flooding my system. The fire in my blood roars for release, for battle.

"Berserkers," Malrik breathes, his silver eyes wide. "Impossible. They were meant to be extinct."

I try to respond but my voice comes out as a growl, deeper and rougher than before. Through our twin-bond, I feel Aspen's own transformation. Ice where I'm fire, but the same primal force reshaping us both.

The ache in my chest intensifies, and I find myself taking an unconscious step toward Kaia. Each movement away from her feels wrong somehow. I notice Aspen drifting closer too, like we're caught in her orbit. Even Finn and Malrik seem to be circling nearer, though they might not realize it.

"Fascinating," Finn says, but his usual humor sounds strained. He's rubbing his chest absently. "I'm guessing this isn't part of the normal realm-hopping experience?"

The corruption of Absentia presses in, thick and wrong. But beneath it, something deeper stirs—a calling that thrums through blood and bond alike. And Kaia... Kaia is the center of it all.

Chapter 9
KAIA

I should be panicking.

We just crossed into a corrupted death realm. The sky is bleeding colors I don't have names for. And the twins? They've morphed into actual berserkers—giants wreathed in fire and frost like something out of a half-remembered nightmare.

But instead of panicking, I'm... staring.

Torric's entire body radiates heat, his skin glowing like forged steel. Aspen's covered in frost that doesn't melt, his eyes edged in ice and fixed on me like I'm the only thing tethering him to reality. Every part of me knows I should look away. I don't.

"So," I say, because silence is worse and my brain is fried. "This is new."

"Berserkers," Malrik says, his voice tight with disbelief. "My father spoke of them, but they were supposed to be extinct. Warriors touched by primal magic, bound to—" He cuts off abruptly, pressing a hand to his chest.

I feel it too, a strange ache that pulses in time with my heartbeat. My shadows coil closer, responding to my unease. Bob takes up a defensive position while Patricia frantically documents the twins' transformation in her swirling script.

"We need to move," Malrik says, already starting forward. "My ancestral home is east. The wards there might still hold, give us somewhere safe to figure this out."

We fall into step behind him, picking our way across terrain that looks like black glass shattered and poorly pieced back together. The sky, if you can call it that, writhes with colors that shouldn't exist, casting sickly light across the jagged landscape. Every surface pulses with corruption, a tangible wrongness that makes my shadows shudder.

"Anyone else feel like their heart's trying to learn interpretive dance?" Finn asks as we walk, grimacing and rubbing his chest.

A growl that might be agreement rumbles from Torric. The sound sends vibrations through the ground, making my wings spread instinctively. Both twins' attention snaps to me immediately, their transformed faces turning with unsettling synchronization.

I try not to stare as we walk, but it's impossible. Torric's transformation slowly recedes, flames sinking beneath his skin but leaving him... different. His eyes still burn gold, his movements more predatory. He's like a living forge, contained but still blazing hot.

And Aspen... God, Aspen with frost still glittering in his hair, blue eyes rimmed with ice. His skin catches light differently, like there's something crystalline beneath the surface. Every time he looks at me, my stomach drops like I'm in freefall.

"Your face is doing the thing again," Finn stage-whispers beside me.

"What thing?" I hiss back, grateful for the distraction.

"The 'I'm totally not checking out the twins' thing. Don't worry, it's adorable."

Heat crawls up my neck. "I have no idea what you're talking about," I mutter, which only makes his grin widen.

Before I can defend myself, something screams in the distance, a sound that should not exist in any realm. My shadows snap to attention, Bob herding the others into defensive formations while Patricia's notes become increasingly urgent.

"We should make camp," Malrik says as darkness creeps across the broken landscape. "The nights here are... dangerous."

We find a relatively defensible spot between two massive rock formations. As everyone settles in, I notice Walter hovering near a twisted flower—if you can call it that. The bloom looks more like a wound in reality, its petals black and weeping. But as Walter bobs closer, something extraordinary happens. Where his gentle presence touches the flower, color bleeds back in. The corruption recedes like ice melting in sunlight, leaving behind a perfect white bloom.

My shadows freeze their various activities to watch. The flower holds its restored form for several seconds before crumbling to ash, but Walter seems undeterred. He's already drifting toward another corrupted plant.

The reaction from my other shadows is immediate and chaotic. They surge forward en masse, attempting to replicate Walter's cleansing. Bob tries to organize them into efficient cleaning squadrons while Patricia takes frantic notes on their attempts. Even Finnick joins in, though his efforts are more enthusiastic than effective.

"Should we tell them it's not working?" Finn asks, watching as my shadows discover that any corruption they manage to temporarily clear simply seeps back in moments later.

"Let them try," I say softly, understanding their need to help, to fix what's broken. "Sometimes hope is worth a little disappointment."

The twins, now almost back to normal size though still thrumming with primal energy, move closer to our makeshift camp. The ache in my chest pulses differently for each of them. With the twins, it's a steady throb, like a warrior's drumbeat calling me to battle. When Finn moves closer, it shifts to something quicker, chaotic but somehow playful. And Malrik... with him it's a deep resonance that seems to echo through my very bones.

"Well," I sigh, watching my shadows continue their determined but futile cleaning attempts, "at least we won't be bored while we wait to die horribly."

"That's the spirit," Finn grins, though it looks strained. "Always look on the bright side of certain doom."

As night settles over this twisted landscape, we huddle closer around a small campfire. The flames cast eerie shadows that dance and writhe, almost indistinguishable from my own restless companions. Even the fire itself feels wrong here, the colors off, the warmth barely reaching my skin.

Torric tears into his portion of food with gusto, still radiating heat from his transformation. "You know," he says between bites, "I always thought being a berserker would involve more, I don't know, berserking. Less weird heart stuff."

Aspen nods, absently rubbing his chest. A fine layer of frost still coats his fingertips. "It's like... a drum. But inside. Does anyone else feel that?"

We all nod, and I notice how we've unconsciously arranged ourselves in a tight circle, with me at the center. Malrik sits to my right, his silver eyes reflecting the firelight as he scans the darkness beyond our camp. Finn's on my left, his usual grin a bit strained as he fidgets with a coin, making it dance between his fingers. The twins have positioned themselves directly across from me, their larger frames like a living wall between us and whatever lurks in the shadows.

"Maybe it's this place," I suggest, trying to ignore how my heart seems to skip a beat every time I catch Aspen or Torric's eye. "Everything here feels... wrong. Like reality is coming apart at the seams."

Malrik shifts beside me. "That's because it is."

Everyone turns to him. His silver eyes are distant, haunted. "Absentia was never meant to be what it became. It was supposed to be a realm between realms—a bridge between life and death." He exhales, his breath misting despite the lack of cold. "But it was corrupted, twisted into something else. A prison for things that couldn't be contained elsewhere. And now the corruption isn't just spreading, it's trying to break what little balance remains."

Something twists in my chest. Not fear. Not exactly. But a pull, like my magic is trying to respond to the mention of balance, like it recognizes something in his words that I don't yet understand.

Aspen watches Malrik carefully. "And what about berserkers?"

Malrik glances between the twins, his expression unreadable. "Berserkers were warriors that walked the edge of balance. Too much rage, and they burned themselves out. Too much control, and their power faded. They needed purpose, something to anchor them. Without it, the magic consumed them." He looks down at his hands. "It always consumes."

A chill runs through me. My shadows stir, restless. They don't like this place.

Torric frowns. "So what are we supposed to do? Just keep walking and hope we don't burn out?"

Malrik looks at me. "Maybe that depends on Kaia."

I stiffen. "Why me?"

He gestures toward my shadows, how they move differently here. Slower. Sharper. Watching.

"They're reacting to this place. Not just to protect you, but because something in Absentia is... responding to you."

I swallow hard. "That's not ominous at all."

Before anyone can say more, the fire sputters and dims.

Finn swears, rubbing his arms. "Why is it colder all of a sudden?"

Aspen's breath mists. "It's not just the fire. The whole area just shifted."

The air presses heavier. My magic coils inside me, twisting in warning as my shadows freeze in place. Something is watching us from beyond the firelight.

Malrik's expression has gone eerily still, his silver eyes fixed on the darkness beyond our camp. "We're not alone," he murmurs.

For a long moment, no one speaks. Then Finn stretches his arms overhead, feigning nonchalance. "Well, whatever it is, let's hope it has bad vision, 'cause I'm calling it a night."

Torric huffs but rises to his feet, shaking out his shoulders like a predator shedding tension. "We set watches?"

"Obviously," Malrik replies, still scanning the distance. "I'll take first."

None of us actually sleeps, though we pretend to. We arrange ourselves in shifts, weapons within reach, eyes only half-closed. Even Torric, who could normally sleep through a battle, keeps twitching at every sound. My shadows maintain a constant perimeter, Bob directing them with silent efficiency.

I lie down, wings curled tight against my back, but I'm hyperaware of every shift in the darkness. The weight of this place, of the watching presence, makes true rest impossible. We're all just waiting, coiled and ready.

Aspen catches my eye from across the fire. His expression says what we're all thinking: whatever's out there isn't going to wait forever.

I get up after an hour of this farce, moving to stand beside Malrik. He doesn't seem surprised.

"You should sleep," he murmurs, not looking at me.

"I can't."

He glances down then, his gaze flickering with something unreadable. "I didn't think you would."

We stand there for a while, side by side, watching the writhing sky above us. The silence between us isn't uncomfortable, it's charged.

"You knew about berserkers," I say finally. "What else do you know about this place?"

Malrik exhales, rubbing a hand down his face. "More than I'd like."

"Tell me."

His lips twitch, but there's no humor in it. "The thing about Absentia is... it doesn't just corrupt. It adapts. It remembers. And if it knows you don't belong, it makes you belong."

I shiver. "That's what this ache is, isn't it?" I press a hand to my chest. "Like it's trying to change us."

Malrik watches me, his gaze dipping briefly to where my fingers press against my skin. Then, slowly, deliberately, he reaches out and rests his palm over my hand.

The moment he touches me, the ache shifts. It's still there, but different, like my magic is stretching toward him, trying to align itself with his.

I inhale sharply. His fingers are warm against mine. His presence steadies me, like an anchor against whatever's happening in this realm.

"Kaia," he murmurs, voice rougher than before.

When I look up at him, I see it—the hesitation, the war between logic and something deeper. Something undeniable.

I don't think. I don't second-guess. I just rise onto my toes, closing the distance between us.

He meets me halfway.

The kiss is slow, not hesitant, just careful. Like he's testing the feel of me in this realm, the shape of this moment. His fingers tighten over mine, then shift, trailing up my arm as he cups my face.

I press closer. His breath hitches. Something in his magic, something deep and ancient, pulls at mine, like a thread being drawn between us.

Then the air around us shudders.

The moment breaks.

Malrik pulls back first, his expression unreadable. But I can feel it, the change in the air, the watching presence pressing closer.

I turn my head, pulse thundering. The fire is still burning, but it feels smaller. The silence around us isn't normal anymore. It's waiting.

I swallow hard.

"Malrik..."

He's already staring into the darkness beyond our camp, every muscle in his body tensed.

"I know."

The darkness beyond our camp writhes, moving in ways shadow shouldn't.

Something is here.

Chapter 10
FINN

I'm pretty sure watching the person you're falling for kiss someone else you're also falling for isn't covered in any self-help books. Then again, maybe I just haven't found the right section: "So You're In Love With A Shadow Queen And A Brooding Prince - Now What?"

From my poorly chosen vantage of fake-sleeping, I watch Malrik kiss Kaia through barely open eyes. Something sharp twists beneath my ribs, not quite pain and not quite longing—more like hunger with teeth. My usual jokes feel stuck somewhere between my lungs and throat, which is probably for the best. Even I can read a room. Usually. Sometimes.

Bob—bless his tiny militant heart—seems torn between approved surveillance and respectful privacy. He settles for what I swear is an embarrassed shuffle before resuming his patrol. Patricia's shadow-notes have taken on a distinctly romantic novel quality, while Finnick appears to be practicing what looks suspiciously like wedding choreography.

Traitors, all of them.

But before I can properly wallow in the irony of my favorite shadows betraying me for the cause of true love, something shifts in the air. The wrongness that's been hovering at the edges of my awareness since we entered this realm suddenly sharpens, like reality itself is holding its breath.

Malrik pulls back from Kaia first, his expression cracking open with a loss that hits me harder than I expect. I know that look. I've felt it every time I've wanted to reach for either of them and stopped myself.

"I know," Malrik says quietly, and for a moment I think he's talking to me before I realize he's responding to something Kaia said.

Then I see it: the darkness beyond our camp isn't moving. It's hunting.

I'm on my feet before I make the conscious decision to move, my usual grin falling away as chaos magic crackles between my fingers. "Not to interrupt the romantic tension," I say, because apparently I physically cannot help myself, "but I think we have company."

The twins snap awake instantly, their transformations already rippling beneath their skin. Torric's shoulders broaden as flames lick along his arms, while frost crystallizes in Aspen's hair. The way they move in perfect sync would be fascinating if I wasn't busy trying not to die.

"You know," I add as shapes begin to emerge from the writhing darkness, "when I said I wanted more excitement in my life, this really wasn't what I had in mind."

Bob snaps into full general mode, coordinating the other shadows into battle formations with military precision. Walter just drifts through the camp like he doesn't have a care in the world. And who knows, maybe he doesn't.

The first creature that steps into the firelight looks like someone tried to sculpt a nightmare out of liquid darkness and gave up halfway through. Its form shifts constantly, as if it can't decide what shape horror should take.

"Well," I manage, "that's delightfully terrifying."

More emerge behind it, each one worse than the last. Their eyes—if you can call them that—fix on Kaia with hungry intensity.

The ache in my chest flares. I move without thinking, placing myself between her and the creatures. Malrik does the same, his silver eyes gleaming with deadly purpose.

"Any chance they're just looking for directions?" I ask, but my voice has lost its usual lightness. The pull toward Kaia is almost painful now, matched only by my need to reach for Malrik.

The creatures surge forward as one, and chaos erupts.

Magic explodes from my hands in wild bursts of color, each blast tearing through the creatures' liquid forms. But they reform almost instantly, like oil flowing back together. The twins are magnificent in their fury—Torric's flames carving paths through darkness while Aspen's ice traps the creatures in crystalline prisons that shatter and reform.

"Is anyone else getting tired of these guys not staying dead?" I call out, ducking under what might be a claw or a tentacle—honestly, their anatomy is questionable at best.

Kaia's wings flare with brilliant light as she takes to the air, her shadows moving like a coordinated army beneath her. Bob's leading the charge with military precision while Patricia appears to be documenting enemy weaknesses. Even Finnick has abandoned his usual chaos in favor of synchronized attack patterns. Carl and Steve surround one of the creatures while Linda tries her best to distract it.

But Walter... Walter just drifts through it all, touching corrupted ground that briefly blazes with cleansing light before the darkness seeps back in. The corruption retreats wherever he passes, but only for moments—like he's testing the boundaries of something larger than himself.

A creature lunges for Kaia, and my heart lodges somewhere in my throat. Malrik's shadows surge up, tangling with the beast while I blast it with enough chaos magic to level a small building. The thing screams—a sound that should not exist in any realm—and dissolves.

For half a second, I think we might actually survive this.

Then I see it—the way the corruption seems to pulse beneath the ground, reaching for Kaia like hungry veins. My warning dies in my throat as one of the shadow creatures clips her wing.

She falls.

The world stops.

I'm moving before I register the decision, chaos magic exploding from me with more power than I knew I possessed. Malrik reaches her first, catching her before she hits the ground. The look on his face—gods, I never want to see that expression again. Not on him. Not for her.

"No, no, no," I mutter, dropping to my knees beside them. Black veins are already spreading across her skin, corruption seeping into her like poison. Her shadows are frantic—Bob trying to organize a defense while Patricia's notes become increasingly desperate. Finnick darts between us all, his usual playful energy transformed into panicked movement.

"We need to—" Malrik starts, but a roar cuts him off.

The sound shakes the very air, and for a moment, I think another creature is about to end us all. But this is different. This feels... ancient. Powerful. Wrong.

A figure drops from the writhing sky, his landing cracking the corrupted ground. A wave of energy pulses outward like Walter's touch but magnified a thousandfold, making the creatures scatter into the darkness as if fleeing something they recognize as deadlier than themselves.

The stranger rises slowly, and there's something about his movements that feels wrong—too fluid, too precise, like he's having to remember how limbs should work. His eyes catch the firelight in a way that human eyes shouldn't, reflecting gold for just a moment before settling into a more natural shade.

Then he sees Kaia.

The change that comes over him steals my breath—not because of what he does, but because of what he doesn't do. He goes completely still, the kind of stillness that belongs to predators and ancient things. The power rolling off him stutters, like a heart skipping a beat. When he looks at her, his expression cracks open with something so raw and complicated that I have to look away.

"I'm here," he says, and his voice carries like harmonics that make my teeth ache. "You're safe now, little star."

The corruption in her veins seems to pause its spread at his presence, or maybe it's responding to the strange energy rolling off him in waves.

"Who—" I start to ask, but Malrik's sharp intake of breath stops me.

"Kieran," he breathes, and there's something in his voice I've never heard before. "The Dragon of the Void."

Oh, I think hysterically as Kieran kneels beside us, that's just perfect. Because we definitely needed to add whatever the void this is to our mess.

But the way he touches her—gentle, reverent, like he's remembering how to handle something breakable—kills the quip on my tongue. His hands glow with light that pulses like breath, like something alive and ancient, not quite light, not quite shadow. There's a story here, written in the tension of his shoulders and the way his hands shake slightly despite their steady glow.

I look at Malrik, finding my own confusion mirrored in his silver eyes. The ache in my chest pulses, drawing me toward both him and Kaia even as this newcomer changes everything.

Well, I think as Kieran begins working magic I've never seen before, at least life's never boring.

Chapter 11
KIERAN

I feel her before I see her. The pull is visceral, a hook beneath my ribs that's been empty for centuries suddenly filled again. When I land, the corrupted ground cracks beneath my feet, power rolling off me in waves that send the shadow creatures scattering. They remember what I am, even if she doesn't.

Little star.

The sight of her steals the breath I don't need. She's grown so much, but something in her face still echoes the child I knew—the same determined set of her jaw even in unconsciousness. Her wings, gods, her wings, shimmer between shadow and light, so similar to how Solveig's did. The corruption spreading across her skin makes my ancient heart stutter.

"I'm here," I manage, though the words feel clumsy in this form. "You're safe now, little star."

Malrik's sharp intake of breath draws my attention. He's grown too, no longer the solemn child who used to pepper me with questions about Absentia's history. The corruption that drove him from his realm has left its mark—not on his body, but in the silver of his eyes—no longer the questioning gaze of a boy, but the blade-edge of a man who's lost too much.

"Kieran," he breathes. "The Dragon of the Void."

The chaos mage beside him radiates wild, unstable power—energy that crackles like a storm barely contained. But there's something in his gaze when he looks at Kaia, something that makes the ancient thing inside me stir with both approval and warning.

Shadows cluster close to her, moving with military precision, far too organized for shadow constructs. There's something in their movements, in the way they orbit her, that echoes a kind of discipline I haven't seen in centuries. One directs the others like a commander. Another scribes strange symbols in the air—shadowy script, new and unknown, but deliberate. It feels like the beginning of a language born from darkness itself.

"The corruption's spreading fast," I say, pushing back centuries of memory. "We need to get her to the sanctuary."

"You have a sanctuary in this realm?" one of the berserker twins asks, flame wreathing his form while his brother watches with frost in his hair. Neither of which should be possible.

"I have many things in this realm." The corruption recoils from my touch, but not fast enough. Another shadow forms, this one carrying the essence of a healer I once knew. "Including ways to slow this poison."

The strange wisp that's been drifting through the corruption pauses near us, its touch leaving brief flares of cleansing light. Something about its power feels familiar, though I can't place why. It hovers near Kaia's head, almost like it's trying to comfort her.

"We need to move," Malrik says, and I notice he hasn't let go of her hand. The realization hits me like ice water, the possessive way he holds her, the tender concern in his silver eyes.

No. This cannot be.

Ancient instinct flares, fierce and territorial. She is mine. The thought rises unbidden, primal and absolute. The dragon within me stirs, threatening to shatter this human form I wear. I force it down, but the rage lingers, cold and sharp beneath my skin.

I gather her into my arms carefully, her wings folding naturally against my chest. The chaos mage moves closer, his face fierce. Something in his protective stance, the desperate worry in his eyes, triggers another wave of cold fury. His gaze lingers on her face with unmistakable devotion.

Two of them? The dragon rumbles beneath my skin, demanding retribution.

The twins flank us, their power humming just beneath their skin.

As we move through the corrupted landscape, something extraordinary happens. New shadows begin to form around her, pulling themselves from the very fabric of this realm. They coalesce slowly, each one distinct. More shadows find their way to her as we continue on, each one a soul I thought lost forever.

I hold her close and try not to think about the last time I saw her, or the night everything changed, when Solveig's desperate magic tore through time itself. The night I failed to protect them both. Solveig died for this future, and yet—watching Kaia fade beneath the same sky—I wonder if we were ever meant to win.

Not this time, I promise silently as another shadow joins her growing legion. This time will be different.

But the way Malrik and the chaos mage move in perfect sync beside me, their concern for her evident in every step, it makes my blood run cold. They move like extensions of one another, both orbiting her even as she lies unconscious in my arms. It is more than friendship or loyalty. The looks they exchange, the way they position themselves, they both claim her in their own way.

The dragon's rage builds. *Mine.* The word pulses with each step.

The sanctuary can't come soon enough.

"Are we there yet?" the chaos mage groans, breaking the silence. "Because if we have to keep trekking through this nightmare wasteland much longer, I might start questioning my life choices."

I don't respond. His magic is wild, unpredictable, but his concern for Kaia is real. I can feel it in the way his energy shifts every time she makes the faintest sound.

"You already question your life choices," Malrik mutters, adjusting his grip on Kaia's hand. He hasn't let go of her since we started moving. The possessiveness of the gesture makes my jaw clench.

The chaos mage flashes a grin, though it doesn't quite reach his eyes. "Fair point. But seriously, any glowing gates, magic doorways, dramatic beams of light ahead? Or are we just walking until our legs give out?"

"Not much farther," I say. The words carry more weight than just distance.

Malrik exhales, his silver eyes flicking toward me. "How bad has it gotten?"

I shift Kaia's weight, ensuring her wings remain tucked safely against her back. "Worse. The corruption spreads faster than it should. The wards hold, but they weaken every time I pull from Absentia."

Malrik nods grimly. "Same as before, then."

"Not exactly." I glance at the growing shadows forming around Kaia, following us like silent sentinels. "The souls are moving toward her. Not just fallen warriors—lost ones. That has to mean something."

The chaos mage scoffs. "Still waiting for someone to explain that one to me."

"It's complicated," Malrik says, his voice tight. "But if they're returning, it means she's more than just a Valkyrie."

"Yeah, I figured that much when she sprouted wings and ruined someone's sense of balance." The chaos mage gestures vaguely. "But, y'know, details would be great."

I don't answer. The path ahead shifts, the air lighter, the corruption thinning. The sanctuary's magic hums beneath my skin, calling me forward.

Malrik's grip on Kaia tightens. "And once we're inside? How do we fix this?"

I exhale, the weight of centuries pressing down on me. "We find out why this is happening now. And then..." My eyes drop to Kaia's unconscious face. "We see if she remembers."

Malrik and Finn exchange a look, but before they can push further, the air shifts again. The shadows ahead flicker, and then, finally, the sanctuary appears, its crystalline structures gleaming against the corruption that surrounds it. As we approach, more shadows pull free from the realm to join us, each one carrying memories that make my chest ache.

Revna meets us at the barrier, her phoenix fire casting warm light across the corrupted ground. Her eyes widen at the sight of Kaia's wings, understanding dawning in their amber depths.

"The Heart calls them," she says softly as another shadow forms. "Just like before, when the balance started to shift."

Corruption pulses darker beneath her skin. A growl builds in my throat. "We need to get her inside. Now."

As we pass through the wards, the whispers begin. Survivors emerge from their homes—shifters, mages, souls I've gathered from across the realms. They line the crystal-lit streets, their voices carrying centuries of hope.

"The Valkyrie returns," someone breathes, and the words ripple through the crowd like wind through leaves. "She's come back to us."

More shadows form with each step toward the castle, drawn by her presence and the murmured prayers of the watching crowd. Each one feels like a memory given form, warriors I watched fall, healers who gave their last breath, guardians who held the line until the very end.

The chaos mage moves closer, his wild magic settling into something protective. His fingers brush against her wing, a gesture so familiar it makes my vision flash gold with rage. "Not that this isn't impressively dramatic," he says, "but she's getting worse."

He's right. The corruption spreads faster now, black veins creeping up her neck despite my attempts to slow them. Her wings shudder with each labored breath, and the shadows surrounding her ripple with shared distress.

"Almost there," I promise, though I'm not sure if I'm reassuring her or myself. I remember the old phrase, the one Solveig used to whisper when the world still made sense: when shadow and light become one, the gates shall remember their purpose.

Malrik's expression darkens as we climb the castle steps. "I grew up here," he says softly. "Before the corruption—before everything twisted—it was the most beautiful place I'd ever known."

"It will be again." The words carry more weight than I intend. Another shadow forms, this one bearing the essence of a guardian I lost in the first wave of corruption. "If we succeed."

Finn looks between us. "Anyone want to share with the rest of the class what exactly is going on here?"

But before I can answer, Kaia's wings flare with sudden light. The corruption recoils as more shadows surge into being around her—dozens now, each one carrying a piece of what was lost. The crowd below gasps in wonder, and I feel the ancient magic stirring beneath our feet.

For the first time in centuries, I dare to hope.

"Get her inside," Revna orders, her phoenix fire already blazing. "I'll hold the barriers."

As we carry her through the castle doors, I try not to think about how many times I've seen hope crumble in the face of corruption. But watching these shadows... her shadows move in perfect unity, seeing the way even the strange drifting wisp seems drawn to her light...

Maybe this time will be different.

It has to be.

The fate of all realms depends on it.

Chapter 12
MALRIK

The castle's halls echo with whispered prayers, but all I can hear is Kaia's labored breathing. Black veins spread across her skin like spiderwebs, and my chest tightens at their familiar pattern. I've seen this before, not just when it started creeping across her skin at the academy, but years ago, watching it consume my father. The memory hits harder now that I understand what it was, what it meant.

I won't let her be taken. Not like the corruption took them from me.

My fingers tighten around Kaia's hand as we follow Kieran deeper into the sanctuary. Each step stirs memories I've spent years burying, running these halls as a child, hiding in alcoves I once thought were secret, trailing my fingers along walls that seemed to pulse with life. Before the corruption drove us out. Before everything changed.

"The healing chambers are ahead," Kieran says, his ancient power rolling off him in waves.

"Through the crystal archway," I finish quietly. His sharp look makes me add: "I remember."

"When you said you were from another realm," Finn says beside me, his usual playful tone tight with worry, "I pictured something less dramatic." His shoulder brushes mine as we walk, a casual touch that sends warmth through my chest despite everything—and I hate how much I need it.

"Everything about him is dramatic," Torric mutters behind us. "You've seen his wardrobe."

I ignore them both, too focused on the way Kaia's wings shudder with each breath. Her shadows ripple with shared distress, both the ones I've grown familiar with and new ones still gathering around her. Bob maintains a careful perimeter while Patricia's frantic documentation feels more desperate than usual.

We pass the great hall where I once sat at my father's feet during council meetings, pretending to understand politics while secretly counting the crystals embedded in the ceiling. The room where my mother taught me to dance, her laughter echoing off walls that no longer gleam. The corridor where I first learned to manipulate shadows, my father's patient guidance making the darkness feel like an extension of myself.

The healing chamber glows with soft golden light when we enter, crystals humming with ancient magic. More shadows appear as we cross the threshold, drawn to Kaia's presence from all corners of the sanctuary.

"Put her here," Kieran instructs, laying Kaia on a crystal bed that pulses with healing energy. Her wings settle naturally against the smooth surface, and I have to force myself to let go of her hand.

"The corruption's spreading faster," Aspen observes, frost forming in his hair as he studies the black veins. "Like it's trying to reach something."

"The Heart," Kieran confirms grimly. "It wants the Heart of Eternity. And it knows she's the tether."

My throat tightens as another memory hits—my mother's voice, urgent and breaking, as she pushed me through a portal. "The Heart must be protected," she'd said. "No matter the cost." Then the portal closed, and she was gone.

A warm hand settles on my shoulder, surprising me. Finn stands closer than I expected, his usual mischief replaced by quiet understanding. "Hey," he says softly. "We're not losing her."

The certainty in his voice makes something in my chest ache. Before I can respond, Kaia's wings flare with sudden light. The corruption recoils as more shadows gather around her, dozens now, drawn from every corner of the sanctuary. Their movements are purposeful, coordinated, like an army remembering its strength.

"It's happening again," I breathe, watching the shadows gather around her. "Just like when my father—" I stop, the words catching in my throat. "When he disappeared."

Kieran's ancient eyes fix on me. "Your father understood, at the end. Before he vanished. Why the corruption wanted Absentia." His gaze drops to Kaia's unconscious form. "She's not just connected to this place. She's bound to it, just as you are."

"Great," Finn says, though his hand hasn't left my shoulder. "No pressure or anything. Just realm-saving destiny and ancient evil. Totally normal Tuesday."

A laugh threatens to break free despite everything. Trust Finn to find humor even now. The corruption pulses darker across Kaia's skin, but before we can act, a familiar wisp of shadow approaches.

Walter settles over one of the black veins, his strange, ethereal form pulsing soft gold where he touches her skin. For once, he's focused—no drifting or chaos, just stillness and light. The sight is unexpected, this strange shadow, usually so detached from everything, now focused entirely on healing.

More shadows surge forward, not chaotically, but in perfect formation. Bob directs them with military precision as they line up, each one touching a different spot where corruption threatens to spread. Patricia's normally frantic note-taking pauses as she joins them, her shadowy form pulsing with gentle light. Even Finnick's chaos stills into something deliberate and focused.

"They're working together," Kieran says softly, ancient eyes tracking their movements. "Different types of shadows, with different sources, somehow united in purpose."

One by one, more shadows come forward, some I recognize from my years in Absentia, others completely new. These others gathering now—new, unfamiliar—seem drawn not by duty, but by something deeper. Recognition. Belonging. Each one adds their light to Walter's, creating a barrier between Kaia and the corruption trying to claim her.

"This is how it starts," I breathe, watching their coordinated effort. "Not just finding them, but bringing them together."

Finn's hand squeezes my shoulder gently. "Leave it to Kaia to turn an army of Valkyrie shadows into a really efficient nursing staff."

Kieran's head snaps up, his ancient eyes suddenly fixed on Finn with unsettling intensity. "What did you just say?"

"Valkyrie shadows," Finn repeats, looking confused at Kieran's reaction. "At least, the original ones are, Bob, Patricia, Finnick, and the others. They're the souls of fallen Valkyrie warriors who bound themselves to Kaia centuries ago. But these new ones gathering here in Absentia, we don't know what they are yet."

A strange stillness comes over Kieran. For a moment, he looks almost shaken. "How do you know this?"

"Kaia told us," I say, watching his reaction carefully. "When her wings first manifested. Her original shadows, the ones she's had since the beginning, are her mother's sisters-in-arms. They chose to bind themselves to her through the Heart of Eternity. These others gathering now seem different, but they're responding to her just the same."

Kieran's gaze returns to Kaia, something complicated and ancient in his expression. "Solveig's sisters," he murmurs, so quietly I almost don't catch it. "They survived after all."

The information seems to transform something in Kieran's approach as he returns his attention to the corruption. His movements become more deliberate, more certain, as if a missing piece has finally fallen into place.

This is more than just healing, it's proof of something I think we've all felt since meeting her. Kaia doesn't just gather people around her; she gives them purpose, makes them stronger together than they ever were alone.

The corruption retreats slowly, unable to break through the unified barrier of shadow and light. It's not a cure, but it's hope. And watching the shadows work in perfect harmony, I finally understand what my father was fighting for before the darkness took him. What my mother sacrificed everything to preserve when she forced me through that portal.

Not just power, but possibility. The chance for something broken to become whole again.

"Stay with us," I whisper, pouring more of my own power into the ward. My shadows join the others, slipping into place as if they've always belonged. "We need you." My voice drops lower, meant only for her. "I need you."

I see it then, the slight movement of her wings, the twitch of her fingers. The shadows continue to gather, drawn to her from every corner of the sanctuary, moving with renewed purpose. Standing in this room where I once sat as a child while my father treated wounded soldiers, I can't help but wonder: what happens when they all return? What happens when the lost are finally found?

The question pulses in my mind, heavy with everything we've seen. Whatever the answer, I'll be there to face it, with her, with Finn, with all of them.

This time, no one gets left behind.

Chapter 13
KAIA

Consciousness returns in fragments, like trying to piece together a shattered mirror. Each shard reflects something different—echoes of feelings, scattered sensations, fractured memories I can't quite grasp. The wrongness running through my body has subsided, thank the void. I thought it was going to kill me.

The first thing I notice, before I even open my eyes, is Mouse pressed against my side, his familiar warmth grounding me. Something washes over me in gentle waves—healing magic maybe, though it feels different than anything I've experienced before. With my eyes still closed, I sense my shadows nearby, their presence stronger than I remember, more tangible somehow. And there are... others? New shadows I don't recognize, their energy hovering at the edges of my awareness, cool and curious against my consciousness.

When I finally force my heavy lids open, I freeze. A man stands nearby—but no, not a stranger. Something about him tugs at me, an invisible thread pulling so hard it steals my breath. Something in his face holds me there, breathless. The pain in my chest builds until it's almost unbearable.

"You're safe," he says softly, and his voice sends fresh waves of agony through me. It's deep and resonant, like the low hum of a distant storm, with an accent I can't place—something that doesn't belong to any realm I know.

My throat locks up when I try to speak. My gaze darts around the unfamiliar room—Malrik stands close, his silver eyes intense with barely contained emotion. Finn hovers near him, his usual grin replaced by genuine concern. The twins maintain a protective stance nearby. But my eyes keep being pulled back to the stranger, like a compass finding true north.

"Why..." I manage finally, my voice cracking. "Why does it feel like I know you?"

Something flickers across his face—an emotion too complex to name. It lands in my chest like recognition that hasn't caught up to memory. The ache in my chest pulses harder.

"Your heart remembers," he says carefully, "even if your mind doesn't yet."

I try to sit up, but my body feels heavy, wrong. Malrik moves instantly to help, his hand steady on my back. Finn appears on my other side, and something about having them both near makes breathing easier.

"Where are we?" I ask, finally taking in the strange room around us. Magic hums in the air, ancient and powerful.

"Somewhere safe," the stranger says. "A sanctuary, hidden from the corruption."

"Hidden isn't the same as protected," Malrik adds quietly, his hand still warm against my back. "The barriers won't hold forever."

"Nothing holds forever," the stranger agrees, and something about the way he says it makes my chest ache sharper. "But they'll hold long enough."

"Long enough for what?" Finn asks, his usual lightness gone.

The stranger's ancient eyes meet mine again, and the pain nearly doubles me over. "Long enough for you to understand what's happening."

"And if I don't want to understand?" The words slip out before I can stop them.

"Some choices," he says gently, "aren't really choices at all."

Not a fan of that.

The pain in my chest spikes again, but this time it's different—not just from looking at him, but from something darker trying to take hold. The wrongness that was in my body earlier pulses once, sharp and cold.

"It's fighting back," the stranger says grimly. "The corruption doesn't want to let go."

"Well," Finn says, his hand finding mine, "that's not ominous at all."

Malrik's grip tightens on my other side, and for a moment, I let myself lean into their strength. Whatever's coming, whatever this all means, at least I'm not facing it alone.

Even if it feels like my heart might shatter every time I look at the stranger with ancient eyes who says he knows me.

"Come on," Finn says, helping me stand. "Let's get you somewhere more comfortable than this creepy healing chamber."

My legs shake embarrassingly, each step slower than the last. The room spins a bit, and I have to lean heavily on Malrik and Finn.

"For void's sake," Torric growls after watching me stumble for the third time. Before I can protest, he scoops me up like I weigh nothing. "This is painful to watch."

"I can walk," I mutter, though we all know it's a lie.

"Sure you can," he says dryly. "And I'm secretly a unicorn."

Aspen's lips twitch as he holds the door. "I always wondered about that rainbow mane."

"Shut up."

The stranger—I still can't think of his name, though it feels like it's right there on the tip of my tongue—follows silently. He moves with an unnatural grace, like something not entirely human, each step deliberate and soundless. He's impossibly tall, all angles and restraint, shadows flickering in his wake like they remember him too. Power rolls off him in waves I can almost see, disturbing my shadows as he passes. Every time he gets close, that ache in my chest pulses harder.

"Second door on the left," he says quietly. His voice sends another wave of pain through me, and I feel Torric's arms tighten slightly.

The bedroom is simple but beautiful, with tall windows letting in soft light. Torric sets me on the bed with surprising gentleness.

"We'll be right outside," Malrik says, but there's a question in his silver eyes.

I nod, understanding what he's really asking. "It's okay. I... I think I need to talk to him."

Finn squeezes my hand once before following the others out. The door closes with a soft click, leaving me alone with the stranger who feels impossibly familiar.

Kieran.

His name finally surfaces, hitting me like a distant memory, like something long-buried clawing its way to the surface.

He exhales slowly, like he's felt it too. "Little star," he murmurs, and the nickname hits like a physical blow. "I've waited so long to find you again."

I swallow hard, my fingers twisting in the bedsheets. "Who... who are you to me?"

Kieran steps closer, his presence both overwhelming and comforting. His movements are measured, restrained, like he's constantly holding back something tremendous. "You are important," he says, voice thick with emotion. "I have searched for you across centuries, through time and death and forgotten realms. I've held onto the hope that one day, you would return."

My breath catches. "Why?"

His gaze darkens with something haunted. "Because you are meant to heal what was broken."

A muscle in his jaw tenses, as if he's debating whether to say more. Then, in a voice barely above a whisper, he speaks:

"You call to the shadows in ways I've never seen before. The fallen ones respond to you. The lost find their way back."

The words resonate deep inside me, something in them familiar yet untouchable. My shadows curl tighter around me, like they're whispering between themselves.

I exhale shakily. "What does it mean?"

His silence is heavy with unspoken truths.

"I don't understand," I whisper. "I'm just... I'm just Kaia."

"No," he says, taking another step closer. "You are so much more."

He looks at me like he's trying to memorize every detail, as if he still doesn't believe I'm real. "I swore I'd find you again. That I'd protect you this time. No matter the cost."

His hand lifts, but he hesitates, as if touching me would shatter whatever fragile reality this is.

And void help me... I want him to.

I want to remember why he feels like something I've lost.

Why his voice feels like home.

And why his presence makes my heart ache like an old wound I'm terrified to reopen.

Chapter 14
ASPEN

I keep my distance. Not because I want to, but because I have to. Every time I see her now, every time I hear her voice, watch her shadows curl around her like something alive, I remember what I am. What I became. The memory of it sits heavy in my chest, a stone that won't dissolve no matter how much I try to rationalize it away.

I should be with her. Holding her. Protecting her. But I can't. Not like this. Not when I still wake up feeling the muscles shifting beneath my skin, my body remembering what it became the moment we stepped into this realm. What I let happen when those creatures attacked. Not when every time I close my eyes, I imagine her blood on my hands—what could have happened if I'd lost control completely.

I exhale sharply, bracing my hands against the stone railing of the balcony. The sanctuary is quiet this late, the sky a deep, endless black, but my mind won't stop running in circles. She almost died. She almost died, and I wasn't strong enough to stop it. The thought circles, like a vulture, refusing to give me peace.

A muscle in my jaw tightens. I squeeze my eyes shut, but it doesn't stop the memories from flooding back. The way she looked at me when I changed, the flash of fear before she shoved it down, swallowed it back like she didn't want me to see. But I did. I saw everything.

I know what I am now—a berserker, a monster, a thing made for vio-lence—and I know she felt it too. She's never said it outright, never looked at me like I was something to be afraid of. But she hasn't looked at me the same since that moment when the ice in my veins turned to something older and darker.

And now... now he's here. Kieran. His presence presses against my senses even from here, dark and unshakable. He moves around her like he already owns a piece of her, like he's been waiting centuries to claim it. And maybe he has. But void help me, I can't watch it happen. Not when I already feel like I'm losing her to something I can't fight.

"You're brooding."

Torric's voice cuts through the silence, rougher than usual, strained with the same tension that's been winding him tighter since we arrived. He leans against the railing beside me, but he's not really looking at me. His golden eyes are locked on the door she's behind. He hasn't taken his eyes off it since we left her with Kieran.

"You should get some rest," I mutter, though I know it's pointless. Torric doesn't rest, not when he thinks someone might need him.

Torric lets out a humorless laugh, running a hand down his face. "I should do a lot of things."

I glance at him, taking in the rigid set of his shoulders, the way his fists clench and unclench at his sides. His entire body is wound like a wire ready to snap. I know exactly where his mind is. It hasn't left the moment she collapsed, the corruption spreading beneath her skin like poison. Or maybe even further back, to memories neither of us can escape.

I hesitate before speaking. "This isn't—"

"Don't," he snaps, cutting me off. His jaw works like he's trying to grind down the words building inside him, but they break free anyway. "Don't tell me this isn't the same. That it isn't happening all over again."

My stomach knots because I can't tell him that. Because I know exactly what he sees when he looks at her lying in that bed. Our sister, a corpse in a battlefield, a promise we made to ourselves never to fail someone like that again. The memory of it washes through me, cold and familiar.

I swallow, my grip tightening on the railing until my knuckles go white. "We didn't lose her, Torric."

"Not yet," he mutters. But his voice is raw. Fractured around the edges in ways only I would recognize.

I shake my head, trying to believe my own words. "She's still here. She's still breathing."

"And what if that changes?" He finally turns toward me, and I wish he hadn't. His golden eyes are sharp with something desperate, something unhinged beneath the surface. "What if next time, she doesn't get back up?"

Something dark claws up my throat, because that thought has been living inside me too. Because it almost happened when the corruption took her down. And no matter how many times I tell myself she's okay, the bond doesn't lie. The hollow stretch of it hasn't faded and the pain started the second she went down in that fight. It was the moment I felt something in me splinter. Something I haven't been able to fix no matter how much ice I call to numb it.

"I wasn't strong enough," I say, the words coming before I can stop them.

Torric stiffens beside me. "Aspen—"

"I wasn't." My voice is quiet, but it feels like a roar inside my head. "She was right there, and I couldn't stop it. I wasn't fast enough, wasn't strong enough, and now—" My breath shudders out of me. "Now I don't know if she even wants me around."

Torric exhales, rubbing the back of his neck. "She doesn't—" He hesitates, searching for the words. "She doesn't blame you."

Doesn't she? I don't say it out loud. I just feel it in every interaction since that moment. Every time she hesitates before looking at me, or her shadows curl toward someone else first. When she leans into Malrik, into Finn, into anyone but me. Maybe she doesn't even realize she's doing it. Maybe she does. Either way, the space between us is growing, and I don't know how to stop it.

"Doesn't matter," I say, forcing the words through the weight in my chest. "I know what I am now."

Torric watches me, silent for a long moment. Then, quietly, he says, "Is that what this is about? The berserker?"

I don't answer. I don't need to. The truth of it is written in every tense line of my body, in the frost that forms unconsciously around my fingers when I think about what happened.

He curses under his breath. "Aspen, you're not—"

"I am." My voice comes out sharper than I intend. I drag a hand down my face, suddenly exhausted by the weight of it all. "I lost control, Torric. I felt it happen. I felt something else take over, something that didn't care about anything but blood."

"I know." He exhales, raking a hand through his hair. "I did too."

His admission makes something twist inside me, something I don't want to name. Maybe we are worse than I thought. Maybe that's what Kaia sees when she looks at us now, something dangerous, something to be wary of. The thought settles like ice in my stomach.

I drop my head against the railing, letting out a slow breath that mists in the air before me. "I don't want to scare her."

Torric leans beside me, his own gaze locked on the sanctuary below. "You don't."

I don't answer, because I'm not sure if I believe him. Because I still remember the way her breath caught when she saw me change, the way her hands shook when she reached for me afterward. The memory of it burns beneath my skin.

And now she's in there with him. Kieran. The ancient one with eyes that see too much and say too little. The one who looks at her like she holds the answers to questions he's been asking for centuries. And maybe I don't deserve to be angry about that. Maybe I don't deserve to be anything at all when it comes to her.

Void help me, the berserker in my blood doesn't give a damn about what I deserve. It only knows one thing: Kaia is ours. But the longer she looks at him like he's the only one who's ever mattered, the harder it is to pretend it doesn't hurt like hell.

Ice crystals spread beneath my fingers, delicate patterns that speak to the storm building inside me. I watch them grow, forcing myself to breathe. To remain in control. To be the calm one, the steady one, the one who thinks before he acts.

But the truth is, I'm none of those things anymore. Not really. Not since I watched Kaia fall and felt something primal and ancient tear through the careful walls I've built around myself.

Not since I realized I might love her in ways I have no right to.

Chapter 15
TORRIC

I push off the railing, exhaling sharply. I shouldn't leave him alone like this, not when he's spiraling, but I don't know how to pull him out of it this time. And I don't think I can do it alone.

I take the stairs two at a time, my mind racing. Malrik. Out of everyone, he's the only one who might be able to cut through Aspen's walls. They don't always get along, but Malrik sees things the rest of us don't. He understands Kaia in ways I don't even want to think about, and Aspen is losing himself because of her. Because of what we've become.

I find him near the sanctuary's entrance, his silver eyes distant as he stares toward Kaia's room. Even now, with everything going on, she's still on his mind—I see it in the way his fingers twitch, restless. His gaze flicks to me the second I step into the room.

"Something wrong?"

"It's Aspen," I say, hesitating just long enough for Malrik's expression to sharpen. "He's... not handling things well."

Malrik doesn't blink. "You mean he's falling apart."

I grit my teeth. "Yeah."

He exhales slowly, standing. "Where is he?"

"Upstairs. He—" I hesitate, rubbing a hand over my face. "He thinks he's a monster."

Malrik's expression doesn't change, but I see the flicker of something behind his eyes. Understanding.

"Of course he does," he mutters. "Because he is."

I stiffen, but before I can snap at him, he shakes his head. "Not in the way you think, Torric. Not in the way he thinks." His silver gaze sharpens. "We're all monsters in our own way. What matters is what we do with it."

I huff out a breath, tension still coiling in my chest. "You gonna tell him that?"

Malrik smirks, but it's sharp, edged in something dark. "I'll make him listen."

I almost feel sorry for Aspen. Almost.

We move through the halls in silence, the shadows flickering against the stone walls. I keep my gaze ahead, focused on the path toward the balcony, but Malrik doesn't let it go.

"You think this is just about Aspen?"

I exhale sharply. "He's the one who's losing it."

Malrik hums like he's unconvinced. "And you're not?"

I cut him a glare. "I'm fine."

His silver eyes flick toward me, unimpressed, cutting straight through the lie. "Sure you are."

I roll my shoulders, tension creeping up my spine. "Aspen's the one who won't talk to anyone. He's the one pulling away."

"And what are you doing, Torric?" Malrik's voice is too even, too measured. "You think you're handling this better just because you're not standing on a balcony, looking like you might snap in half?"

My jaw tightens. "This isn't about me."

He scoffs. "If you say so."

I grit my teeth, shoving a hand through my hair. "I didn't come find you for a therapy session, Malrik."

"No," he says, stopping at the base of the stairs. "You came to find me because Aspen is feeling the exact same thing you are. And you're too damn stubborn to admit it."

The words hit like a gut punch, and I hate that he's right. The ache in my chest hasn't let up since the moment Kaia collapsed. It's only gotten stronger, worse, like something is missing. Like something is breaking inside me, piece by piece.

Malrik watches me for a long moment. "You know why that is, don't you?"

I shake my head, pushing past him. "We're wasting time."

Malrik doesn't follow immediately. When he speaks again, his voice is quieter, but no less certain.

"This isn't just about Aspen, Torric."

I don't answer, because I don't want to hear it. Aspen is the one breaking. And I don't know how to stop it.

I find him on the balcony, gripping the railing like it's the only thing keeping him upright. His knuckles are white, his breath controlled too carefully.

"She's not yours, you know."

Malrik's voice is casual, but Aspen goes rigid. I feel it too, something sharp and defensive twisting in my gut.

Aspen exhales slowly. "I know."

Malrik steps closer. "Do you?"

Aspen doesn't answer.

Malrik doesn't let it go. "You think you've lost her."

Aspen laughs, but it's empty. "Haven't I?"

And damn it, that question does something to me. Because it's not just Aspen who feels it. It's me. Every time Kaia's shadows curl toward someone else first. Every time she hesitates before meeting my gaze. Every time I think about the moment she collapsed and I wasn't fast enough.

It's been clawing at me since that night in the corrupted forest. Since the berserker inside us awakened and we let the monsters out.

I thought whatever this was between us would snap into place after that, that it would settle the ache I've felt since the moment I met her. But it hasn't. It's only gotten worse.

Malrik leans against the railing, his silver eyes unreadable. "You felt it the second she went down, didn't you?" His voice is quieter now, sharper. "Like something inside you broke."

I don't breathe. Because yes. I did.

Aspen swallows. His voice is rough when he finally speaks. "What are you saying?"

Malrik glances between us. "You both feel the connection to her. But it's incomplete."

A cold weight settles in my chest.

Aspen tenses beside me. "What do you mean?"

Malrik exhales, shaking his head. "You think this is just about Kaia? That it's just her fate being decided?" He levels us both with a look. "You felt it. You both did."

Neither of us answer. We don't have to.

Malrik nods like he already knew. "The ache in your chest? The pull that's only getting stronger? It's not just in your head." His gaze sharpens. "It's a bond. An ancient one."

I stiffen.

Aspen swears under his breath, dragging a hand down his face.

Malrik keeps going. "She doesn't just need one of us. She needs all of us."

A flicker of movement catches my eye, Walter, that strange shadow who's been following Kaia, drifts between us like smoke. He pauses, bobbing in the air as if considering something, before splitting into multiple copies of himself. Each shadow-Walter hovers near one of us before merging back together with what feels suspiciously like satisfaction.

Malrik's words about needing all of us, combined with Walter's perfect demonstration of many becoming one, hit me like a punch to the gut. The shadow is literally showing us what Malrik just explained, multiple bonds forming into something greater.

And suddenly, everything clicks.

The ache.

The pull.

The thing that never settled.

Kaia isn't just ours.

We are hers.

Chapter 16
KIERAN

Kaia stands on the balcony, staring out at the storm rolling over the distant mountains. The wind pulls at her hair, stirring her shadows, making them drift and shift with purpose. She's tense. I can see it in the way she grips the stone railing, in the rigid set of her shoulders.

She knows I'm here.

She's known since I stepped into the room.

But she doesn't turn.

"Tell me what you're not saying."

Her voice is steady, but I feel the weight beneath it, the demand wrapped in frustration.

I hesitate, though I shouldn't.

I've carried this story for centuries, repeated it so many times it should slip from my lips as easily as breath.

And yet, something about telling her feels... different. Heavier.

More than truth. More than memory.

Still, I keep my voice controlled.

She doesn't need my emotions.

She needs clarity.

"It wasn't just about power," I say finally.

"It was about balance."

Kaia glances at me, eyes sharp, searching for something in my expression. I make sure she doesn't find it.

I clasp my hands behind my back, keeping my posture stiff. "We didn't understand it at first. We didn't think it mattered."

She turns fully now, arms crossing over her chest. "You say that like it's just history. Like it doesn't mean anything to you."

I hold her gaze, unflinching. "It is history."

She lets out a quiet laugh, but there's no humor in it. "No, it's not. Not to you."

She's perceptive. Too perceptive.

I push forward before she can pry at my armor.

"You were never supposed to be alone," I tell her. "The Valkyries were a balance to this world, not just warriors, not just ferriers of the dead. You weren't meant to fade." I pause, inhaling deeply. "And yet, you did."

Kaia's shadows pulse faintly, curling closer to her body. She doesn't speak.

So I continue.

"When the war came, the realms were divided," I say, my words careful, measured. "Absentia had already begun to collapse from the inside. Your people were fighting, but they were outnumbered. We—" My throat tightens. I force myself to keep my tone even. "We tried to help."

Kaia tilts her head slightly, and I brace for the inevitable.

"You failed."

The words shouldn't sting. I've told myself this story so many times, relived it more times than I can count. But hearing it from her lips? From the one I couldn't save?

I swallow hard. "Yes."

I don't tell her how many times I searched for her, only to find more of her people dead. I don't tell her about the nightmares, the battles, the screams that still echo in my head. I don't tell her that even then, I felt something—the bond, the ache of what was lost—even though I didn't understand it at the time.

Instead, I give her the facts.

"The realms surrounding Absentia saw what happened. They saw an entire people eradicated. And they made a vow—never again."

Kaia's fingers twitch at her sides, but she doesn't interrupt.

"The seers from the eastern realms foresaw it," I continue, shifting my stance. "That one day, the last Valkyrie would return, and when she did, she would either restore balance—or unravel it completely."

Kaia exhales slowly. "And you believe it's me."

"I know it's you."

She lets out a breath that isn't quite a laugh, shaking her head. "Right. Because fate has already decided for me, hasn't it?"

I don't respond.

Because I don't know what to say.

I've spent centuries waiting for her. But I've also spent centuries convincing myself that this was inevitable. That I was inevitable.

She takes a slow step toward me, tilting her head slightly. "You're telling me this like it's just a history lesson."

I hold her gaze. "It is history."

Her lips press together. I can see her working through her thoughts, sifting through my words, picking apart what I won't say.

But I won't give her more than this.

I can't.

She turns back toward the mountains, shadows still moving restlessly around her, as if they too are unsatisfied with my answer.

The wind shifts, carrying the scent of coming rain.

She speaks without looking at me. "And the berserkers?"

I exhale slowly, my jaw tightening. "They disappeared with your people."

She stiffens, her fingers tightening around the stone railing.

I step beside her, staring out at the same distant storm. "The Nightwraiths overwhelmed them," I say, my voice quieter now, but no less steady. "The Valkyries didn't just fall—they became something else. Something worse. And the berserkers... they were warriors, but they weren't prepared for the scale of it. No one was."

Kaia's breathing is slow, controlled. But I can see it, the tension in her shoulders, the way her nails dig into her palms.

I should stop.

But I don't.

"They vanished fighting what your people became," I continue. "And when the last of them was gone, the realms finally understood, true extinction isn't just about loss. It's about consequences."

She turns to me then, her expression unreadable. "And now what?"

I meet her gaze. "Now we make sure it doesn't happen again."

She studies me for a long moment, but I can't tell what she's looking for.

Finally, she nods once and steps back.

Her shadows follow her.

She's closing off.

And I let her.

Because this conversation, this truth, is already more than I meant to give her.

So when she turns and walks away, I don't stop her.

I only watch her go.

Because I don't deserve to follow.

Chapter 17
KAIA

Morning comes too quickly, sunlight slicing through unfamiliar windows. My shadows stir restlessly at my feet, their movements sharper than usual. Bob takes up a defensive position while I dress, his inky form rippling with tension. Patricia hovers nearby, cataloging every corner of my new quarters with suspicious efficiency.

The sanctuary feels different in daylight—less oppressive, but no less alien. I don't remember anything before waking in the healing chamber, so every corridor we pass feels like treading between worlds. Ancient magic hums against my skin, making my shadows twist and coil with recognition even as I struggle to understand why. Steve and Carl dart between my ankles in erratic patterns, their excitement betraying my own carefully masked curiosity.

The low buzz of conversation reaches me before I see the dining hall. Heavy oak doors stand open, releasing the scent of fresh bread and something spiced and unfamiliar. My stomach clenches with hunger, but when I step into the doorway, silence falls like the blade of an executioner.

Dozens of unfamiliar faces turn toward me. Battle-hardened warriors with scars like roadmaps across their skin, weapons propped against chairs like casual extensions of themselves. Some wear practical leathers studded with metal; others bear formal robes with sigils I don't recognize. Morning light streams through stained glass, fracturing across the room in jew-el-toned patterns. But it's their expressions that make my throat tighten, a mixture of awe and something that looks unsettlingly like expectation.

My shadows coil tighter against my ankles. Mouse presses against my calf, his warmth a silent reassurance.

"Little star." Kieran appears beside me, his movement so fluid it seems he's stepped directly from the air itself. That strange ache flares beneath my ribs at his proximity, the same inexplicable pull I've felt since waking in this place. His offered arm hangs between us, an invitation wrapped in ancient power. "Let me introduce you to everyone."

"I've got her," Finn interrupts, materializing on my other side with his trademark grin plastered across his face. But his eyes carry an unmistakable edge as they meet Kieran's. "Unless you think formal introductions should come before caffeine?"

The room's tension shifts, electric and dangerous. My shadows freeze, waiting. Older warriors exchange glances while others grip their weapons tighter, reading the power dynamics with practiced ease. Bob shifts into what I recognize as battle-ready formation, while Patricia's frantic notation speeds up. Even Mouse's tail stiffens against my leg.

"She should sit with us," a voice calls from somewhere in the back, formal and weighted with authority. "The balance clearly requires—"

"Balance can wait until after breakfast," Finn interrupts, his cheerful tone slicing through the tension like a blade wrapped in silk. His fingers find mine, warm and steady. "Come on, Trouble. We saved you a seat."

The silence feels heavier with each step across the stone floor. Every eye follows our movement—some curious, others calculating, a few openly hostile. The dining hall smells of woodsmoke and metal polish and that underlying current of ancient magic that seems woven into the very stones. Bob tracks every face we pass, while Patricia's shadowy form darts between warriors as if taking inventory of potential threats.

"Don't mind them," Finn murmurs, leading me past a table where scarred hands pause mid-reach for bread. "They're just excited to meet their mystical savior." His voice drops lower, with a hint of wickedness that tugs at something in my chest. "Though I bet none of them expected said savior to travel with an army of dramatic shadows and a judgmental cat." Mouse rumbles something that might be agreement.

A few gasps ripple through the room at his casual tone. I bite my lip to keep from smiling, grateful for his defiant normalcy in this sea of reverence and suspicion.

Our table comes into view, and my heart stutters at the sight. A space has been preserved between Malrik and where Finn was clearly sitting before, as if they've been holding my place all along. But something's definitely shifted since yesterday. Aspen's gaze skitters away from mine, his fingers tracing patterns of frost against his mug. Torric watches me with an intensity that makes my skin prickle, heat radiating from him in almost visible waves.

The ache in my chest sharpens suddenly, a strange pressure that makes me press my hand against my sternum. I've felt this ever since stepping into this realm, but it's stronger now, with all of them so close, like my body is trying to tell me something my mind can't grasp.

"You feel it too," Torric says quietly, his golden eyes fixed on my hand against my chest.

I frown, confused by his certainty. "Feel what?"

Before he can answer, someone calls from near the front: "She belongs at the high table with the Guardians."

I glance toward where Kieran stands with others who radiate the same ancient power he does. Their table sits on a raised platform, clearly designed to separate them from everyone else. Morning light catches on the silver and gold threads woven through their formal attire, making them shimmer like living constellations against the practical leathers and battle-worn armor surrounding them.

"She sits with us," Malrik says quietly, but his voice carries like shadow given sound. The darkness around him deepens slightly, and the authority in his tone brooks no argument. My shadows respond instantly, stretching toward him like they recognize something in his power that speaks to their own nature.

A man rises from near the high table, his weathered face twisting with disdain. The decorative sword at his hip suggests ceremony rather than combat, despite the jagged scar bisecting his jaw. "And who are you to decide where she belongs?" His voice drips with contempt as his gaze dismisses Malrik entirely. "Some academy shadow-wielder playing at power?"

The temperature in the room drops so suddenly my breath fogs. Malrik's expression remains unchanged, but the shadows around him sharpen like living blades. Several nearby warriors subtly shift their chairs back, recognizing the gathering storm. Finn's hand tightens around mine, a warning or reassurance—I'm not sure which.

"Mind your tongue, Callum." Kieran's voice slices through the tension. He steps forward, his presence commanding immediate attention. Light seems to bend around him, drawn to the ancient power coursing beneath his skin. "You stand before Malrik Duskbane, rightful heir to the throne of Absentia. The last true prince of the shadow realm."

A ripple of shocked whispers sweeps through the room. Weapons clatter against tables as hands go slack with surprise. Callum pales slightly, the scar along his jaw standing out stark against his skin. I watch the revelation land, feeling a twist of satisfaction at seeing Malrik finally acknowledged for who he is, even as I wonder why he's kept his identity so carefully guarded from everyone else here.

My shadows surge toward Malrik with protective curiosity. Walter, ever the unpredictable one, drifts closer to Malrik's shoulder, pulsing with an odd purplish light I've never seen before.

"That's impossible," Callum stammers, his arrogance cracking like thin ice. "The royal line vanished when Absentia fell."

"Not vanished," Kieran corrects, his ancient eyes fixed on Malrik with something that might be respect or calculation—with him, it's impossible to tell. "Hidden. Protected. Waiting for the proper moment to reclaim what was taken." His gaze shifts to me, weighted with meaning I can't decipher. "Some connections run deeper than even the oldest records suggest."

Callum sinks back into his seat, thoroughly silenced. The other Guardians watch with new interest, their expressions shifting from dismissal to careful assessment. Warriors throughout the hall exchange meaningful looks, reevaluating everything they thought they knew about the quiet shadow-wielder in their midst.

I slide onto the bench between Malrik and Finn, feeling the weight of too many secrets pressing against my chest. The strange ache intensifies, resonating like a plucked string. I press my hand against it again, wincing slightly.

"It's the bond," Torric says quietly, leaning across the table. His golden eyes carry an intensity that makes my breath catch. "That feeling in your chest. It's been there since Absentia, hasn't it?"

I stare at him, momentarily speechless. "What bond?"

Malrik's silver gaze meets mine. "An ancient connection. Between all of us." His voice drops lower. "That's what you feel, what we all feel. It's been growing stronger since we got here."

Finn looks between us, confusion clear on his face. "Hold up. What exactly are we talking about here?"

"The reason we can't stay away from each other," Aspen says softly, finally meeting my eyes. "The reason we all feel it when one of us is in danger. It's not just coincidence, Kaia. It's something older."

My shadows twist anxiously, matching the knot forming in my stomach. Another revelation about myself I didn't choose. "And when exactly were you planning to tell me about this... bond?"

"We only recently understood it ourselves," Malrik says, his tone carefully neutral. "And we needed to be certain."

The implications crash over me in waves. The constant ache. The way I feel drawn to each of them differently but insistently. The way my shadows react to their presence. "So what does it mean?"

Malrik's eyes flick to Kieran, who watches us from the high table with ancient patience. "It means we're connected in ways even Kieran might not fully understand."

"Great," Finn mutters, but his usual humor sounds strained. "Magical mystery bonds on top of everything else. Just what we needed."

My shadows curl around my ankles, uneasy and alert. Around us, warriors and Guardians observe every move I make, weighing me against expectations I don't understand. And now this, a bond I never chose but apparently can't escape.

I reach for the coffee, needing something, anything, to ground me in this moment. My fingers brush Malrik's as we both reach for the same mug. The contact sends a jolt through my chest, his magic resonating with whatever this bond is in a way that makes my shadows flare.

"I think we need to talk," I murmur, just loud enough for our table to hear. "About all of this. No more secrets."

Four pairs of eyes meet mine—silver, green, ice blue, and molten gold—each carrying knowledge that tangles with my own growing confusion.

"Yes," Malrik agrees quietly. "We do."

Chapter 18
KIERAN

I feel their stares before they speak, the weight of centuries of Guardian politics pressing in as I follow them into the council chamber. The breakfast drama was inevitable. Callum has always been too eager to assert authority he doesn't possess.

"You can't be serious about the Duskbane heir," Callum starts the moment the doors close. His voice carries that familiar blend of arrogance and fear that's always made him dangerous. "He abandoned Absentia."

"He was a child," I say sharply, memories resurfacing with painful clarity. The mysterious disappearance of the royal family, a single heir spirited away in the chaos. My fingers press against the smooth stone table. "The only survivor of the royal line."

"Exactly why he should have stayed," Mira interjects, her silver hair catching the light as she paces between the ancient pillars. Her footsteps echo against the marble floor, each one precise and measured like her words. "Absentia needed its prince."

"Absentia needed him alive," Revna counters from her seat by the window. At least someone here has sense. The sunlight makes the scars on her hands almost luminous, badges of honor from battles these younger Guardians have only read about. "What good is a vanished prince to a fallen realm?"

Callum's mouth twists, his disdain poorly concealed. "He seems quite... comfortable with our Valkyrie," he says, the possessive term making something dark and ancient stir beneath my skin.

"She is not *our* anything," I say, my voice dropping to a dangerous whisper. The temperature in the room plummets several degrees as my power ripples outward. "Choose your words with more care, Callum."

He steps back instinctively, a flicker of genuine fear crossing his face before he masks it. But the damage is done, I've seen it, and we both know it. The other Guardians shift uncomfortably, sensing the edge of my control fraying.

I wrestle my emotions back into place, burying the things I don't want to examine too closely. The things I've been struggling not to dwell on since I first saw them together.

The bond. The way their shadows reach for each other without conscious thought. The way she looks at him, at all of them, like they're pieces of her soul she didn't know she was missing.

My chest tightens with an ache that's grown all too familiar. I mask it with practiced indifference.

"The records—" Callum begins again.

"—mention connections even the oldest seers didn't fully understand," I interrupt, keeping my voice steady despite the storm brewing beneath my skin. "Malrik Duskbane is exactly where he needs to be."

"But why now?" Mira asks, pausing mid-step. She turns to face me, her expression tight. "Why return now, when the barriers are barely holding?"

"The scrolls—" Callum starts again, but Revna snorts, the sound sharp as breaking glass.

"Enough with the scrolls and ancient texts. You weren't there, Callum. None of you were." Her eyes meet mine, ancient and unwavering. "Only Kieran and I remember what it was really like. What we lost."

Revna moves to stand beside me, her presence as steady as it's been for centuries. She was there when Solveig made her choice, when everything changed. She's been there for every endless year of searching since.

"She was just a child," I say quietly, the words scraping my throat. "Only six years old when Solveig sent her forward."

"And now she returns with not one, but multiple bonds forming," Mira observes, her tone carefully neutral though her eyes betray her wariness. "That's... unprecedented."

"She has a shadow prince, a chaos mage, and two berserkers bound to her soul," Callum says, like he's listing crimes. "How can we be sure she's even still—"

"Choose your next words very carefully," I cut in, my voice dropping dangerously low. The temperature in the room plummets. "That's Solveig's daughter you're questioning."

Revna straightens, her movement drawing all eyes. "The bonds are not a weakness," she says firmly. "They're part of this. Can't you feel it? The way everything is weaving itself together?" She looks at me. "The lost prince returns just as she does. The berserkers awaken. None of this is coincidence."

"I think," Revna adds, her eyes glinting with that familiar determination that's gotten us through worse, "it's time we spoke with all of them. Together."

I exhale slowly. She's right, of course she's right. She usually is, though I rarely admit it aloud.

"Have them brought to the Hall of Echoes," I say, ignoring the way my chest aches at the thought of facing this. "All of them."

Mira and the other guardians move toward the door. Their silver-threaded ceremonial garments shimmer with subtle runes, fabric whispering against the stone floor as they exit. Revna and I hang back. I've known her long enough to recognize when she has something to say that the others shouldn't hear.

"When were you going to tell me?" Revna asks quietly once they're out of earshot. When I don't answer immediately, she adds, "About your bond. To her."

I exhale slowly. "I've always known."

She studies me for a long moment, waiting. Her patience has always been her greatest weapon against my silence.

I drag a hand through my hair. "When I first met her, I felt it. The connection. But she was so young, and she didn't understand. And then..." My throat tightens. "Then she was gone."

"And now she's back," Revna says, voice steady.

I nod, jaw clenching. "And she's forming bonds with them."

Revna exhales sharply. "You thought it would just be you."

I don't answer. Because yes. That's exactly what I thought.

"That's not how it works," Revna says, watching me carefully. "Not for Valkyries. Not for her."

My fingers tighten into a fist at my side. "I know that now."

And that's the problem.

For centuries, I carried the certainty of our connection—the knowledge that we were meant to find each other again. It was supposed to be me and her. A reunion of souls. A return to what was stolen from us.

But now?

Now she looks at me and sees a stranger.

Now she's bonding with others.

And I can feel it.

The connections growing one by one, tightening around her like threads of fate. Each bond reinforcing something different. The strength of the berserkers. The shadows of Malrik. The chaos of Finn.

And me.

Still here. Still bound. But no longer the only one.

Revna studies me in silence, her eyes as sharp as the truth she's been waiting for me to admit. Finally, she says, "You're afraid you'll lose her."

A bitter laugh escapes me. "I already have."

She frowns. "She's still yours, Kieran."

I shake my head. "Not like I thought. Not like before."

Revna sighs. "You thought she would come back, and the bond would be exactly as it was before. Just the two of you."

I nod, throat tight.

"But that's not how the bond works for Valkyries," she reminds me gently. "It was never meant to be just one. Each connection strengthens different aspects of her power. It's balance, not competition."

Balance.

The word grates against something deep inside me.

"It's not just about fate choosing companions," Revna continues. "It's about what she needs. And Kaia?" She meets my eyes squarely. "She's not just a Valkyrie. She's the last Valkyrie."

I clench my jaw. I know.

I hate how right she is.

"The Hall of Echoes will make her see," Revna says. "It was built for this. Where Valkyries once acknowledged their bonds, where fate aligned them with those meant to stand beside them. She won't be able to deny it once she steps inside."

I exhale slowly, nodding. "That's why I chose it."

And that's why I hate it.

Because once she enters that chamber, it will all become real.

Her bonds.

The ones with them.

And the one with me.

The Hall looms ahead, its entrance framed by towering runes that glow faintly, thrumming with magic older than most of the sanctuary itself. The air shifts as we approach—heavy with memory, thick with power.

The Hall of Echoes is unlike any other place in the sanctuary. It doesn't just hold history, it preserves it. Magic lingers here, etched into the stone, woven through the air. It's where Valkyries once gathered to make important decisions. Where the royals gathered after, seeking wisdom.

And where bonds were acknowledged.

Revna exhales beside me. "It still feels the same."

It does. Too much the same.

The chamber is vast, with arched ceilings that seem to stretch beyond reality, shimmering with threads of magic from realms long since lost. Shadows flicker along the walls, but they aren't just shadows.

They're memories.

Echoes of the past.

Faint figures drift in and out of sight, remnants of those who stood here before us. Valkyries. Their companions. Their warriors.

The energy here is alive, waiting.

Revna places a hand against one of the glowing runes. "Once she enters, she won't be able to deny it."

I nod, the weight of it settling in my chest.

The Hall will show her the truth.

And I'm not sure any of us are ready for what comes after.

Chapter 19
KAIA

Breakfast is quiet, but not in a peaceful way.

It's the kind of quiet that feels too careful, too forced. Like everyone's pretending things are normal when they absolutely aren't. The weight of what we learned about the bond sits heavy between us, unspoken but impossible to ignore.

Finn is the only one keeping things from falling into full-blown awkward silence, mostly by shoveling food into his mouth and making dramatic noises about how "deprived" he was last night.

Malrik just drinks his coffee, watching him like he's debating whether to hex him into silence or let him continue.

Aspen and Torric, on the other hand, are not watching anything.

Torric hasn't said a word all morning, which isn't entirely out of character, but it's the kind of silence that feels heavier than usual. Like something is sitting on his chest and he's refusing to acknowledge it. Aspen is worse. He's just picking at his food, barely eating, shoulders stiff with tension I can almost see rippling beneath his skin.

I don't like it.

My shadows don't either.

Bob drifts closer to Aspen and Torric, hovering over them with unmistakable suspicion, his shadowy form almost military in its posture.

Patricia's usual frantic note-taking slows as if even she's taking inventory of the tension. Finnick bounces anxiously between all of us, his usual chaotic energy subdued into nervous movement. Walter just hovers near the ceiling, pulsing with that strange purplish light.

Finn is the first to crack under the weight of it. He leans forward, lazily spearing a piece of fruit from my plate. "So, what's the plan today?"

Malrik doesn't look up. "Survive."

Finn hums like he's considering that answer. "Not really my strong suit."

Torric exhales through his nose, but still doesn't speak. Aspen just blinks down at his food like he's waiting for it to say something first.

I set my fork down with more force than necessary, the sound of metal against ceramic making Aspen flinch. "Okay, what's going on?"

Aspen doesn't react, but Torric glances at me. "Nothing."

I narrow my eyes. "Try again."

Aspen exhales slowly, still not looking up. "We're fine, Kaia."

I hate that answer.

It's dismissive, controlled, too even—the way Aspen only ever gets when he's holding something back. My hand itches to reach for his, but there's something in the deliberate space he's keeping between us that stops me.

"You're fine?" I repeat, voice sharper than I mean for it to be. "That's my line. And if I know it's bullshit, so do you."

I take a breath, forcing myself to stay calm even as my shadows ripple with my frustration. "That's why you haven't spoken all morning? That's why you're both acting like you don't even want to look at each other?"

Aspen's fingers tighten around his fork. Torric shifts like he's debating answering but then doesn't. The bond in my chest pulses with something that feels like dread, or maybe anticipation.

Before I can press further, a shadow falls over the table.

A woman with an athletic figure and cropped black hair stands at the edge of our group, her Guardian attire pristine, her expression neutral. But her silver eyes linger on me for a beat too long before she speaks, studying my face like she's measuring me against someone else.

"Kieran has requested your presence," she says, voice smooth but firm. "All of you."

The shift in energy is immediate. The tension morphs into something else entirely. I glance at Finn, who raises a brow but doesn't say anything. Malrik doesn't react visibly, but his shadows deepen around his feet.

Torric leans back in his chair, arms crossing over his chest. "Requested our presence for what?"

The woman barely acknowledges the question, her silver gaze fixed somewhere over his shoulder. "You are to meet him in the Hall of Echoes."

I wait for someone to react, but none of them seem to recognize the name. Except Malrik, whose expression darkens slightly, shadows coiling tighter.

Finn leans toward me, whispering just loud enough for everyone to hear. "That sounds ominous. Is it ominous?"

I shrug, my shadows mimicking the gesture. "It's got 'Echoes' in the name, so probably."

The woman remains unfazed but tilts her head slightly, like she's deciding whether or not to humor him. "That depends."

Finn perks up. "On what?"

She finally looks at him. "On how well you handle the truth."

Finn blinks. "Nope. Don't like that." He shoves the last of his toast in his mouth as he stands. "Come on, Trouble. Let's go find out just how doomed we are."

The woman turns, headed for the far doorway. "Follow me."

Finn sighs dramatically, pushing away from the table. "Summoned before I could even finish breakfast. This is oppression."

I roll my eyes and stand, my shadows gathering around me like a second skin. The others follow, and I don't hesitate before slipping between Aspen and Torric.

They don't acknowledge it, but they don't pull away either. Their magic hums against my skin, Aspen's cool presence, Torric's steady heat, and the bond in my chest responds with a dull ache that feels both uncomfortable and right.

The halls are quiet as we follow the Guardian through the sanctuary, the air shifting the deeper we go. With each turn down another corridor, the stone beneath our feet grows older, worn smooth by centuries of footsteps. The magic changes too, no longer the gentle hum I've grown used to, but something deeper, more primal. It feels heavier, charged with history, like the magic here isn't just present—it's waiting. My shadows ripple with each step, responding to power that seems to seep from the walls.

Torch flames flicker in ornate bronze holders, casting dancing shadows that feel almost alive. The air grows cooler, carrying the scent of ancient stone and something that reminds me of ozone before a storm, of power gathering.

No one speaks much.

Finn, normally incapable of letting silence exist, makes a few halfhearted jokes, but they don't land the same way. His voice seems to get swallowed by the weight of the air around us. Malrik hasn't said a word since we left the dining hall, his silver eyes tracking shadows I can't see. And Aspen and Torric... they still aren't looking at each other.

I stay between them, keeping my pace even with theirs, but it's impossible to ignore how tense they are. They don't touch me, they barely acknowledge my presence. The space between us feels charged, like static building before a lightning strike.

It's like they're holding something back, and I hate that I don't know what it is.

But now isn't the time to push.

I turn my attention to the Guardian who walks a few steps ahead. Her stride is confident and controlled, like someone who doesn't doubt where she stands in the world. She doesn't look back, but her voice carries easily when she finally speaks.

"I'm Mira, by the way," she says, still facing forward. "Second to Kieran."

I blink, something cold settling in my stomach at the casual way she says his name.

Finn quirks a brow, glancing at me before grinning. "Wow. Second to Kieran? Sounds important."

Mira doesn't react to his teasing, her spine straight as a blade. "It is."

The way she says it, so smooth and certain, irritates me immediately. Maybe it's the confidence. Maybe it's the way she hasn't looked at me once since she started speaking.

Or maybe it's the way she's clearly implying something.

Second to Kieran.

Does she mean politically? Strategically? Or something else entirely?

I keep my expression neutral, but something about her tone sticks in my ribs like a thorn. "Second in what, exactly?"

Mira finally glances over her shoulder, her silver eyes lingering on me. "In everything that matters."

I don't know what pisses me off more—the answer, or the fact that I have no idea if she's deliberately messing with me. But before I can come up with something appropriately cutting, Malrik speaks, his tone flat.

"We're here."

I tear my gaze from Mira, and my breath catches.

The Hall of Echoes.

The entrance is massive, carved from ancient stone that seems to pulse with its own heartbeat. Runes line the towering archway, glowing faintly with old magic—not the steady shine of modern enchantments, but something wild and untamed. They shift and dance as I watch, forming patterns that tug at something deep in my memory before dissolving again. The doors stand open, revealing the vast chamber beyond.

Through the archway, I catch glimpses of soaring columns that disappear into shadows far above, their surfaces etched with spiraling patterns that seem to move when I'm not looking directly at them. The air that drifts out feels different—heavy with memory and magic so thick I can almost taste it, like metal on my tongue.

The moment I see it, something in my chest pulls. The sensation is physical, like a hook behind my sternum drawing me forward. My skin prickles with goosebumps, and my shadows coil tighter around me, responding to whatever power waits inside.

Not the bond.

Something else.

Something older.

Something that feels like coming home and stepping into darkness all at once.

I swallow hard as I step forward, but Finn grabs my arm, stopping me before I can cross the threshold. His hand is warm against my suddenly chilled skin.

"Wait." His voice is softer than usual, his joking edge gone. "Does anyone else feel that?"

I do.

The pull is stronger now, making my heart race and my breath catch. The runes pulse in time with my heartbeat, or maybe my heart is matching their rhythm. I can't tell anymore. My shadows writhe restlessly, caught between drawing closer to the doorway and shrinking back from whatever waits inside.

And I don't think I'm ready for what's waiting there.

Finn, Aspen and Torric take a few hesitant steps inside, and when nothing happens, they continue on. Their footsteps echo strangely, as if the sound is coming from much further away than it should. Malrik hangs back, his silver eyes distant, seeing something beyond the present moment.

"I used to come here, as a child," he says with a softness I've rarely heard from him. The words seem to ripple through the air, carrying echoes of childhood memories I can almost feel. "My father held meetings in this room. He said... he said he always found the answer here."

His silver eyes meet mine, filled with an understanding that makes the bond in my chest ache. "Perhaps you will too, Kaia. Perhaps we all will."

With a small smile, he squeezes my hand. His touch grounding me against the pull of ancient magic as he walks into the room, leaving me there to think about what that might mean for all of us.

The runes pulse once more, beckoning, waiting for me to step through and face whatever truths the Hall of Echoes holds.

My shadows press close as I take a deep breath and follow them into the chamber, feeling like I'm crossing a threshold I can never un-cross.

Chapter 20
KAIA

The moment I step fully into the chamber, the world changes. What seemed vast from the doorway now feels infinite inside, towering columns disappear into shadows far above, their surfaces etched with spiraling patterns that shift when I'm not looking directly at them. The air is thick with magic, pressing against my skin like a physical weight.

My shadows coil tightly around me as I take it all in, the ancient power of this place humming in my bones. The Hall of Echoes isn't just a name, whispers seem to drift through the air, fragments of conversations long past, remnants of those who stood here before.

Before I can process it all, something slams into me.

It's not physical, not even entirely magical, but it drags me down like a riptide, knocking the breath from my lungs. My knees give out before I can stop them, the stone floor cold against my palms as I catch myself.

Pain explodes in my chest.

Not an injury. Not magic.

Something else.

Something worse.

It's the same ache I've felt since arriving in this realm, the one that started as a dull pull and has only grown stronger. But now, it's unbearable, pressing against my ribs like it's trying to tear me apart from the inside out.

My shadows curl around me instinctively, but it doesn't help. Bob tries to form a protective barrier while Patricia's frantic movements blur together. Even Mouse presses against my leg, his violet eyes wide with concern, but none of it stops the pressure building inside me.

I hear movement, a curse muttered somewhere behind me, but it's distant, unimportant. The only thing that matters is the weight pressing into me, the way my lungs feel like they can't fully expand, the way the ache is sharpening instead of fading.

"Kaia."

Kieran's voice is sharp, his presence suddenly in front of me, kneeling. His golden eyes burn with something I can't name—concern, but also anticipation. "Breathe."

I try, but the pressure in my chest is suffocating.

Revna steps closer, her eyes scanning me carefully before her expression tightens. "It should have stabilized by now."

"What should have stabilized?" Finn demands, stepping forward.

"The magic, the bonds," Kieran says tightly. "This Hall was built to reinforce connections."

Finn frowns. "Then why does she look like she's about to pass out?"

I grit my teeth, pressing my palm against my ribs. "Because something is wrong."

The ache should be fading.

I don't know how I know that, but I do.

This place, this Hall, is doing something to me, something to all of us. The energy here presses against my skin, wrapping around something deep inside me, something I don't understand but feels like it has always been there.

The pull gets stronger.

It's unbearable, like my body is splitting apart at the seams. I feel them. Not individually at first, but then the bonds snap into focus one by one, each with its own distinct sensation burning through me.

Kieran's bond hits first, ancient and golden, like sunlight breaking through storm clouds. It carries wisdom and power that feels older than time itself, steady and unwavering. But there's something else there too, a familiar ache, like we've done this dance before.

Malrik's connection flows like liquid shadow, cool and deep. It resonates with my own shadows, which writhe and reach for his instinctively. His bond feels like midnight and starlight, like secrets whispered in darkness. My shadows coil tighter, recognizing their prince even as I struggle to process what's happening.

Finn's bond crackles with barely contained chaos, wild and bright and dangerous, like lightning captured in a bottle. It fizzes through my veins like champagne, making my skin tingle with untamed magic that somehow feels perfectly right despite its unpredictability.

The twins' bonds hit together—Aspen and Torric's connections intertwined but distinct. Aspen's feels like spring steel, flexible but unbreakable, while Torric's burns like banked embers, all controlled power waiting to ignite. Their berserker strength hums through the connection, raw and primal.

My shadows dance erratically around me, responding to each new bond as it locks into place. Bob seems particularly agitated, his usually rigid form rippling with tension. Patricia's shadowy movements become frantic, like she's trying to document everything happening all at once. Mouse just presses closer, his violet eyes fixed on me.

The Hall itself seems to pulse in response, the ancient runes flaring brighter with each connection that solidifies. The air grows thicker, heavy with power that swirls visibly around us like golden mist. The stone beneath my hands warms, thrumming with energy that seems to reach up through my palms and into my chest, anchoring each bond in place.

I can see the others feeling it too. Kieran's muscles flex and shiver beneath his skin. Malrik's shadows writhe around him, reaching toward mine. Finn's chaos magic sparks visibly in the air around him, while the twins' branded runes transform—Aspen's ice rune frosting over completely, Torric's fire rune burning through his shirt like molten light.

The realization sends a wave of panic through me.

This isn't supposed to be real.

I've been pretending this ache I felt was something I could ignore, something I could fight.

But now I feel them. All of them.

Tangled threads pulling tighter, locking into something solid, unbreakable. Each connection distinct but harmonious, like pieces of a puzzle I didn't know needed solving. They don't compete, they complement, strengthening each other in ways I don't understand but can feel deep in my bones.

My stomach twists with both terror and something dangerously close to belonging. I try to shove it down, try to push it away, but the Hall isn't letting me. It's cementing something that I am not ready for.

"Make it stop," I whisper, pressing my forehead against the cold stone. "Make it stop."

No one answers.

Because they can't.

The bonds are real. I can't pretend anymore.

Kieran exhales sharply, his eyes glinting with ancient power. His voice is lower when he speaks, strained in a way I've never heard from him. "It's done."

The words send a bolt of white-hot rage through me. He brought us here knowing exactly what would happen. Knowing it would force these bonds into place whether we were ready or not. My shadows sharpen in response, their edges becoming lethal.

I don't move.

I don't breathe.

My hands curl into fists against the stone floor, anger burning hotter than the pain of the bonds.

And then, just as suddenly as it started, the pain fades.

Not completely, not all at once, but enough that I can take a breath without feeling like my ribs might shatter. The rage, though—that doesn't fade at all.

My hands are still shaking as I push myself up, but now it's as much from anger as from the aftermath of what just happened. I barely register the way Finn moves forward like he's debating whether or not to help me, my glare fixed on Kieran.

Torric takes a step back, his expression carefully blank. Aspen is looking anywhere but at me.

No one speaks.

No one knows what to say.

And then, as I force myself to my feet, my body stiffens.

Because something is still missing.

The ache that should be gone isn't.

It's less, but it's not fixed.

And I know, deep down, why.

Because one of them isn't here.

Revna exhales quietly, rubbing her temple. "There's another."

The weight of those words settles over the room like a heavy stone.

Kieran doesn't move, doesn't blink, but I feel the sharp pulse of his magic. "No," he says, but this time it's not denial—it's dread.

I want to feel satisfied at his obvious discomfort, at this unexpected complication to whatever he planned. But I'm too angry, too overwhelmed by everything that's just been forced upon us.

The Hall didn't just confirm the bonds that were here.

It confirmed the one that's missing.

And I think, wherever they are—

They just felt it too.

Walter drifts silently between us, his strange purplish light pulsing faster than usual. He seems drawn to the empty space where something—someone—should be, hovering there like he's trying to fill it. But he can't. None of us can.

The rage builds inside me like a gathering storm. My shadows respond, their edges becoming razor-sharp, coiling tighter with each breath I take. Mouse presses against my leg, a silent guardian as my fury threatens to spill over.

The Hall of Echoes suddenly feels too small, too confining, the ancient magic pressing against my skin like an unwelcome touch. I force myself to stand straighter despite the trembling in my limbs.

Kieran takes a step toward me, his golden eyes unreadable. "Kaia—"

I hold up my hand, cutting him off. I don't trust myself to speak. The bonds pulse inside me, unwanted and forced into place by his machinations. If I open my mouth now, I might unleash something we can't take back.

Instead, I turn away, every muscle in my body rigid with restraint. My shadows lash in tight, controlled spirals—betraying the chaos I refuse to show. Bob moves ahead of me, clearing a path to the door, while Patricia's frantically writing shadow follows at my heels.

The others watch me go, their newly forged bonds to me vibrating with tension. I can feel their confusion, their concern, their uncertainty.

Let them feel it.

Let Kieran wonder what I'm thinking.

Let him worry about what comes next.

Right now, I need distance before I do something I'll regret.

The ancient stone seems to whisper beneath my feet as I walk away, leaving them all standing in the echoing silence of a Hall that has taken something precious from us all.

Our choice.

Chapter 21
DARIAN

Fuck.

Chapter 22
KAIA

My shadows coil tight and sharp around me, responding to my fury. Even Mouse's usual calming presence can't soothe the storm brewing inside me.

"You knew," I say, my voice deadly quiet as I finally break the silence. "You knew exactly what this place would do."

Kieran meets my gaze steadily, but there's something ancient and tired in his golden eyes. "Yes."

The simple admission makes my shadows lash out before I can stop them. "Why?" The word comes out raw, scraping my throat. "Why would you do this?"

"Because we needed—"

"Don't," I cut him off. "Don't you dare talk about need. About balance or ancient wisdom or whatever other excuse you've prepared." My hands shake as I step closer. "Tell me how these bonds were really meant to form."

His jaw tightens, but it's Malrik who answers, his voice soft with realization. "Love," he says, and the word seems to echo in the ancient chamber. "They were sealed through love. Through choice." His silver eyes meet mine. "That's what I've been feeling. What we've all been feeling, but couldn't understand."

"The bond forms naturally," Kieran admits reluctantly. "Growing stronger as hearts align. The final sealing..." He pauses, looking away. "It was meant to happen during lovemaking. A choice made in perfect trust and devotion."

The truth of it nearly brings me to my knees. What should have been beautiful, sacred even, twisted into this forced connection. My shadows writhe with shared grief and fury.

"You stole that from us," I whisper. "You took something that was supposed to be about love and turned it into another chain."

"Kaia—" Finn starts, his voice uncharacteristically gentle.

"No." I turn back to Kieran. "You didn't just force these bonds. You took away our chance to choose them. To let them grow naturally. To fall in love on our own terms."

The silence that follows feels heavy enough to crush stone.

"Do you have any idea what you've done?" My voice shakes with barely contained fury. "These bonds—they're not just magic. They're not just convenient connections you can force into place when it suits you."

My shadows surge with my anger, and I catch Bob actually positioning himself between me and Kieran like he's ready for battle. Patricia's frantic note-taking has turned sharp and aggressive, while Mouse's growl vibrates through the stone floor.

"The timing—" Kieran starts, but I cut him off.

"The timing?" I laugh, but there's no humor in it. "You mean your schedule? Your plans? Because that's all that matters, right? Not the fact that these bonds are supposed to be sacred."

Malrik steps forward, his silver eyes intense. "The ancient texts spoke of bonds formed over years. Of connections that grew stronger with each shared moment, each choice to stay." His voice carries the weight of generations of shadow realm knowledge. "They were never meant to be forced."

"But they were always meant to form," Kieran counters, though his voice lacks its usual certainty.

"Eventually," I snap. "Through trust. Through actually falling in love. Through choosing each other every single day until the bond grew strong enough to seal itself." My hand presses against my chest where I can feel them all now, these connections I didn't ask for. "Not like this. Never like this."

Finn moves closer, his usual playful demeanor gone. "So what happens now? These bonds—they're permanent, aren't they?"

"Yes." Kieran's answer falls like a stone. "Once sealed, they can't be broken."

The anger burns hotter. "Of course they can't. Because why would you give us any choice at all?"

"Kaia—" Aspen starts, but I shake my head.

"Don't. Just... don't." I turn back to Kieran. "You talk about fate and duty like they justify everything. But you just turned something beautiful into another weapon. Another tool."

The silence that follows feels sharp enough to draw blood.

My chest is tight, my shadows still pulsing with restless energy, but it's the rage burning beneath my skin that keeps me upright.

I need to get out of here.

I turn sharply, not waiting for anyone to say anything else. No one tries to stop me as I storm toward the exit, though I can feel their eyes on my back, heavy with things they want to say but know better than to voice right now.

The corridors blur together as I move, each step fueled by too many emotions, all of them threatening to consume me.

Rage.

Betrayal.

A grief so heavy and unexpected it nearly brings me to my knees.

I don't stop walking until I find myself somewhere unfamiliar. Which is pretty much everywhere here.

The air shifts. The oppressive weight of the sanctuary eases, and for the first time since entering this cursed place, I can breathe.

I glance around, my heartbeat slowing as I take in the space.

A garden.

Not like the rest of the sanctuary, which is bathed in shadows and cracked with signs of corruption. This place is untouched.

Flowers bloom in rich shades of violet and deep blue, their petals shifting faintly in the soft breeze. Tall trees stretch overhead, their leaves rustling in a way that feels almost like a whisper. A small pool of water sits in the center, so clear it looks like glass.

This place is... wrong.

Not in the way the sanctuary is wrong, not like the twisting shadows and corrupted magic.

It's wrong because it shouldn't exist.

The land outside is rotting, infected with whatever sickness is spreading through this realm. And yet, here, the air is clean, the earth is whole. Nothing should be this untouched.

I exhale shakily and step forward, my fingers brushing over the petals of a nearby flower.

"I wish Seren were here," I murmur, the words barely more than a breath.

The wind stirs, the magic in the air shifting.

But it's not Seren who answers.

"It seems you and I had the same thought."

I turn sharply, shadows flaring around me before I even register who's standing at the edge of the garden.

Revna.

She watches me with an expression I can't quite read, her silver-streaked hair catching the soft glow of the garden's magic. She's not wearing her Guardian armor, but she doesn't need it. There's something about her presence that feels just as commanding without it.

She tilts her head slightly, studying me. "I was hoping we could talk."

I narrow my eyes. "If this is about Kieran, I don't want to hear it."

Her lips twitch slightly, not quite a smile. "It is. And you do."

I cross my arms, biting down my instinct to snap at her. I don't want another lecture on duty or fate or any of the other excuses Kieran is bound to throw at me later.

Revna steps forward, but she doesn't get too close. "I've known Kieran for centuries," she says, her voice even, steady. "I've known him as a warrior. As a leader. As a friend."

I don't answer.

Because I know where this is going, and I don't want to hear it.

She watches me carefully, like she knows exactly what I'm thinking. "And I've known that he's loved you every moment in between."

My breath catches, but I force myself to keep my expression neutral. "Love?" I scoff. "Love isn't forcing a bond. Love isn't taking away someone's choice."

"No," Revna agrees. "It isn't."

That throws me. I expected her to defend him, to tell me why he did what he did, why I should forgive him. Instead, she just watches me with that same measured calm.

I shake my head. "Then why are you here?"

"Because you need to understand something, Kaia." She steps forward again, and this time, I don't move away. "For centuries, Kieran held onto one thing—one belief that kept him going when the rest of the world burned around him."

She tells me anyway.

"He believed it was just the two of you."

The words hit harder than I want them to.

"He thought your bond would be singular, unbreakable. He believed, with everything in him, that it was meant to be just you and him." She exhales softly. "And when he realized it wasn't? That you had others?"

"He couldn't handle it," I finish for her.

Revna doesn't deny it.

I let out a slow breath, shaking my head. "That doesn't change what he did."

"No," she agrees. "It doesn't."

She doesn't try to justify it. Doesn't try to make excuses for him. And somehow, that makes this conversation worse.

Because I wanted to fight.

I wanted to argue.

But she isn't here to fight. She's here to tell me the truth.

I exhale, my hands tightening at my sides. "What am I supposed to do with that?"

Revna watches me for a long moment. Then, softly, she says, "That's up to you."

I look away, my eyes tracing the flowers at my feet, the small pool of still water, the trees stretching above us.

It was supposed to be just the two of us.

And now?

Now, I don't even know what's real anymore.

Chapter 23
FINN

The tension in the Hall of Echoes lingers long after Kaia storms out.

No one moves. No one speaks.

I feel the bond now—really feel it. Like something has snapped tight inside me, threading through my ribs, settling deep in my chest where it pulses with a life of its own. But it's not just my emotions churning through me anymore. Kaia's anguish crashes through the connection in waves, raw and devastating. Her rage burns like acid, but beneath it... beneath it is a grief so profound it steals my breath.

I press a hand against my chest, trying to steady myself against the onslaught. My chaos magic sparks erratically, responding to the storm of emotions I can't control—mine, hers, all of it tangled together until I can barely tell where I end and she begins.

And judging by the way the others look, the rigid tension in their shoulders, the pain bleeding through their carefully controlled expressions, I'm not the only one drowning in it.

"You had no right." Torric's voice breaks the silence, low and dangerous. His fire rune still glows beneath his shirt, the brand visible through the singed fabric. "No fucking right."

Aspen steps forward, and for once his calm facade is completely shattered. Frost patterns spread across his arms where his ice rune flares, the cold radiating from him in waves. "We trusted you," he says, each word sharp as winter. "Kaia trusted you. And you took that choice from her. From all of us."

Torric's fists clench so tight his knuckles go bone-white, trembling with barely contained fury. "You don't even know half of what she's been through. How many choices were stolen from her. And you did this anyway?"

Malrik hasn't stopped watching the door Kaia disappeared through. Doesn't look away, doesn't move to follow her, doesn't do anything. Just stands there like a statue, his silver eyes unreadable while his shadows writhe restlessly around his feet.

And Kieran—Kieran, the one person who knew exactly what this place would do, hasn't moved at all. Just stands there like he's carved from stone, golden eyes fixed on nothing.

I exhale through my teeth, shoving a hand through my hair. Usually, this is where I'd crack a joke. Make everyone remember how to breathe. Step in when things feel too heavy and remind people that the world hasn't actually ended.

But right now? I don't feel like breathing. I feel like putting my fist through something.

And unfortunately for Kieran, he's the closest available target.

I take a step forward, slow and deliberate, chaos magic crackling faintly around my fingers. His golden eyes finally snap to me, and I see him brace himself. He knows what's coming.

"Tell me something," I say, my voice lighter than I feel. "At what point did you decide this was a brilliant idea?"

Kieran doesn't answer.

"Was it before or after you realized Kaia was going to hate you for it?" I press, letting the words slip out smooth and easy, like I'm not two seconds from putting him through the nearest wall.

"Finn," Malrik warns, but I barely glance at him.

"No, really," I continue, tilting my head with mock curiosity. "Because I'd love to know what was running through that ancient brain of yours when you decided to trap us all in this." I gesture vaguely at the space between us, at the weight sitting in my chest like a stone, at bonds none of us were ready for.

"The bonds were already forming," Kieran says quietly, his voice carrying centuries of exhaustion. "You all felt it."

"And that gives you the right to force it?" Aspen demands, his voice sharper than I've ever heard it. Ice crystals form in the air around him as his power responds to his anger. "To take away our chance to let it happen naturally?"

Torric takes a menacing step forward, heat radiating from him in waves. "You knew what this would do to her. To all of us. And you did it anyway."

Kieran's hands flex at his sides, but his voice remains steady. "The bonds were always meant to form."

I let out a sharp laugh that echoes off the ancient stones. "Right, right. *Meant to.* And that makes it okay?"

His jaw tightens almost imperceptibly. "It was already happening."

"Yeah?" My magic flares brighter, chaotic energy dancing between my fingers. "Well, guess what? Now Kaia hates you. So tell me, Kieran—was it worth it?"

Silence.

A muscle in Kieran's jaw twitches. His hands curl into fists at his sides, golden magic rolling through the air like distant thunder. I don't back down.

Because here's the thing. I don't care what fate wants. I don't care that these bonds were "meant to happen." I care that Kaia didn't get to choose them. That something beautiful—something sacred—got twisted into another chain around her neck.

And now? Now she's hurt, pissed, and looking for a way out that doesn't exist.

"Someone should go after her," Malrik says finally, his voice carefully controlled.

Torric exhales sharply, flames flickering around his shoulders. "Not me. I'm likely to set something on fire right now."

Aspen runs a hand through his hair, frost still clinging to his fingertips. "She needs space."

Kieran's hands twitch like he wants to move, wants to follow her, but knows better. The golden light in his eyes dims slightly—regret, maybe, or just exhaustion.

I sigh dramatically, throwing my hands up. "Fine. I'll do it."

Malrik gives me a look, shadows coiling tighter around him. "You sure that's wise?"

I shrug, forcing my usual grin even though it feels like broken glass. "Nope. But someone has to, and I'm apparently the least likely to get murdered on sight."

"Finn," Aspen calls as I turn toward the exit. His voice is tight with concern, ice crystals still floating around him like tiny stars. "Be careful. She's not just angry. She's hurt."

I nod, more serious than usual. "I know."

The bond in my chest thrums with Kaia's pain, her rage, her grief. It's like carrying someone else's broken heart alongside my own.

"And Finn?" Torric's voice stops me at the threshold. When I look back, his fire rune pulses once, bright and fierce. "If she wants to burn this whole place down... well, I've got plenty of fire to spare."

Despite everything, I feel my grin turn genuine. "I'll keep that in mind."

And with that, I turn and head toward the garden, chaos magic sparking anxiously around me.

Time to see if Kaia's in the mood to murder me. With my luck, she probably is.

Chapter 24
Kaia

I feel him coming before I hear his footsteps. The bond pulses with his presence, a chaotic energy that somehow feels steadying despite everything else churning inside me. My shadows ripple in recognition, but I don't turn around.

"If you're here to defend him," I say quietly, "don't."

"Wouldn't dream of it." Finn's voice carries that familiar lightness, but underneath I can feel the turmoil he's trying to hide. "Pretty sure he deserves everything you're feeling right now. And then some."

I let out a shaky breath, staring at the impossibly clear water of the pool. "You can feel it too, can't you? All of it?"

"Yeah." He moves closer, careful but not hesitant. "Gotta say, you've got quite the emotional range there, Trouble. The rage is impressive, but it's the heartbreak that's really doing me in."

"I'm not heartbroken," I snap, but we both know it's a lie. The bond makes lying impossible now.

"No?" His reflection appears beside mine in the water as he settles at the pool's edge. "Because what I'm feeling through this thing suggests otherwise."

My shadows coil tighter, restless and agitated. Mouse presses against my leg, a warm anchor in the storm of emotions. "I don't want to talk about it."

"Good thing I'm not here to make you talk." He drops down to sit beside me, his usual manic energy somehow muted. "I'm just here to remind you that you're not alone in this mess."

"Even though none of us had a choice?"

"Especially because none of us had a choice." His green eyes meet mine in the reflection. "Look, what Kieran did? It was wrong. But these bonds? They were already there, Kaia. We all felt it building. He just..." He runs a hand through his auburn hair, frustration bleeding through the connection. "He took away our chance to choose when. How."

I close my eyes, fighting against the fresh wave of grief that threatens to overwhelm me. "It was supposed to be beautiful."

"It still can be."

"How?" The word comes out raw, scraping my throat. "How can it be beautiful when it was forced on us?"

"Because the bond forming and what we choose to do with it are two different things," Finn says softly, and something in his voice makes me look at him directly. He's watching me with none of his usual mischief, just quiet understanding that aches through our connection. "He might have forced the timing, but he can't force what happens next. That's still ours."

My shadows drift toward him unconsciously, drawn to the steady warmth beneath his chaos. Even Bob seems to relax slightly, though he maintains his protective stance.

"I can feel all of you," I whisper, pressing a hand to my chest where the bonds pulse like separate heartbeats. "All the time. Your emotions, your energy... it's overwhelming."

"Tell me about it." Finn's laugh is gentle but strained. "Your rage alone could power half the sanctuary right now. Not that I blame you."

"How are you so calm about this?"

He shrugs, but I feel the carefully controlled panic beneath his casual demeanor. "Someone has to be. And since you're busy plotting murder, Malrik's doing his brooding statue impression, and the twins look ready to tear the place apart..."

"And Kieran?"

"Is definitely aware of how badly he screwed up." Finn's tone darkens. "Trust me on that one. The guilt coming off him is practically choking."

I sink down beside him, close enough that our shoulders brush. The contact sends a jolt through the bond, like completing a circuit I didn't know was broken. My shadows curl around us both, seeking comfort in his presence.

"I don't know how to do this," I admit quietly. "How to handle feeling everyone all the time. How to trust any of it when it started like this."

"We figure it out together." His hand finds mine, fingers interlacing. The simple touch grounds me in a way that surprises us both. "Day by day. Choice by choice. Until maybe one day it feels less like a chain and more like..."

"More like what?"

"More like coming home."

I turn to look at him properly, meeting his gaze. There's a vulnerability there I've never seen before, raw and unguarded in a way that makes my breath catch.

"Kaia," he says, his voice dropping to something softer, more real. "What we have—what we've always had—it's not defined by this bond. It's not created by it. You know that, right?"

Before I can answer, he shifts closer, one hand cupping my face with surprising gentleness. "Close your eyes."

"Finn—"

"Trust me. Please."

I do, and suddenly I'm overwhelmed by sensations that have nothing to do with magical bonds. The warmth of his skin against mine. The steady rhythm of his breathing. The scent that's uniquely him, smoke and starlight and something indefinably wild. But more than that, I feel his emotions washing over me without the filter of magic. Admiration. Affection. A fierce protectiveness that steals my breath.

"This," Finn murmurs, his thumb tracing my cheekbone, "this is us. No bond. No magic. Just you and me, Trouble."

And then he kisses me.

It's like the world explodes into color. Every nerve ending comes alive, singing with something that has nothing to do with forced connections and everything to do with choice. I've been kissed before, but never like this. Never with such tenderness and passion intertwined, never with someone who makes me feel like I'm coming apart and being rebuilt all at once.

When we finally break apart, both breathless, Finn rests his forehead against mine.

"That," he says, wonder bleeding into his voice, "is what we are without any bonds at all. Beautiful. Powerful. Real."

And then something shifts between us.

The bond—still raw and unwanted—suddenly doesn't feel like a chain. It feels like recognition. Like something that was always there finally has permission to exist.

I don't mean to open myself to it. Don't mean to let him deeper. But Finn is already there, waiting, and somehow it doesn't feel so terrifying anymore.

The rush is indescribable. Like diving into a sea of starlight, every cell in my body singing with joy and connection that feels earned rather than stolen. I can feel Finn's wonder echoing my own, our emotions amplifying and reflecting until I'm not sure where I end and he begins—but for the first time, that doesn't terrify me.

I'm trembling in his arms, steady and strong, and I can feel his heart racing in perfect sync with mine.

"Holy shit," he breathes against my hair, voice shaky with awe. "That was..."

"Different," I finish, understanding flooding through both of us simultaneously. "The bond—it feels different now."

"Because we chose it," Finn says, pulling back to meet my eyes. "In that moment, we chose each other. Not because of the bond. In spite of it."

My shadows dance around us, lighter somehow, more playful than they've been since we arrived. Even Mouse seems less tense, his violet eyes warm with approval.

"I think," Finn continues, that familiar mischievous grin finally return-ing, "we might just be unstoppable when we stop fighting what we actually want."

I laugh, actually laugh, for the first time since stepping foot in this realm. "Is that your solution to everything? Stop fighting and start kissing?"

"Hey, it worked, didn't it?" He waggles his eyebrows, but there's real tenderness underneath the humor. "Besides, I've got about four more people to convince, so I better perfect my technique."

The thought of Finn trying to kiss his way through everyone's anger makes me snort with laughter. "I'd pay to see you try that approach with Torric."

"Please. The man's basically a walking furnace. One good kiss and he'd melt like butter."

"You're ridiculous."

"You love it." He says it lightly, but there's a question underneath. A hope.

I meet his gaze, feeling the bond hum between us. Not forced now, but freely given. "Yeah," I say softly. "I do."

The ache in my chest doesn't disappear, but it shifts into something warmer. Something that feels less like a wound and more like possibility.

Chapter 25
KIERAN

I shouldn't be here.

The thought loops through my mind, but the bond doesn't care. It pulls with relentless insistence, dragging me toward her like a tide I can't escape. Every instinct screams at me to give her space, to let her process what I've done without my presence poisoning the air further.

But I can't stay away.

I keep to the shadows beyond the garden, hidden among the twisted trees that somehow still grow in this corrupted place. The sanctuary's dim torches flicker over the impossible oasis where Kaia sits with Finn, golden light catching in her hair, dancing across the restless movement of her shadows.

She doesn't push him away when he settles beside her.

Doesn't tense or retreat.

She leans into him.

Something sharp twists in my chest—not jealousy, exactly, but something rawer. More complicated.

At first, it's subtle. A whisper of warmth creeping through the bond, easing the rigid tension that's held my shoulders locked since the Hall. The relief isn't mine—it's hers. Kaia's emotions trickle through our connection like water through cracked stone, and despite everything, despite the fury I can still taste at the edges of her consciousness, there's something else.

Contentment.

The warmth spreads through me, settling in places I didn't realize were cold. For a moment, I almost forget why I'm lurking in the shadows like some lovesick fool, because feeling her at peace, even if it's not because of me, is worth the ache in my chest.

But then the bond shifts.

Her emotions deepen, intensify. Affection bleeds through the connection, soft and genuine, followed by something that makes my breath catch.

Want.

It starts as a flutter, barely noticeable, but it builds with each passing second. Heat spreads through my stomach as Kaia's desire flows through the bond, and I have to grip the bark of the nearest tree to steady myself.

She's not thinking of me.

The realization hits hard, but the bond doesn't care. It forces me to feel every flutter of her pulse, every spark of attraction she feels for the man beside her. My body responds like her desire is my own—muscles tensing, breath coming shorter, hardening with want that isn't mine to claim.

I should leave. Should tear myself away from this torment and let her have this moment without my unwanted presence contaminating it.

But I can't move.

Finn's hand finds her face, gentle and sure, and even from this distance I can see the way Kaia melts into his touch. The bond thrums with her anticipation, with the growing heat between them, and my treacherous flesh betrays me completely.

Then Finn kisses her.

The bond explodes.

A sound rips from my throat—half growl, half groan—as the full force of Kaia's pleasure crashes through me. My knees buckle, and I catch myself against the tree, bark splitting beneath my grip as I fight to stay upright.

The connection is merciless. Every sensation Kaia feels becomes mine—the warmth of Finn's lips, the way her heart races, the liquid heat that pools in her belly. My vision blurs as arousal slams through me, my body responding to her pleasure like it's my own touch bringing her such joy.

I can't breathe. Can't think. Can only feel as the bond forces me to experience every second of her choosing someone else.

Heat coils at the base of my spine, muscles going rigid as I fight against the overwhelming rush of sensation. My pulse hammers so hard I can feel it in my skull, and the ache between my legs becomes almost unbearable.

This is what I've reduced myself to. Standing in the shadows, getting off on the woman I love kissing another man.

"Well, that's fucking pathetic."

I whirl around, heart slamming against my ribs, my body still betraying me even as I try to compose myself.

Malrik stands a few feet away, arms crossed, silver eyes gleaming with sharp amusement as he takes in my disheveled state. Of course he followed me. Of course he'd witness this humiliation.

I clench my jaw, forcing my breathing to steady, willing my body to stop reacting to emotions that aren't mine.

He smirks, but there's no warmth in it. "Are you really going to stand here and get off watching her kiss someone else?"

A snarl tears from my throat before I can stop it, golden magic crackling around me in warning. But Malrik doesn't flinch. He never does.

"You're feeling it, aren't you?" His voice is conversational, almost curious. "Every second of what she feels for him."

I don't answer. What could I possibly say?

His laugh is low and cutting. "This is rich. The great Kieran, brought low by a bond he forced into existence."

"Shut up, Malrik." The words come out rougher than intended.

"Why? Not enjoying the connection right now?" He takes a step closer, shadows writhing around his feet. "That bond you decided we all needed, whether we wanted it or not?"

The blood pounds in my ears, but I can still hear him perfectly. Still feel the lingering heat of Kaia's desire threading through my veins like poison.

"Tell me," Malrik continues, his voice dropping to something softer but infinitely more dangerous, "how does it feel knowing she's not just accepting Finn, but choosing him? Actively wanting him?"

I turn away, but there's nowhere to go. Nowhere to hide from the truth he's throwing at me.

"You really thought she'd always be yours, didn't you?" His words are surgical in their precision. "Thought if you waited long enough, fate would hand her back to you. That you wouldn't have to fight for her, wouldn't have to earn her."

The air feels too thin. I can barely draw breath past the tightness in my chest.

"You spent centuries waiting for her to be yours," Malrik says, and now his voice carries something almost like pity. "But did you ever stop to think that maybe you were supposed to be hers instead?"

The question lands like a blade between my ribs. Because the answer is no. In all my planning, all my certainty about destiny and bonds meant to be, I never considered that I might have to prove myself worthy of her choice.

I can still feel her through the bond. The lingering warmth of her joy, the satisfaction that comes from being truly seen and accepted. And none of it, not one single spark, is directed at me.

Malrik watches me for another moment, then shakes his head. "That bond was supposed to be your greatest strength. But right now? It's just your fucking curse."

He melts back into the shadows, leaving me alone with the wreckage of my assumptions.

I don't move. Can't move. My pulse still throbs painfully, my breath still comes in ragged gasps, and the ghost of Kaia's desire still burns through my veins like a fever I can't break.

The cold air does nothing to ease the ache.

Nothing can.

Because for all my waiting, for all my faith in what was meant to be, I never considered the one possibility that could destroy everything I'd built my existence around.

Kaia might not choose me at all.

And now I'll feel it all—every time she chooses someone who isn't me.

Chapter 26
MALRIK

The bond still lingers in my veins like a phantom touch, curling through my chest with echoes of emotions that aren't mine. But unlike Kieran, I know how to control myself. I compartmentalize, lock it away, deal with it later when I'm not surrounded by witnesses to my unraveling.

I turn away from the trees where I left him—still caught in his own personal hell, still standing there hard and shattered by the bond he forced on all of us.

Pathetic.

I don't need to see the wreckage on his face to know he's breaking. The bond made sure we all felt it—Kaia's joy, her pleasure, the way she melted into Finn like he was gravity itself. The difference is, I don't let it consume me.

I understand what she needs. What they both need. And my own complicated feelings about wanting them both more than I ever thought possible? That's my problem to sort through, not theirs.

I shove my hands into my pockets as I move through the stone corridors of the sanctuary, ignoring the old ghosts that press at the edges of my consciousness. This place carries too much history, too many memories of the boy I used to be before everything went to hell.

I don't linger. Don't stop to examine the familiar architecture or the way shadows fall differently here than anywhere else. Don't give in to the pull of a past that belongs to someone else entirely.

This was my home once.

Now it's just another cage with prettier bars.

I take the longer route through the training grounds, avoiding the main passages where I might encounter anyone else from our group. The torches burn bright against ancient stone, flickering in the humid air that seeps through open archways.

It's unsettling how much of this place still feels familiar despite the years I've spent trying to forget it. The way my footsteps echo in certain corridors. The particular scent of old magic and older secrets that clings to everything here.

I should be used to ghosts by now. I carry enough of them.

But this place is different. This is where I learned what it meant to become one.

I'm rounding the next corner, lost in thoughts I'd rather not examine, when I find Mira leaning casually against the stone railing, watching me with that same unreadable expression she always wears.

She doesn't speak at first, just tilts her head slightly, her silver eyes glinting in the firelight.

"You always did like lurking in the shadows."

Her voice is smooth, edged with something familiar. Something almost reminiscent.

I lift a brow. "And you always did like watching from a safe distance."

Her smirk deepens. "I prefer to assess the battlefield before I step onto it."

I know what she's doing. Mira has always been drawn to power—not to people, not to love, not to loyalty. Power. And now, she's trying to see how much of it I still have.

She pushes off the railing, taking a step closer. "You're restless."

I don't respond.

Her gaze flicks over me, sharp and searching. Not in attraction, in evaluation.

"Was it hard for you, Malrik?"

I let out a slow breath, my patience thinning. "Be more specific."

Her smirk lingers, but there's something speculative in her eyes. "The bond."

I don't react, but I know she sees the tension in my shoulders.

She takes another step, close enough that I can feel the warmth of her magic, smooth and contained. "You felt it too."

It's not a question.

I meet her gaze, cold and unmoving. "Everyone in the bond did."

She hums, dragging a hand through her dark hair. "And yet, you're the only one who walked away with your dignity intact."

A slow, amused chuckle builds in my chest. "Are you asking if I got hard over Kaia kissing Finn?"

She shrugs, but her silver eyes don't leave mine. "I wouldn't judge."

I shake my head, leaning against the nearest pillar. "No. But I did feel it."

She watches me for a beat, her expression assessing, calculating. "And?"

I tilt my head, studying her in return. "And what?"

Her lips curve, but it's not playful. It's testing. "And how did it make you feel?"

I let the silence stretch before I answer.

"Like I already knew."

She blinks, but I don't elaborate.

Because I did know. Kaia isn't some prize to be won. She's not some fragile thing waiting to be claimed. She's choosing. And I? I'm waiting for her to choose me too.

Mira steps closer, close enough that I know this isn't just conversation anymore. Her gaze lingers on mine, her pupils dilating slightly.

She lifts a hand, trailing one finger along the sleeve of my shirt, a test. One to sate her curiosity.

"What are you doing, Mira?" My voice stays steady, but I don't move away.

She tilts her head, considering me. "Testing a theory."

"About?"

"Power." Her silver eyes catalog the changes in me, the sharper edges, the way shadows respond to my presence now like they recognize something that wasn't there before. "You're different than you were as a boy."

She traces her fingers down my forearm, just the barest brush of contact, waiting to see if I'll react. If I'll let her.

I don't.

I catch her wrist before she can move any further, grip firm but not unkind.

She exhales softly, her smirk deepening. "Interesting."

My jaw tightens. "Is it?"

She watches me, something calculating in her expression. "Most men would have reacted by now. One way or another."

My grip tightens, just for a second, before I release her. "I'm not most men."

For the first time, something flickers across her face, something almost like genuine interest. But it's gone before I can name it.

She exhales softly, stepping back. "No. You're not."

I give her a slow, humorless smile. "Was that your conclusion?"

She tilts her head, studying me one last time before turning to walk away. "Among others."

I close my eyes, inhaling deep, letting the silence settle.

This place is trying to pull me back into old patterns. But I'm not the boy who left this realm in desperation and shame.

And I'm sure as hell not the prince they lost.

Chapter 27
KAIA

The world around me shifts.

I know this is a dream—I always know.

But this one feels different.

I'm standing in a place I don't recognize, though something about it tugs at the edges of my mind like a half-forgotten song. Shadows coil around my feet, not just stretching but clinging, their tendrils wrapping like searching fingers, like they're trying to tell me something I'm not ready to hear. The cracked stone beneath me pulses faintly, as if it carries a heartbeat, as if it remembers things I've forgotten.

The air hums with something ancient, something hungry.

The sky above is endless black, no stars, no moon, just a vast and empty void that presses down on me like a weight I can taste. The silence isn't peaceful—it's waiting. Watching.

A flicker of movement catches my eye, something small, bobbing just above the ground.

Walter.

But his usual lazy drifting is gone. His form wavers in and out of focus, like a candle struggling against wind. He moves toward me with hesitant urgency, his strange purplish glow flickering as he hovers near my shoulder. He's trying to warn me.

I take a step forward, but the ground beneath me isn't solid. It shifts like sand made of shadows, not quite earth, not quite anything. Each step feels like walking on the surface of a frozen lake where the ice grows thinner with every breath.

Then I see him.

A figure stands in the distance, half-swallowed by shifting mist.

I can't make out his face clearly.

I can't even tell if he's real.

But I feel him.

Something inside me snaps taut, an invisible wire pulled tight around my ribs. My breath stutters in my throat, the bonds that should be settled inside me shuddering like struck tuning forks.

The others—Finn, Malrik, Aspen, Torric, even Kieran—they all fell into place, their connections forming and locking into something solid, undeniable.

But this? This bond still bleeds.

It aches.

Like something vital is missing. Like something is trying to crawl home through broken glass.

I take another step forward, my pulse hammering against my skull, my body knowing something my mind refuses to accept.

The shadows part just enough for me to glimpse him clearly.

Dark hair that catches light it shouldn't have. Sharp features carved from marble and regret. Eyes like storm clouds before lightning strikes.

A voice echoes through the space, low and rough, but the words dissolve before they reach me, slipping through my fingers like smoke.

Walter flickers beside me, his glow dimming to almost nothing. He bobs once—frantic, urgent—then vanishes entirely.

I know him.

But I don't.

The recognition slams into me like a fist to the chest. My lungs seize, my body reacting to something my mind can't grasp. There's history here, written in the space between us, carved into the way he stands like he's holding himself together by will alone.

I know that face.

I know the weight in those eyes.

But before I can reach him, before I can even whisper the name burning on my tongue, the darkness pulls.

And everything shatters.

I wake with a gasp that tears from my throat like a scream I couldn't release. My entire body is rigid, every muscle locked like I've been struck by lightning. My heart pounds so violently it hurts, the incomplete bond in my chest pulling, *demanding*, refusing to be ignored.

The room is dark, but I can feel warmth beside me, solid and real. Finn's arm tightens around my waist as I jolt awake, his breath warm against the back of my neck. His body anchors me, pulls me back from whatever edge I was standing on.

I press my fingers against my sternum, willing the ache to fade.

It doesn't.

It gets *worse*.

Across the room, Malrik shifts restlessly, his jaw clenched even in sleep. Aspen and Torric both tense, their bodies responding to something their unconscious minds recognize. Kieran's bond flares—just for a heartbeat, sharp and distant—before settling back into careful control.

Finn stirs, his fingers searching across my skin even before he's fully awake.

The dream clings to me like cobwebs, thick and suffocating, refusing to fade. I should wake Finn, tell him, let him distract me with his chaos and warmth. But I can't move.

Can't breathe.

I squeeze my eyes shut, but it doesn't help. My mind is racing, chasing fragments of recognition that slip away the moment I try to hold them.

I felt him.

The bond is there. Its been there all along, just out of reach, lingering in the space between what is and what's been stolen from me.

And whoever he is, wherever he is, he felt it too.

I know it the same way I know my own heartbeat.

The same way I felt each of my other bonds snap into place like pieces of a puzzle I didn't know I was solving.

Whoever he is, he's waiting.

And I'm running out of time to find him.

Chapter 28
KAIA

The morning is too bright.

It shouldn't bother me. The sanctuary's halls are always bathed in soft golden light filtering through enchanted crystals embedded in the walls. But today it feels harsh, intrusive, like it's trying to scrape me awake when my mind is still tangled in dream-smoke and shadows that won't let go.

I don't remember falling asleep again after the nightmare, but when I finally pry my eyes open, Finn's arm is draped across my waist like he's afraid I might disappear. His warmth is steady, his breathing slow and even against my neck. My shadows drift around the room—twice as many as when I first stepped into this cursed realm. Bob notices my attention and immediately starts herding the smaller ones into formation like a drill sergeant with unruly recruits.

As if military precision will solve anything.

For a few heartbeats, I let myself stay here. Let myself breathe. Let myself pretend the world isn't unraveling faster than I can hold it together.

Then the ache in my chest pulses, sharp and demanding, dragging me back to reality.

The dream. The missing bond. The stranger with storm-cloud eyes who felt like coming home and losing everything all at once.

I press my fingers against my sternum, willing the hollow space inside me to stop *bleeding*. But whoever he is, wherever he is, he felt it too. I know it like I know my own heartbeat. Like I know the exact moment each of my other bonds snapped into place.

He's out there, waiting.

And I don't know if I'm supposed to find him, or if he's already hunting me.

Finn stirs beside me, letting out a low groan before his grip tightens around my waist.

"Five more minutes," he mumbles into my shoulder. "Or twenty. Maybe forever."

I snort despite myself. "Planning to become one with the mattress?"

"Not my fault you're perfect for cuddling," he mutters, lips brushing against my neck in a way that sends heat curling down my spine. For a moment, I let myself sink into the sensation, eyes fluttering closed as warmth spreads through me like honey.

But then reality crashes back—the ache in my chest flaring, guilt twisting my stomach at enjoying this when someone else is waiting for me in whatever void dreams are made of.

Finn must feel me tense because he sighs against my skin and pulls back. "Right. Functioning adults. I keep forgetting."

"We've never been functioning adults," I point out, grateful for his easy reading of my mood.

He grins, stretching as he rolls out of bed. "Come on, Trouble. Let's see if breakfast comes with less existential crisis today."

Highly doubtful.

But I get up anyway, pulling on leather pants that fit too well to be coincidence and ignoring the way my shadows seem more agitated than usual. Carl actually salutes me as we pass, while Mouse circles Finn like a suspicious chaperone.

The dining hall buzzes with morning energy when we arrive. Long tables stretch across the room, filled with warriors and scholars and people who look like they actually got sleep. The air is thick with roasted meat and fresh bread, but my stomach churns, still twisted up in dream-fragments and missing pieces.

Aspen and Torric sit rigid as statues, their eyes tracking my approach. Malrik lounges beside them with studied casualness, though the tension in his silver gaze tells me he's still processing last night's revelations.

Finn drops into his seat with his usual sprawl of limbs. I slide in next to him, forcing myself to focus on tea and normalcy and anything but the way my chest feels like it's caving in.

Then the room *shifts*.

Conversation doesn't stop, exactly, but it changes pitch. A collective intake of breath, like the hall itself is bracing for impact.

I glance up—and freeze.

Mira glides through the crowd like she owns every inch of stone beneath her feet. Confident. Poised. Making a beeline straight for Kieran.

I don't react.

Not at first.

Kieran's eyes find mine for a heartbeat before shifting to the woman approaching him. Something sharp coils in my stomach when she stops beside him, resting her hand on his arm with casual possessiveness.

He barely acknowledges her initially, but when she leans in close, murmuring something meant only for his ears, his mouth curves into a slow smirk.

Something inside me *cracks*.

I don't understand the feeling, not entirely. It's not like I haven't seen people flirt with him before. We're bonded by force and circumstance, nothing more.

Except apparently, I *do* care.

Mira's laugh is soft and knowing, her fingers trailing down his forearm. She presses closer, claiming space I didn't even know I wanted to protect.

Something ugly and possessive sparks in my chest.

Not the bond. Not magic. Something rawer.

Finn's fork scrapes porcelain as he leans in, voice dropping conspiratorially. "Uh-oh."

I exhale sharply, forcing my gaze back to my tea. "What?"

His grin is pure delight. "You jealous, Trouble?"

I scoff. "Of *Mira*? Please."

"Sure." He props his chin on his hand, watching me like I'm the most entertaining thing he's seen all week. "So that white-knuckle grip on your cup? That's just... enthusiasm for breakfast?"

I flex my fingers, realizing I'm moments from shattering ceramic. "I don't care what Kieran does."

Finn hums like he's never heard a bigger lie.

I try to ignore it. Try to ignore the way my shadows are coiling tighter, the way Bob is radiating disapproval toward Kieran and Mira, the way Patricia's frantic note-taking has turned sharp and aggressive.

I'm fine.

Absolutely fine.

Except when Mira laughs again, her palm pressing flat against Kieran's chest, I am absolutely, definitively, *not* fine.

The sharp *clink* of my cup hitting the table echoes across our section.

Malrik's knowing gaze finds mine. Aspen and Torric both tense, attention bouncing between me and the scene unfolding across the room.

Finn just leans closer, voice rich with teasing delight.

"Kaia, darling—" His smirk widens. "You look ready to commit murder."

I grit my teeth. "I'm not."

He gestures toward where Mira is now trailing her nails down Kieran's forearm. "Uh-huh. And that's what—performance art?"

My shadows bristle.

Fine. Maybe I'm not fine.

But I'm not jealous.

I just really, *really* don't like her.

I don't notice at first when my shadows begin moving. I'm too busy glaring at my tea like it holds the secrets of self-control. They slip away from me, purposeful and silent, not the usual emotional flickering but something with *intent*.

The hall gradually quiets as people notice.

I'm still contemplating my beverage when Finn makes a strangled sound beside me.

"Oh my *gods*," he wheezes, shoulders shaking with laughter. "Kaia, you absolute legend."

I frown. "What?"

Aspen sits frozen, fork halfway to his mouth, eyes wide. Torric sets his cup down like he's defusing a bomb. Malrik just sighs and takes another sip of coffee.

"What the hell—" Mira's voice cuts through the room, sharp with indignation. "Some kind of shadow parade?"

I look up.

And *oh*.

Two perfect columns of my shadows are marching through the crowd like they're on military parade. Bob leads one formation, Linda commands the other, both moving with the grim determination of soldiers on a sacred mission.

They reach Mira before I can process what's happening.

Without hesitation, they lift her straight off the ground.

Mira lets out an undignified *squawk*, arms windmilling as shadows hoist her into the air. The entire dining hall falls silent.

She blinks, clearly not comprehending. "Excuse me?!" she sputters, still not taking it seriously. "If you wanted me gone, you could have just *asked*."

Finn collapses against me, tears streaming down his face. "This is the greatest moment of my entire life."

Mira starts struggling in earnest, but my shadows don't falter. They carry her through the room with perfect coordination, past gaping warriors and stunned onlookers, straight toward the exit. Bob and Linda working in flawless synchronization like they've drilled this exact scenario.

Dead silence.

Malrik sets down his cup with deliberate calm. "She should feel honored," he observes, completely deadpan. "They don't usually provide personal escort service."

Torric coughs to hide a laugh. Aspen just drags his hands down his face.

Finn wipes tears from his eyes, still wheezing with laughter. "Survival Tip #4," he manages between gasps. "If Bob disapproves, you're probably about to die or fall in love. Possibly both."

I open my mouth to deny involvement, but Finn beats me to it.

"Your jealousy is *showing*, Trouble."

I glare at him. "I'm not jealous."

He points toward where Mira is actively cursing out my shadows as they cart her through the doorway. "Right. Total coincidence."

I stare into my tea like it might offer absolution. "No idea what you mean."

Kieran's voice carries across the room, entirely too amused. "Definitely not jealous at all."

From the hallway: "KAIA, CALL THEM OFF!"

I take a deliberate sip of tea, refusing to look up.

"Must be talking to someone else."

Chapter 29
Kaia

My shadows are still basking in their victory.

Bob actually struts as he leads the others in what can only be described as a triumph parade around our end of the table. Even Patricia, usually laser-focused on her documentation, keeps recreating the exact moment Mira's face shifted from confusion to pure outrage. Finnick has appointed himself chief dramatist, complete with shadow-flailing and what I'm pretty sure are interpretive dance moves.

"They're never going to let this go, are they?" I mutter, watching Steve and Carl stage an increasingly elaborate performance where they carry Linda around like she's royalty.

"Not a chance." Finn grins, stealing bread from my plate with zero shame. "Bob's probably commissioning a commemorative plaque. 'The Great Mira Ejection'—catchy, right?"

I glare at him, but there's no heat in it. Mouse, draped across my lap like a satisfied cat, makes a sound that's definitely laughter.

Malrik takes another careful sip of coffee, but I catch the way his mouth quirks. "Linda's tactical coordination was particularly impressive. Textbook execution."

"Of course you'd analyze shadow military strategy," Torric snorts, though his golden eyes spark with amusement. "Next you'll be grading their formation techniques."

The warm glow in my chest—pride, satisfaction, maybe a hint of possessiveness I'm pretending doesn't exist—begins to settle. Then the hollowness *punches* through. That familiar ache. The bond that refuses to complete itself, hanging in my chest like an open wound.

The magic in me doesn't respond with comfort.

It responds with *panic*.

Chaos magic explodes through me without warning, wild and vicious, scattering my shadows like startled ravens. The cup in my grip *cracks*, tea leaking across the table in dark rivulets that look too much like spilled blood.

"Fuck," I gasp, hands shaking as I try to hold myself together. Bob snaps into crisis mode, marshaling the others into damage control while Patricia's frantic scribbling turns sharp with worry.

Finn's fingers find mine beneath the table, anchor-steady. "Talk to me, Trouble."

Before I can answer, movement at the high table steals my attention. A figure in battle-worn leather armor bends low, whispering urgently in Kieran's ear. The transformation is instant, his entire frame goes rigid, amusement dying like a snuffed candle.

The bond between us *jolts*, electric where it should be warm.

Mouse's ears flatten as Kieran rises, his gaze cutting across the room to find mine. The playful energy dies completely, replaced by something that tastes like dread on the back of my tongue.

"Well," Finn mutters, grip tightening. "We're fucked, aren't we?"

Kieran strides toward us in silence, but I feel his urgency like lightning under my skin. My shadows abandon their celebration, clustering close with sudden wariness. Even Finnick drops his theatrical nonsense, snapping into formation beside Bob.

"War Room. Now." His voice could cut glass. Those ancient eyes sweep over our group before locking on mine again, and I see something flicker there, not just alarm, but something rawer. Like he can feel me coming apart and has no idea how to stop it.

Aspen sets his cup down almost too gently. "What's happened?"

Kieran's already turning away, shoulders carved from stone. "Not here."

Another wave of chaos magic *tears* through me, foreign and violent, nothing like the controlled chaos that belongs to Finn. This feels like something trying to claw its way out from inside my bones. My shadows writhe in response, agitated by power that doesn't belong.

"Easy," Finn murmurs, hand warm against my spine. "Just ride it out."

Mouse presses against my leg as we follow Kieran through corridors that suddenly feel too narrow, his violet eyes sharp with concern. The missing bond pulses like an infected wound, responding to whatever tension is building in the air around us.

The War Room buzzes with grim energy when we arrive. Revna stands rigid beside the ancient table, silver armor catching torchlight, maps spread before her like battle scars. Symbols mark locations I don't recognize, but they feel important. Dangerous.

"Tell them," Kieran commands, and something in Revna's expression goes knife-sharp.

"Our scouts in the northern mountains sent word." Her voice stays level, but there's steel underneath. "Alekir's forces are mobilizing. And they're not alone."

The name hits like ice water in my veins. Bob immediately shifts into defensive positioning while Patricia's notes become increasingly frantic, pages flipping with supernatural speed.

"Not alone how?" Malrik's question carries weight I don't understand, like he already knows the answer will be terrible.

Revna's gaze finds his, something dark passing between them. Shared knowledge. Shared fear. "The corruption isn't just spreading anymore. It's *changing* people."

"Into what?" The question slips out before I can stop it, though I'm not sure I want the answer.

"Something else," Kieran says quietly. "Something that shouldn't exist."

The foreign chaos magic *rips* through me again, buckling my knees. Finn catches me before I can fall, but I feel his alarm through our bond like a live wire.

"We move now," Kieran continues, eyes fixed on me with uncomfortable intensity. "While we still have the advantage."

"What advantage?" I ask, fighting to stay upright. "What exactly do we have that he doesn't?"

His expression goes granite-hard. "You. Bonded. Here. Stronger than you've ever been."

But am I? The incomplete bond *screams* in my chest, a constant reminder of everything that's broken, everything that's missing. And this chaos magic tearing through me, I'm not controlling it. It's controlling me.

Aspen shifts beside us, his usual stillness cracking. There's something in his face—knowledge, maybe, or fear—that makes my anxiety spike higher.

"Aspen?" I start, but he's already moving toward the door, movements too controlled, too careful.

"Need air," he says without looking back, but it sounds more like *escape* than breath.

Mouse makes a distressed sound, ears tracking Aspen's retreat. Bob starts to follow, then hesitates, torn between duties.

The others remain focused on maps and battle plans, but something *pulls* me toward Aspen. Not the bond exactly, something deeper. Instinct maybe, or the certainty that whatever he knows, whatever he's running from, it's about to change everything.

"Be right back," I murmur to Finn, who squeezes my hand once before letting go.

As I slip out after Aspen, shadows trailing like worried children, one thought hammers through my skull:

Whatever he's hiding, I need to know it. Because this isn't just about missing bonds or uncontrolled magic anymore.

This is about keeping us all alive long enough to figure out what the hell we're fighting for.

Chapter 30
ASPEN

The war room presses in on me from all sides.

Too many voices. Too much tension. Too much *everything* crackling through the air like lightning waiting to strike.

I slip out, my steps deliberately measured despite the urge to run. The moment the door closes behind me, I exhale like I've been holding my breath for hours. My skin still hums from Kaia's wild magic, from the chaos tearing through her that I can't fix, from bonds that ache with incompleteness and the weight of everything spiraling beyond my control.

From *her*.

My feet carry me toward the library without conscious thought. It's quiet there. A place where knowledge sits patient on shelves, where answers exist even if I can't always find them. Maybe if I sit still long enough, I'll figure out what the hell is happening to me.

But the moment I cross the threshold, I know I'm not alone.

The bond *shifts*.

She followed me.

Of course she did.

I don't turn around immediately, even though I can feel her presence settling just inside the doorway like warmth against my back. I close my eyes, dragging my composure back into place before facing whatever this conversation is going to cost me.

"You bolted pretty fast back there." Her voice is careful, testing.

I exhale through my nose. "Needed space to think."

Silence stretches between us. Then, quieter: "Want me to leave?"

Yes.

No.

Gods, I don't know.

"Do whatever you want, Kaia." The words come out rougher than I intend.

I hear her move closer, boots soft against stone. "You've been pulling away from me."

I force something that might pass for a laugh. "Not pulling away. Just..." I drag a hand down my face. "Trying to figure things out."

"What things?"

I finally turn to meet her gaze, and the openness there nearly undoes me. She's looking at me like I'm still worth something, like I'm still the man she trusted before everything changed.

Like she can't see the monster I'm becoming.

I lean against the nearest bookshelf, arms crossed defensively. "I don't know if I can control it anymore."

Understanding flickers in her violet eyes. "The berserker."

One sharp nod. "What happened when we stepped into Absentia, that wasn't *me*, Kaia. It was something else wearing my face. And I don't know if I can stop it from happening again."

She studies me with that unnerving focus of hers, shadows drifting around her ankles like curious cats. Something unreadable passes through her expression before she steps closer, eliminating the careful distance I've been maintaining.

I should back away.

I don't.

Instead, I go perfectly still as she reaches up, pressing her palm flat against my chest, right over my hammering heart. The touch is gentle but deliberate, warmth seeping through fabric to settle in my bones.

"You're still you," she says simply.

I swallow hard. "You can't know that."

Her fingers curl into my shirt, grip firm. "I do."

The certainty in her voice makes my breath catch. She means it—I can feel it through the bond, solid and unwavering. But she doesn't understand what I saw in that moment when the berserker took over. What I felt when control slipped away like water through my fingers.

"I could have hurt you." The admission scrapes my throat raw. "Could have killed you."

She doesn't even blink. "But you didn't."

"That's not the point." I shake my head, frustration bleeding through. "It wasn't *me* that held back. It was you. Your presence, your magic, something about you kept me tethered. But what happens when that's not enough?"

Her expression softens, and somehow that's worse than fear would be. Because she's not afraid of me. Not the way she should be. Not the way I'm afraid of myself.

She presses her palm more firmly against my chest. "Then let me be your anchor again."

I blink. "What?"

"If I could pull you back once, I can do it again." Her voice carries absolute conviction. "Let me be that for you."

My hands clench at my sides. "I don't want to *need* you for that."

A breath that's almost laughter escapes her. "Too bad."

I search her face for doubt, for the self-preservation that should make her run from someone like me. Find nothing but stubborn determination and something that looks dangerously like trust.

Just Kaia, offering me what I can't ask for.

Hope.

Choice.

Her.

Her voice wavers for the first time. "I need you too, Aspen."

Everything in me goes still.

She doesn't look away, even as vulnerability cracks her careful composure. "I need you, and that terrifies me." Her grip on my shirt tightens. "Because I don't know how to do this—how to trust these bonds, how to let people in. But I know I choose you. And if I have to fight for you, I will."

Something breaks open in my chest. "You shouldn't have to fight for me."

Her expression turns fierce. "That's not your decision to make."

The air between us changes, charged with something electric. I'm suddenly aware of everything—her scent, dark and sweet and uniquely hers, the way her fingers feel curled in my shirt, the space that's somehow both too much and not nearly enough.

Behind her, I catch the soft ripple of shadows retreating, giving us privacy. Even her magic understands this moment is ours alone.

For once, I stop thinking. Stop fearing. And I let myself want her

Then she tugs me forward.

And I'm lost.

Her mouth meets mine desperate and demanding, and whatever control I've been clinging to *shatters*. My hands find her waist, pulling her against me as I walk her backward until she hits the bookshelf. She gasps but doesn't retreat. Instead she presses closer, body melting into mine like she's been waiting for this as long as I have.

A sound rumbles from my chest, half growl, half surrender. Her nails scrape against my neck, and fire races down my spine. I deepen the kiss, one hand tangling in her hair, the other gripping her hip like she might disappear if I let go.

The bond flares between us, not the forced connection from the Hall but something chosen, something *earned*. The berserker inside me stirs, not with rage but with something infinitely more dangerous.

Want.

Need.

Mine.

I break away just enough to rest my forehead against hers, both of us breathing hard. My hands shake where they hold her, the intensity of what I'm feeling almost too much to contain.

"Still think you're a monster?" she whispers, breath warm against my lips.

My grip tightens involuntarily. "Not when I'm with you."

Her eyes flash with something wild and wonderful. Then she's pulling me back down, sealing whatever I might have said with another kiss.

One I'd tear apart worlds to protect.

Chapter 31
ASPEN

The moment our lips meet again, I come undone.

Not like the berserker, not losing myself to rage. This is different. Deliberate. A choice I'm finally brave enough to make.

Her hands slip beneath my shirt, fingertips tracing fire across my skin. Through our bond, I feel her raw need wrapping around me like a current I don't want to escape. The careful distance I've been maintaining dissolves like ice in sunlight.

I should pull back. Should think this through.

Instead, I press her closer, letting instinct win.

My pulse hammers in my ears, indistinguishable from the magic crackling between us. It feels dangerous. It feels right. I want to run from the intensity. I want to drown in it until I forget why I was ever afraid.

"Aspen." Just my name, breathed against my mouth. But it sounds like absolution.

I pull back enough to see her face—pupils blown wide, lips parted, flush spreading across her cheeks. Beautiful in a way that aches, that breaks something open inside me I didn't know was sealed shut.

For the first time, I stop fighting what I want.

"You're sure?" My voice doesn't sound like mine.

She reaches for the hem of my shirt, fingers brushing bare skin. "I've never been more sure of anything."

The bond flares so bright it's almost painful. Emotions cascade through me—hers, mine, impossible to separate. Trust. Want. A bone-deep certainty that shatters my last defenses.

She peels my shirt away like she's unwrapping something precious. The way she looks at me, like she sees past the monster I'm terrified of becoming, like she knows something about me I've forgotten, steals my breath.

I hate how vulnerable it makes me feel. I need it more than air.

When I kiss her again, it's softer. Deeper. My hands find her waist, slipping beneath her shirt to trace warm skin. She shivers, and the sensation shoots straight through our connection, making me force myself to slow down.

"Not here," I murmur against her lips. "Not against a bookshelf."

A smirk tugs at her lips. "Too undignified?"

"You deserve better than hard wood and dust." The double meaning hits me a second too late.

She laughs, soft and bright, and something frozen in my chest cracks open. Melts.

"There are worse things," she teases, but takes my hand, letting me lead her deeper into the library to an alcove where cushions and rugs create a sanctuary.

Her shadows flow around us as we move, creating a barrier between us and the world beyond. Mouse takes position at the entrance, violet eyes watchful and protective.

The bond flickers with sudden uncertainty, panic from one of us, maybe both, then settles into something deeper. More primal.

Mouse turns away. The shadows thicken.

Kaia pulls me down, and I follow. We're a tangle of limbs and quiet laughter. No rush this time. Only certainty.

I brush her hair back, trying to memorize everything, the curve of her cheekbone, the scatter of freckles across her nose, the exact shade of violet in her eyes.

"I've wanted this," I admit, the words pulled from somewhere I keep locked away. "Wanted you. Since the first time I felt you through the bond."

Her eyes soften as she traces my jawline. "Show me."

Those two words undo me completely.

I bend to kiss her neck, her collarbone, the hollow of her throat. Her shirt disappears. Mine follows. The first press of skin against skin nearly stops my heart. The bond surges, magic crackling between us like lightning gathering strength.

"Tell me what you need," I whisper against her skin.

"You," she says without hesitation. "Just you."

I don't deserve that kind of certainty. That kind of trust.

Our remaining clothes vanish beneath trembling hands. We're not graceful—elbows bump, laughter spills, clothes tangle. But none of that matters. What matters is the way she arches when I find a sensitive spot. The small sounds she makes when I kiss along her inner thigh. The way her shadows dance with her pleasure.

Her scent surrounds me—storm and salt and sweetness. Her taste on my tongue. The heat of her skin beneath my hands.

And then—panic. The berserker stirs, feral and possessive. I freeze.

"Aspen?" Kaia's voice anchors me. Her hand on my cheek, steady and warm. "Stay with me."

"I don't want to hurt you," I grit out, fear rushing back like a tide. The berserker wants to claim, to mark, to possess.

She sits up, taking my face in her hands. "You won't."

"You can't know that."

"I can. I do." Her eyes hold mine, fearless. "I trust you, Aspen. I need you to trust yourself."

How can she ask that? Trust myself when everything in me is a battle between control and chaos?

But before I can respond, she kisses me—fierce and sure. The bond flares, steadier than before. The berserker snarls once, then settles. Recognizing something it can't fight. Something it doesn't want to.

She pulls me back to her, wrapping her legs around my hips. Our eyes lock, and something passes between us—understanding deeper than words.

"Stay with me," she whispers.

"I couldn't leave if I tried," I answer, the honesty scraping my throat raw.

Then I enter her, and the world falls away. There's only sensation. Only Kaia.

She arches, whispering my name like a vow. The bond flares in response, weaving around us like something alive. For the first time since the berserker awakened, I don't feel torn apart.

Actually, that's not true. I feel more fragmented than ever—torn between the need to claim and the fear of losing control, between surrendering to the bond and maintaining some piece of myself.

But as we move together, finding a rhythm as natural as breathing, something unexpected happens. The fragments don't fight each other anymore. They realign into something new. Something stronger.

Her hands map my back, tangle in my hair. My lips never leave her skin for long—tasting, memorizing, claiming.

The berserker inside me stirs, but not with rage. With fierce, protective devotion that coils low and goes still. As if it's finally found its purpose. As if it has nothing left to fight.

The magic between us pulses wild and erratic. Her shadows stretch and curl with her pleasure. Bob and Linda form protective circles. Mouse watches with ancient patience.

The bond between us flickers—and then blazes brighter than before, sending shockwaves through both of us.

"Open your eyes," I tell her when I feel her getting close, when I feel myself teetering on the edge. "Look at me."

She does, and the vulnerability I see nearly breaks me. No one has ever looked at me like this—like I'm her anchor, like I'm worthy of trust.

I don't deserve it. I'm not worthy of it.

I am.

We're shaking—together, unraveling. The magic builds. The bond pulses. Time vanishes.

And then it shatters.

Not just climax—though that crashes through us both. The bond itself fractures, splintering into a thousand pieces before reconstructing in a heartbeat. The sensation is so intense I cry out—part pleasure, part pain, part something I have no name for.

"Aspen," she gasps, body tightening around mine. Her shadows flare wild and bright, plunging us into darkness for three heartbeats.

When sight returns, everything is sharper. Her eyes. Her skin. The gold and silver threads of magic binding us together.

The shadows around us pulse with her pleasure. Mouse's eyes glow brighter. Even Walter spins in lazy circles above us.

"I feel you—everywhere—" she breathes.

"I know. I feel you too."

The sensation crests again—pleasure spiraling into something transcendent. I feel the fall, losing the last threads of control—but there's no fear now. No need to hold back.

Because as I fall into her, she falls into me. As I claim her, she claims me. Equal. Complete.

The moment crashes over us, and I surrender—not to darkness, but to her. The bond blazes, blinding and brilliant, weaving us together in ways that can never be broken.

Except—there's still something missing. Not between us, but beyond us. A hollow space. A bond left open. A presence yet to arrive.

I don't have time to question it before aftershocks claim us both.

We lie tangled afterward, skin damp, hearts racing. I shift to pull her against my side, unwilling to let go. Her shadows settle around us like a warm blanket.

"The bond," I murmur, tracing patterns on her skin. "It's different now."

She nods, eyes heavy but clear. "Stronger."

"Steadier." The berserker inside me has calmed like a storm finally passing. Not gone, but no longer fighting to break free. No longer something to fear.

She brushes her fingers along my jaw. "You feel... settled."

"I am." The truth surprises me. I press my lips to her forehead. "You were right."

"About?"

"About being what I need."

She smiles—slow, a little smug. "Does that mean you'll stop hiding from me?"

"I wasn't hiding," I protest weakly.

Kaia raises an eyebrow.

"Fine. I was hiding. But no more."

She nestles deeper into my embrace, fingers tracing idle patterns over my heart. "Good. Because we need you." A pause. "I need you."

Words rise in my throat—words I'm not ready to say but feel with every fiber of my being. Instead, I press them into her skin with my lips. Against her temple. Her cheek. The corner of her mouth.

Mouse appears at the edge of our makeshift bed, keeping watch. The other shadows form protective circles around us, guarding this moment of peace.

Beyond our alcove, war is gathering. But here, with Kaia warm and trusting in my arms, none of that matters.

Here, I am whole. I am hers.

For the first time since the berserker awakened, I feel peace. But that's a lie—I'm terrified of how much I need her. Of what I'd become if I ever lost her.

But tonight, that fear is distant. Secondary to the peace flowing through me, through us. Through a bond that finally feels like home.

Chapter 32
FINN

The war room is silent.

Not the comfortable kind of silence. Not the 'we've made a great battle plan and are now basking in our brilliance' kind of silence. No, this is the kind of silence that stretches too long, too loaded, too... *deeply, deeply uncomfortable.*

I shift where I stand, dragging a hand down my face. Yep. Still hard. Still *very much* feeling *everything* Kaia and Aspen just did. The bond has no chill. No shame. No mercy.

And I know, *I know* the rest of them feel it too.

Kieran is at the head of the table, bracing himself against the wood like it's the only thing keeping him standing. His jaw is so tight I swear he's seconds away from breaking his own teeth. Malrik, for all his usual composure, looks *mildly* less smug than usual. Torric is standing stiff as a board, arms crossed over his chest like if he just folds himself tightly enough, he can pretend this didn't happen.

But it *did*.

And the bond made damn sure we got every single detail.

I can still taste her on my tongue—salt and sweetness that isn't mine to claim. The phantom press of skin against skin. The echo of pleasure that wasn't mine rippling through me like I swallowed lightning.

My body can't tell the difference. My heart—

Nope. Not going there.

Fucking hell.

I glance around for an escape route, but nope—no exits, no mercy, and to make things worse, Walter is just floating nearby like the smug little shadow menace he is.

I swear to the gods, he's *smirking* at me. Or whatever passes for a smirk when you're a cosmic intern made of shadow stuff and existential dread.

My eyes flick back to Kieran. He looks like he's two seconds away from snapping a chair in half with his bare hands.

Finally, I can't take it anymore. The silence, the tension, the *hard situation* (pun absolutely intended). I clear my throat, shifting uncomfortably as I adjust my stance.

"Well," I say, my voice a little hoarse, "this is awkward."

No one responds.

Malrik inhales sharply through his nose, then turns on his heel and *walks out.*

Torric follows, his movements tight, like he *hates* everything about this moment.

Honestly, same.

Kieran doesn't move. Doesn't react.

Walter bobs beside him, vibrating like he's *thriving* in the discomfort. Little bastard.

"Should we, uh, talk about the weather instead? Sunny with a chance of magical sex echoes?" I try again.

Nothing. Not even a glare.

Something shifts in the bond—a click, a lock turning. The sensation floods through me like freezing water, dousing the heat with something worse.

The phantom taste of her vanishes from my mouth.

I'm alone in my skin again.

And somehow, that's so much worse.

Kieran's fingers dig into the wood of the table, leaving actual indentations.

Oh.

I feel it then—the bond between Kaia and Aspen, cementing into place. Stronger than before. Different than before.

And it *hurts*. Not jealousy exactly. Something more... displaced.

Like a house I helped build... and then someone else got handed the keys.

Like when my sister moved out and took her half of our shared record collection.

Except this isn't records. This is my—

Not mine. Never was. Never will be.

"Right then," I mutter, the joke dying in my throat. "I'll just—"

I don't finish the sentence. Don't need to. No one's listening anyway.

I sigh dramatically, adjusting my pants before muttering, "Gonna need a cold bath after that one."

Kieran's head snaps up, those predator eyes locking on me. Something cold and dark flickers across his face, and for a brief, bizarre moment, I want him to say something. Anything. To acknowledge that whatever just happened in the bond affected us both.

Instead, he just looks through me like I'm already gone.

Fine. *Fine.*

I stroll out of the war room, whistling a tune that sounds hollow even to my own ears.

The hallway isn't much better. The stone walls feel too close, the air too thick with magic that isn't mine. I'm fine. Totally fine. It's not like I wasn't expecting this. It's not like I thought—

A shadow detaches from the wall, following me. Patricia, with her little shadowy notebook and too-observant eyes.

She floats alongside me, furiously scribbling notes, tilting her formless head as she studies me like I'm some fascinating specimen. She holds up her notebook, tapping insistently at a graph that seems to be tracking my emotional state.

I blink at her. "What?"

She points at me, then at her notebook again, gesturing emphatically at what looks like a statistical analysis of... my emotional state? Great. Even Kaia's shadows are psychoanalyzing me now.

"Nope," I say, popping the 'p' with extra emphasis. "No data. No statistics. No... whatever this is. I'm good."

Patricia tilts her head, clearly unconvinced. She scribbles something else, then holds it up—a rudimentary drawing of a face that looks suspiciously like mine, with arrows pointing to the eyes and chest with little notations.

"Bye, Patricia!" I wave, walking faster.

She hovers for a moment longer, then melts back into the shadows with what feels like disapproving energy trailing behind her.

I round the corner, making sure I'm alone before I let my shoulders slump.

Then straighten them immediately. Because I'm fine.

The truth is, I'm not fine. Not even a little bit.

The bond between Kaia and Aspen feels... right. Settled. Like it was always meant to be that way.

I check the walls for more shadows. Count the torches. One, two, three—fuck, my hands are shaking.

Because none of us got a real choice, did we? Not after the Hall of Echoes. Not after Kieran forced the issue.

"I mean, I chose Kaia. Chose her that night she fell asleep surrounded by her shadows, if I'm being honest with myself—which I'm absolutely not going to be. But the others? Kieran took that choice away from them."

Took it away from her.

No, that's not fair. Maybe she would have picked Aspen anyway. Maybe she would have—

I didn't want this. Didn't want to feel it. Didn't want to know what it's like when they—

But I did. I felt every second. How he touched her. How she responded. How the bond between them locked into place like the final piece of a puzzle I'm not part of.

I'm not jealous.

I'm fucking devastated.

Wait, no. I'm not. I'm just tired. Mildly annoyed. Perfectly healthy emotional response to magical voyeurism.

I press my back against the cold stone wall, letting my head thump against it. Once. Twice. The third time actually hurts, which feels oddly appropriate.

"I made my choice that night she fell asleep surrounded by her shadows," I whisper to the empty hallway. "Watching her finally look peaceful, realizing I'd do anything to keep her that way. I just didn't realize how fast the world would take that choice away from her."

The bond pulses once, quiet and distant. Not gone, but settled. Stabilized.

And somehow, that's scarier than if it had disappeared entirely.

Because now? Now it feels like watching the tide go out, knowing the wave that's coming back will drown everything in its path.

I push off the wall, shaking out my arms like I can physically cast off the feeling crawling under my skin.

"Yeah, sure, magical soul-bond sex echo," I mutter to myself, forcing a grin that feels brittle. "Just what I needed to get through the day. That and maybe three bottles of wine."

Actually, fuck the wine. I need something that won't make me think. Something that won't remind me of bonds and choices and everything I'm apparently not part of.

I head for the kitchens instead.

Twenty minutes later, I'm emerging with an armload of travel cakes, dried fruit, and what might be chocolate but could also be some kind of preserved meat. My arms are so full I can barely see over the pile, which is probably why I nearly walk straight into Malrik as I turn the corner.

He's standing there like he was waiting for me, silver eyes dark with something I recognize because I'm feeling it too. We're both breathing a little too hard, both still processing what we just experienced through the bond.

His gaze drops to my ridiculous haul of food, one eyebrow arching. "Finn, what—"

"What?" I say, stuffing a crumbling square into my mouth before any of it can fall. "Survival Tip #2. Don't forget the snacks. Ancient evil is exhausting work."

For a heartbeat, neither of us moves. The air between us crackles with tension—not just the shared aftermath of Kaia and Aspen's intimacy, but something else. Something that's been building since that kiss we shared, since all the moments we've been dancing around each other.

"Don't," I warn, but my voice comes out rougher than intended.

"Don't what?" His tone is carefully controlled, but I can see the crack in his composure. The way his hands are clenched at his sides like he's fighting not to reach for something.

"Whatever you're thinking. Whatever you're about to say."

He steps closer, close enough that I can feel the heat radiating off him. "You think you know what I'm thinking?"

"I think we both just got a very detailed reminder of what we're not getting," I snap, then immediately want to take it back because that's too honest. Too raw.

Something flickers in his silver eyes—understanding, maybe. Or recognition. "Finn—"

"No." I step back, but there's nowhere to go. The wall is right behind me, and he's right in front of me, and suddenly the hallway feels too small for both of us. "I can't do this right now."

"Do what?"

"Pretend like that didn't just happen. Pretend like we don't both want—" I cut myself off, shaking my head.

"Want what?" He's closer now, close enough that I could reach out and touch him if I wanted to. Which I absolutely do not want to do.

Liar.

"You know what."

His eyes drop to my mouth for just a second, but I catch it. The tension between us ratchets higher, dangerous and electric.

"We should talk about this," he says quietly.

"Should we? Because I'm pretty sure talking is the last thing on either of our minds right now."

The silence stretches between us, loaded with everything we're not saying. Everything we felt through the bond. Everything we want and can't have and are too fucked up to figure out.

Finally, Malrik steps back, giving me room to breathe.

"This isn't over," he says, and it sounds like a promise and a threat all at once.

I push past him, shoulder brushing his in a way that sends sparks down my spine. "Sure it isn't, prince."

But as I walk away, I can feel his eyes on me until I turn the corner.

The shadows around me shift and fade, leaving me alone with the taste of something I can't name and the certainty that I'm in way over my head.

Chapter 33
DARIAN

I should be checking the perimeter wards.

Or cataloging supply routes. Or doing literally anything that resembles the strategic planning Alekir expects from his perfectly controlled operative.

Instead, I'm sitting on the floor of an abandoned storage room like some broken toy someone forgot to put away.

My knees are drawn up, shirt clinging to my back with sweat that won't dry no matter how long I sit here. The stone wall offers nothing—no comfort, no answers, no absolution for what I've become. Just cold granite that reminds me how far I've fallen from the pristine Light Faction student who used to have a future.

I haven't slept. Or maybe I haven't woken up yet. Hard to tell the difference when every moment feels like I'm still trapped in that cell, still wearing invisible shackles, still hearing the echo of a scream that never quite left my throat.

The corruption writhes beneath my skin, restless and hungry. It wants something I can't give it. Or maybe it wants something I won't admit I want to give it.

Either way, we're at an impasse.

I drag my hands through my hair, noting distantly that they're shaking. Pathetic. The great Darian Luthar, reduced to trembling in storage rooms like a—

The bond *explodes* through me.

No warning. No gentle buildup. Just raw, overwhelming sensation that hits like lightning striking water.

Her.

I'm not seeing it—I'm *feeling* it. Every nerve she has becomes mine. The stretch, the pressure, the way her breath catches on a sound that's half-sob, half-surrender. My body responds before my mind can catch up, arousal slamming through me so hard my vision blurs.

It's not mine. None of it's mine. But my traitorous flesh doesn't care.

Her pleasure builds through the bond, bright and devastating, and I'm drowning in it. In the way she gasps. In the trust she's giving to someone who isn't me. In the *choice* she's making with every movement, every touch, every broken sound.

And then she breaks.

The orgasm crashes through our connection like a tidal wave, dragging me under. My body seizes, back arching off the wall as I come harder than I have in months. Unwanted. Involuntary. Utterly, completely mortifying.

I bite down on my sleeve to muffle the sound that tears from my throat—part groan, part sob, all humiliation.

When it finally stops, I'm left gasping on the floor, pants ruined, shirt soaked through with sweat and shame.

Alone.

Thank every god in every realm, *alone.*

The aftershocks fade slowly, taking the heat with them. What's left behind is worse than emptiness. It's the crystal-clear understanding that I just experienced the most intense physical pleasure of my life because of someone else's choice to be intimate with someone else.

Someone who isn't me.

Someone who will never be me.

I sit there for a long moment, staring at my hands, trying to process what just happened. "Well," I mutter to the empty room, voice hoarse. "That's a new low. Even for me."

The walk to the baths feels like a parade of shame.

Every person I pass seems to stare too long. A guard nods in my direction but I pretend not to see him. One of Alekir's advisors starts to approach and I turn down a side corridor so fast I nearly trip over my own feet.

My shirt clings to my back, my pants are a disaster, and I'm pretty sure I look exactly like what I am: someone who just had an unwanted magical sex dream that wasn't even his own.

The baths are mercifully empty. I strip with mechanical efficiency, letting the ruined clothes fall to the floor like evidence of a crime I didn't commit but somehow feel guilty for anyway.

The water is hot enough to scald, which feels appropriate. I scrub my skin until it's raw, trying to wash away the phantom sensation of pleasure that wasn't mine. Trying to erase the memory of what it felt like when she chose someone else.

It doesn't work.

Nothing ever works.

By the time I'm clean and dressed in fresh clothes, I look like myself again. Controlled. Composed. The perfect image of a man who definitely didn't just fall apart on a storage room floor.

I find Thorne in the planning room, bent over maps that won't save any of us.

"You look terrible," he observes without looking up.

"Charming as always." I settle into the chair across from him, grateful my voice sounds steady.

"Rough night?"

I almost laugh. "Something like that."

He glances up then, taking in whatever expression I'm failing to hide. "The bond?"

I don't answer immediately. Instead, I look out the narrow window at the bleak landscape beyond. Somewhere out there, she's probably still glowing with satisfaction. Still wrapped up in someone else's arms. Still choosing everyone but me.

The thought should hurt more than it does.

Instead, it just feels... final.

Like the end of a story I never got to finish.

My Little Shadow. She doesn't even know I still think of her that way. Doesn't remember what it meant.

"I felt her choose," I say quietly, the words tasting like ash.

Thorne sets down his pen. "Darian—"

"No pity." My voice comes out sharper than intended. "I knew what I was when I made the deal. This is just... confirmation."

He studies me for a long moment. "You could still—"

"Could still what?" I meet his gaze, letting him see whatever's left of the man I used to be. "Win her back with my sparkling personality? Seduce her with my unwavering loyalty to the man who wants to destroy everything she cares about?"

The silence stretches between us.

"She chose," I repeat, softer this time. "And it wasn't me. It will never be me."

And for the first time since this whole nightmare began, that feels like the truth.

It should be liberating.

It's not.

Chapter 34
TORRIC

Packing should be simple.

Clothes. Weapons. Whatever supplies I need to not die in whatever hellscape we're walking into. Done.

Instead, my hands move without thought—rolling fabric, checking straps, adjusting weight—while my brain runs in circles, desperate to find something solid.

The bond won't shut up. Every few seconds it pulses, reminding me what just happened. What I *felt* when Kaia and Aspen—

Fuck.

I slam the pack harder than necessary, the sound echoing off stone walls. My fire rune burns beneath my shirt, responding to frustration I can't shake loose.

Kaia chose Aspen.

Not fate. Not prophecy. Not some cosmic arrangement none of us had a say in.

Her.

The thought sits in my chest like a coal I can't spit out. For months I've been telling myself this bond thing was inevitable. That whatever happened between us didn't matter because destiny would sort it out anyway. That I didn't need to risk anything because it was all predetermined.

Bullshit.

She chose him. Which means she could choose any of us.

Or none of us.

My hands freeze on the pack's straps. The possibility I've been avoiding crashes over me—what if I've been waiting for something that was never mine to begin with? What if all my careful distance, all my reasons for not pushing, not claiming space, not being another complication in her already complicated life... what if it just made me invisible?

The fire rune flares, heat spreading across my chest. I need to move. Need air. Need something other than this room and these thoughts eating me alive.

The main hall buzzes with preparation when I arrive. Kieran's people loading packs, sharpening weapons, moving with the focused energy that comes before walking into danger. But I barely register any of it.

Because Kaia's there.

Standing too close to Aspen, their heads bent together over some map or supply list. She's smiling at something he said—that soft, unguarded expression I haven't seen directed at me in weeks. The easy familiarity between them makes my stomach clench.

I should look away. Walk past. Mind my own damn business.

Instead, I stand there like an idiot, watching them. Watching *her*.

The hollow ache in my chest spreads, settling into my bones like cold I can't shake. This is what I get for being a coward. For assuming she'd just... wait for me to figure my shit out.

"You know she chose us long before we came here, right?"

Malrik's voice cuts through my spiral. I turn to find him leaning against a pillar, arms crossed, watching me with those unreadable silver eyes.

"What?" The word comes out rougher than I meant.

He nods toward Kaia and Aspen. "You're standing there like she just picked her favorite and threw the rest of us away."

My jaw tightens. "Didn't she?"

"You're an idiot."

"Thanks for the pep talk, prince."

But Malrik doesn't rise to the bait. Instead, he pushes off the pillar, stepping closer. "She chose all of us, Torric. Before the bonds. Before the Hall of Echoes. Before any of this became inevitable." His voice drops. "The only question is whether you're going to choose her back."

Something in my chest shifts, not the bond, something deeper. "And if she doesn't want me to?"

"Then you're an even bigger idiot than I thought."

Before I can snap back, Kaia glances up. Her violet eyes find mine across the room, and for a heartbeat, everything else disappears. No Aspen. No crowd. No complicated magical bonds tying us all together.

Just her, looking at me like I still matter.

The moment stretches, charged with possibility I've been too afraid to acknowledge. Then her mouth curves into a small smile. Not the soft one she gave Aspen, but something fiercer. Something that's just mine.

My fire rune pulses once, heat spreading through my chest. But this time it doesn't feel like frustration.

It feels like coming alive.

Maybe Malrik's right. Maybe she has been choosing me all along.

Time to stop being a coward and choose her back.

The fire inside me doesn't just burn now. It points. And this time, I'm following.

Chapter 35
KAIA

I'm supposed to be packing.

Instead, I'm standing in my room, staring at my empty travel bag like it might spontaneously fill itself through sheer force of wishful thinking.

"Okay," I mutter, hands on my hips. "Clothes. Weapons. Whatever else people need to not die horribly. How hard can this be?"

Apparently, very hard.

Every time I turn around to grab something, I forget what I was reaching for. The silver pendant Kieran gave me keeps catching the light wrong, making me dizzy. And my shadows—usually so helpful—are acting like caffeinated squirrels.

Bob hovers near the window, his usual commanding presence replaced by what I can only describe as pacing. Patricia's frantic note-taking has reached new heights of chaos, her shadowy quill practically smoking. Even Mouse seems agitated, circling my ankles with uncharacteristic urgency.

"What's gotten into you guys?" I ask, finally managing to stuff a spare shirt into my bag.

Carl zooms past my head, trailing what looks suspiciously like one of Torric's leather bracers. Steve follows, clutching a book that definitely belongs to Malrik. Finnick brings up the rear with something that glints like Kieran's ceremonial dagger.

"Are you—are you *stealing* again?" I demand, but they're already gone, vanishing through the walls like guilty children.

Bob remains, radiating disapproval so intense I can practically feel it.

"Don't look at me like that," I tell him. "I didn't tell them to steal anything."

He flickers once—sharp, impatient—then drifts toward the door.

"I'm coming, I'm coming." I grab the rest of my essentials, shoving them haphazardly into the bag. "Though I still don't understand why everyone's acting so—"

My hand freezes on the Heart of Eternity.

The moment my fingers touch the pendant, Mouse *hisses*. An actual, audible hiss that makes my blood run cold. Bob snaps to attention, positioning himself between me and the necklace like a tiny shadow bodyguard.

"What the hell?" I whisper.

Patricia abandons her notes entirely, hovering near the Heart with obvious distress. Even Carl pokes his head through the wall, vibrating with anxiety.

I try to lift the pendant. Mouse *growls*.

"Okay, okay." I drop my hands, stepping back. "Message received. No Heart of Eternity on this trip."

The relief that washes through my shadows is palpable. Mouse immediately settles, purring against my leg. Bob returns to his usual stoic composure. Patricia dives back into her documentation with renewed vigor.

I stare at the pendant, its familiar weight suddenly feeling like a burden I can't bear to carry but can't bear to abandon. "If you don't want me taking it..." I murmur, then an idea strikes me.

Moving to the ornate wooden chest near my window, I lift the false bottom—a hiding spot I discovered weeks ago. The Heart settles into the hidden compartment with a soft *click*, like it belongs there. Safe. Protected. Waiting.

But the wrongness doesn't fade. If anything, it gets stronger.

I finish packing in a daze, my shadows clustering closer than usual. Something's missing. Something important. But every time I try to focus on what, the thought slips away like water through my fingers.

The sanctuary's courtyard buzzes with departure preparations when I finally make it downstairs. Horses stamp and snort, their breath misting in the morning air. Warriors check weapons and supplies with practiced efficiency. Everything looks normal.

So why does it feel like I'm forgetting something crucial?

"There she is," Aspen calls, his relief obvious. "I was starting to think you'd decided to stay behind."

"Never." I force a smile, shouldering my pack. "Just had some... packing complications."

Torric glances at my bag, then at the shadows clustering around my feet. "Let me guess. Your personal army decided to help?"

"Something like that."

Kieran approaches, his golden eyes scanning the group with military precision. "We leave now. The northern routes won't stay clear much longer."

"Right." I look around the assembled riders, mentally checking off faces. Kieran, obviously. Aspen and Torric, mounted on matching bay horses that somehow suit them perfectly. Malrik on a sleek black mare that seems to absorb light. A handful of Kieran's most trusted warriors.

Everyone's here. Everyone's ready.

So why does the courtyard feel... empty?

"Problem?" Malrik asks, noticing my hesitation.

"No, just—" I shake my head, trying to dislodge the nagging sensation. "Just making sure we have everything."

Mouse chirps from my shoulder, but it sounds strained. Worried.

Patricia's note-taking becomes increasingly frantic, her shadowy form darting between the horses like she's conducting some kind of invisible census. Bob maintains his guard position, but there's a tension in his stance that wasn't there before.

They know something I don't.

"Kaia." Kieran's voice carries a note of impatience. "Mount up."

Right. The horse situation.

I approach the large bay gelding they've assigned me, trying to project confidence I absolutely don't feel. Horses are big. Horses have opinions. Horses can sense fear, and right now I'm pretty sure I smell like a walking anxiety attack.

"Easy," I murmur, reaching for the reins.

The horse snorts, eyeing me with what I swear is judgment.

"She's fine," Aspen says, moving to help. "Just needs—"

The wind shifts.

Not weather wind. Magic wind.

The air thickens, charged with power that makes my shadows ripple and my skin prickle with recognition. Above us, something moves across the sun—large, graceful, impossible.

Wings.

"Holy shit," someone breathes.

A massive winged horse descends from the sky, coat black as midnight, eyes the same violet as mine. Power radiates from her in waves, ancient and wild and somehow familiar.

The moment I see her, memory crashes over me like a tide.

My parents, their hands guiding mine as I stroke a smaller version of this magnificent creature. "She will wait for you, little star. Until you're ready."

"Enif," I whisper.

She lands with impossible grace, folding wings that shimmer with starlight. When she kneels before me, the gesture feels like a coronation.

"A Valkyrie steed," Kieran breathes, his composure finally cracking. "They were supposed to be extinct."

"Apparently not," I say, reaching out to touch Enif's muzzle. She's warm and solid and real, and the moment our skin makes contact, something settles in my chest. Like a piece of myself I didn't know was missing finally clicks into place.

Mouse purrs approval, rubbing against Enif's neck like they're old friends. My other shadows cluster close, their earlier agitation replaced by something that feels almost like relief.

I swing onto Enif's back, marveling at how right it feels. Her wings spread slightly, catching the light, and I can't help but grin.

"Show-off," Aspen mutters, but he's smiling.

"Says the man with the magical ice powers," I shoot back.

Torric shakes his head. "At this point, I'm not even surprised anymore."

"We should move," Kieran says, though his eyes linger on Enif with something like wonder. "The longer we delay—"

"Wait." The word slips out before I can stop it.

Everyone turns to look at me. I scan the group again, that nagging wrongness finally crystallizing into something I can name.

"Where's Finn?"

Chapter 36
FINN

The silence in this corridor is different.

Not the comfortable kind that settles between jokes, or the expectant pause before I say something brilliant and slightly inappropriate. This is the hollow kind. The kind that echoes back everything you don't want to hear.

I'm perched on a stone ledge that overlooks the sanctuary's eastern wall, legs dangling like I'm twelve years old again, hiding from responsibilities that feel too big for my hands. The departure preparations buzz in the distance—voices calling, leather creaking, hooves striking stone. All the sounds of people who belong somewhere, doing something that matters.

I should be down there.

I'm not.

Because about an hour ago, I felt Kaia and Aspen's bond lock into place like the final tumbler in a lock I'll never have the key to. And now? Now the phantom taste of her is gone from my mouth, the echo of shared pleasure has faded from my skin, and all that's left is the cold understanding that I just experienced the most intimate moment of someone else's life.

Someone who isn't me.

Someone who chose someone else.

"Should've brought popcorn to the soul-bond climax," I mutter to the empty air, but the joke falls flat even to my own ears. Nothing's funny when you're the punchline.

My chaos magic sparks restlessly around my fingers, little bursts of color that die as quickly as they form. Even my power seems confused about what to do with all this... *feeling*. This stupid, messy, inconvenient ache that won't go away no matter how many times I tell myself it doesn't matter.

It does matter. That's the problem.

The bond is still there, humming in my chest like a wire that's been pulled taut but not snapped. I can feel the others, Kaia's contentment, Aspen's quiet satisfaction, even the distant pulse of Kieran's ancient magic. We're all connected, all part of this grand mystical design.

So why do I feel so alone?

Footsteps echo down the corridor, measured and familiar. I don't turn around. Don't need to. There's only one person who moves through shadows like he owns them, who finds hiding spots like he invented them.

"Did you draw the short straw," I ask without looking back, "or just get bored of brooding in doorways?"

Malrik doesn't answer immediately. Just stands there, close enough that I can feel his presence like a question mark against my back. When he finally speaks, his voice is quieter than usual.

"You weren't at the courtyard."

I shrug, still staring out at the darkening sky. "Didn't want to spoil the magical sendoff. Nothing ruins group photos like the guy who's having an existential crisis."

Silence. The kind that suggests he's not buying my bullshit.

"Besides," I continue, forcing levity into my voice, "someone had to make sure this place doesn't fall apart while you're all off playing hero. I'm really more of a behind-the-scenes kind of guy anyway."

"No," Malrik says simply. "You're not."

The certainty in his voice makes something twist in my chest. I finally turn to look at him, taking in the way shadows cling to his shoulders like they can't bear to let him go, the silver eyes that see too much.

"What do you want, Malrik?"

He steps closer, close enough that I have to tilt my head back to maintain eye contact. "I felt it too."

My breath catches. "Felt what?"

"The bond locking. The ache of being outside it." His voice drops lower, more intimate. "The way it felt like watching the door close on something you didn't know you wanted until it was gone."

The words hit like a punch to the gut. "Yeah, well," I manage, my usual grin feeling more like a grimace, "you don't seem the type to come in your pants from someone else's orgasm."

I expect him to flinch. To step back. To give me the distance I'm begging for without actually asking.

Instead, he says, "And yet here I am."

I stop breathing entirely.

The air between us shifts, thickening with possibilities I've been shoving down for weeks. Months, maybe. The way his eyes linger on my mouth when he thinks I'm not looking. The careful distance he maintains, like he's afraid of what might happen if he gets too close.

"I don't know what to do with all of this," I admit, the words scraping my throat raw. "With her. With you. With any of it."

"You don't have to know," he says, stepping closer. "You just have to stop running."

Something breaks inside me. It's not clean, not pretty, but like ice cracking under too much pressure.

I surge forward, closing the distance between us, and kiss him.

It's not gentle. It's angry and desperate and too honest, tasting like all the words I've been swallowing for months. For a heartbeat, he goes perfectly still, and I think I've made a catastrophic mistake.

The bond between Kaia and I pulses once in my chest. A reminder of what I can't have, that she chose someone else—

Then his hand cups my jaw, holding me in place as he deepens the kiss with a precision that steals my breath. The bond's ache fades, smothered by something else entirely. Something that's just mine. It's not rushed or frantic like mine was. It's deliberate. Devastating. Like he's been thinking about this for a very long time.

I fumble, overwhelmed by the sheer *intent* behind his touch. The way he's not just kissing me but *claiming* something, staking a quiet flag in territory I didn't know was disputed.

He walks me back until my shoulders hit the stone wall, but it's not about dominance. It's about grounding me. Anchoring me to something solid when everything else feels like it's spinning apart.

"If you're going to walk away again," I breathe against his mouth, "do it now."

His silver eyes meet mine, and something shifts there—decision, maybe, or surrender.

"No," he says quietly. "Not this time."

The kiss that follows is different. Slower. Deeper. I can taste the promise on his tongue, feel it in the way his fingers thread through my hair. My chaos magic responds, sparking between us in little bursts of light that make the shadows dance.

His shadows reach for mine, twining together like they've been waiting for permission. The sensation is intoxicating, not just physical contact but something deeper, more fundamental. Like recognizing a piece of yourself you didn't know was missing.

I arch into him, desperate for more contact, more connection, more *anything*. His mouth finds my throat, and I make a sound that's embarrassingly close to a whimper.

"Finn," he murmurs against my skin, and the way he says my name, like it's important, like it matters, nearly undoes me completely.

My hands fist in his shirt, pulling him closer even though there's no space left between us. Heat builds where our bodies press together, the kind of tension that makes breathing optional and thinking impossible.

He lifts his head to look at me, and what I see in his expression makes my heart stutter. Want, yes, but something else too. Something that looks dangerously like care.

"We should—" I start, but he silences me with another kiss, softer this time but no less devastating.

When we finally break apart, we're both breathing hard. He rests his forehead against mine, his hands still tangled in my hair.

"We should go," he says quietly, but he doesn't move away.

"Should we?" My voice comes out rougher than intended.

Instead of answering, he straightens my shirt with careful hands, his touch lingering longer than necessary. The simple gesture feels more intimate than everything that came before it.

"We're still going to pretend nothing happened, aren't we?" I ask, though I'm not sure I want the answer.

"Only if you ask me to."

I don't answer. Can't answer. Because the truth is, I don't want to pretend. I want this, whatever this is, to be real.

We walk back toward the courtyard together, not touching but close enough that I can feel the heat radiating from his skin. There's a new tension between us now, quiet and dangerous and completely undeniable.

And for the first time since the bond locked without me, I don't feel quite so alone.

Chapter 37
KAIA

The rhythm of Enif's hoofbeats against the mountain path should be soothing.

It's not.

We've been riding for hours, the sanctuary shrinking to a distant speck behind us, but something feels wrong. Not the usual wrongness of riding into danger—I'm getting used to that. This is different. Personal.

I shift in my seat, Mouse's warm weight across my shoulders the only thing keeping me grounded. My shadows coil restlessly around Enif's legs, their movements sharp and agitated in ways that mirror the knot forming in my chest.

"Easy," I murmur to them, but they don't settle.

Because they feel it too.

Kieran leads our formation, his golden eyes scanning the horizon with military precision. Torric and Aspen flank me on either side, close enough to protect but not so close as to crowd. Everything looks normal. Everything *should* be normal.

Except Finn is nowhere near me.

He rides at the back with Malrik, and for the first time since I've known him, he's not talking. Not grinning. Not making ridiculous observations about the landscape or trying to name the clouds. He just... rides. Silent. Distant.

And he won't look at me.

I try to catch his eye, craning my neck to see past Torric's broad shoulders. But every time I look back, Finn's gaze is either fixed on the horizon or locked in quiet conversation with Malrik. Their heads bent together, voices too low to carry.

The sight makes something cold settle in my stomach.

My shadows sense it before I do, the shift in dynamics, the way the air between us all feels charged with unspoken tension. Patricia abandons her usual frantic note-taking to drift toward the back of our group, returning moments later with what I swear is shadowy concern radiating from her form.

"What?" I whisper, but she just flickers and rejoins the others.

Even Bob seems agitated, marching back toward Finn and Malrik's position before returning to hover near my ankle with obvious displeasure. His usual military bearing is replaced by something that looks suspiciously like worry.

Mouse shifts against my neck, his violet eyes reflecting my unease. "Something's changed," I murmur to him, low enough that the others can't hear.

He doesn't disagree.

The wrongness builds as we ride, settling into my bones like a fever I can't shake. I keep replaying the morning's departure, looking for clues I might have missed. Finn had been there, helping with supplies, making his usual jokes about our chances of survival. But now that I think about it, had he looked at me? Really looked?

Or had he been avoiding eye contact even then?

My chest tightens with a realization that hits like ice water: I can't remember the last time Finn sought me out. The last time he appeared at my shoulder with a grin and some ridiculous observation. When did he stop gravitating toward me like he used to?

When did they both stop fighting for the seat next to me?

The memory hits without warning—that night in my room, after everything with the bonds and the Hall of Echoes. Finn's easy laughter as he sprawled across my bed. Malrik's careful distance that somehow felt more intimate than touch. The way they'd both looked at me like I was the center of their world.

Now Malrik rides beside Finn, their conversation quiet but intense. And I'm here, surrounded by the others but feeling more alone than I have in months.

"Did I do something wrong?" The question slips out before I can stop it, barely audible over the wind.

Aspen glances over, his ice-blue eyes sharp with concern. "What?"

I shake my head, heat flooding my cheeks. "Nothing. Just... thinking out loud."

But Aspen doesn't let it go. He guides his horse closer, close enough that our legs nearly brush. "Kaia." His voice is gentle but insistent. "What's wrong?"

How do I explain the growing certainty that I've lost something I didn't know I was supposed to fight for? That whatever connection I thought I had with Finn and Malrik has somehow shifted, leaving me on the outside looking in?

"They're different," I say finally, nodding toward the back of our group. "Finn and Malrik. Something's... changed."

Aspen follows my gaze, his expression thoughtful. When he looks back at me, there's understanding in his eyes that makes my chest ache.

"People change," he says quietly. "Relationships evolve. That doesn't mean you've done anything wrong."

"Doesn't it?" The words taste bitter. "I mean, look at them. When's the last time you saw them that comfortable with each other? That... synchronized?"

As if summoned by my observation, Finn's laugh carries forward on the wind. Not his usual bright, attention-seeking laughter, but something quieter. More intimate. Shared.

With Malrik.

Not me.

My shadows coil tighter, responding to the spike of something I don't want to name. It's not jealousy—not exactly. It's more like the hollow ache of being forgotten. Of realizing you were never as important as you thought you were.

"Maybe," I whisper, more to myself than to Aspen, "they never needed me at all."

"Stop." Aspen's voice cuts through my spiral with gentle firmness. "That's not true, and you know it."

"Do I?" I laugh, but there's no humor in it. "Because from where I'm sitting, it looks like they've figured out they're perfectly fine without me."

Mouse makes a soft sound of distress, pressing closer to my neck. My shadows flutter anxiously, Bob actually abandoning his post to drift back toward me in what looks like an attempt at comfort.

"Your shadows don't think so," Aspen observes, a small smile tugging at his lips. "And they know you better than anyone."

Before I can respond, Kieran raises a hand, signaling for us to halt. Below us, a clearing opens up in the mountain forest, the perfect place to rest and water the horses.

As we dismount, I watch Finn and Malrik swing down from their saddles together, their movements unconsciously coordinated. Finn says something that makes Malrik's lips quirk in what might be amusement, and the casual intimacy of the moment hits me like a physical blow.

They're not avoiding each other anymore.

They're gravitating toward each other.

And I'm not part of that equation.

I slide down from Enif's back, my legs unsteadier than they should be. The bond in my chest pulses—not with pain, exactly, but with a hollow ache that feels like absence. Like reaching for something that's no longer there.

Torric appears at my elbow, his golden eyes scanning my face with characteristic directness. "You look like someone stole your favorite dagger."

"Do I?" I force a smile. "Must be the altitude."

He doesn't buy it for a second, but before he can push, Finn approaches. My heart does a stupid little leap of hope—maybe I was wrong, maybe nothing's changed, maybe—

"Kaia." His voice is carefully neutral. Polite. "You should eat something. Long flight ahead."

He hands me a piece of travel bread, our fingers not quite touching, and something in my chest cracks. This is Finn—chaotic, tactile, never-met-a-boundary-he-wouldn't-cross Finn—being careful not to touch me.

"Thanks," I manage, accepting the bread.

He nods and turns away, back toward where Malrik is examining our route on an ancient map. No lingering grin. No ridiculous comment about the bread's personality or the way the sunlight hits my hair.

Just... politeness.

I watch him go, noting the way his shoulders relax as he rejoins Malrik's side. The easy way they fall into conversation. The space they create that doesn't include me.

Mouse nuzzles my cheek, his warmth a small comfort against the growing cold in my chest.

"They used to fight for my attention," I whisper to him, the words barely audible. "Now I think they're fighting to forget me."

The worst part? I can't even blame them.

Maybe this is what I deserve for taking so long to figure out what I wanted. For being too scared to choose, too paralyzed by the fear of hurting someone to risk reaching for what I actually needed.

Now it looks like the choice has been made for me.

And I'm not part of it at all.

Chapter 38
KIERAN

The golden light of dusk stretches everything into distortion.

Long shadows cling to the mountain path like fingers reaching for something they'll never grasp. The air itself feels unstable, caught between day and night, neither one thing nor another. Much like everything else lately.

I ride at the edge of our formation, close enough to maintain the illusion of leadership but far enough that I don't have to watch. Don't have to see the careful way Aspen checks on her, or the protective stance Torric maintains at her flank, or the way Malrik and Finn have somehow found their rhythm without me.

Without *her*.

The bond pulses in my chest, dormant but present. A reminder of what I've lost. What I never truly had. I could reach for it—test the connection, see if she'd respond—but I don't. Reaching means vulnerability, and I've been burned enough for one lifetime.

My shadows ripple restlessly around my horse's hooves, responding to tension I can't quite control. They want to surge forward, to wrap around her like they used to, but I hold them back. She doesn't need my shadows. She has theirs.

She has *them*.

Walter materializes beside me, his small form bobbing gently in the space between my horse and the rocky outcropping. He doesn't speak—Walter never speaks—but his presence carries a weight of understanding that I'm not ready to accept.

"Not now," I mutter, but he persists, drifting closer until he's nearly touching my boot.

Something inside me snaps.

My shadows explode outward without warning, a violent surge of power that sends Walter tumbling through the air. He recovers quickly, ever graceful, but the hurt in his strange little form is unmistakable.

"I said not now," I growl, louder than I intended.

The others glance back, concern flickering across their faces. Kaia's violet eyes find mine, and for a moment I see something that might be worry. But then Torric says something that makes her laugh, and her attention shifts away.

Always away.

Walter hovers at a safe distance now, watching me with those inscrutable not-eyes. The reproach in his silence is worse than any words could be.

I force my shadows back under control, wrapping them tight around myself like armor. Like chains.

The memory hits without warning—her at six years old, bouncing on her toes as she asked if I could really turn into a dragon. The way she'd clapped and laughed when I shifted for her, creating shadow shapes to chase me through the air while I showed off with aerial acrobatics. Her shadow magic had danced with mine that day, perfect harmony between two powers that recognized each other.

When she hugged my scaled neck and demanded I promise to come back, I thought that moment would anchor us forever. That being the first to see her magic, to play in that meadow where wonder mattered more than fear, would mean something when she returned.

Now I watch her surrounded by others who understand her in ways I never will. Aspen, who grounds her chaos. Torric, who burns away her doubt. Malrik, who matches her shadows with his own royal darkness. Finn, who makes her laugh even in the depths of Absentia.

And me? I'm the one who forced the bonds before they were ready. The one who stole her choice. The one who stands apart, watching her heal from wounds I helped create.

She doesn't need you, I think bitterly. *She's got them. All of them.*

The path ahead curves around a bend, and that's when I see him.

Callum emerges from the mist like a wraith, his Guardian attire pristine despite the rough terrain. There's something about his approach—too calculated, too perfectly timed—that sets my teeth on edge.

"Commander," he says, inclining his head with military precision. "I bring word from the advance scouts."

The others tense, hands moving instinctively toward weapons. But there's no immediate threat in Callum's posture, just that familiar blend of competence and barely concealed ambition I've grown to distrust.

"What word?" I ask, though part of me already knows I won't like the answer.

"The eastern pass is compromised. Corrupted creatures moving in organized patterns." His silver eyes flick briefly to Kaia before returning to me. "I've mapped an alternate route through the southern valleys. Safer, but it will add two days to our journey."

Torric frowns. "Two days we don't have."

"Better than walking into a trap," Callum replies smoothly.

But something about his arrival grates against my already frayed nerves. Maybe it's the way Kaia immediately moves forward to listen, or how the others defer to his expertise without question. He's too composed, too helpful, arriving exactly when we need guidance.

Another voice she'll trust more than mine, I think bitterly.

Kaia moves forward, studying the map Callum produces from his pack. "This route," she says, tracing the path with her finger, "it takes us closer to the old battlefields."

"Unavoidable, I'm afraid," Callum replies. "But the corruption there is dormant. Safer than the active threats to the east."

I watch this exchange, noting how easily she trusts him. How quickly the others gather around his map, hanging on his words. It's not strategic thinking that makes my jaw clench—it's the sick certainty that I'm watching myself get replaced again.

By someone younger. Clearer. Less broken by centuries of failure.

"We follow the original route," I say, cutting through their discussion.

Callum's expression doesn't change, but something flickers behind his eyes. "Commander, with respect, the intelligence suggests—"

"I don't care what your intelligence suggests." My voice carries more edge than I intended. "We don't have time for detours."

The silence that follows is heavy with unspoken tension. I can feel the others' confusion, their concern at my apparent dismissal of sound tactical advice. Even Kaia looks at me with something that might be disappointment.

Let them think I'm being unreasonable, I tell myself. *Maybe I am. I just—don't trust him. Not when she's already listening to him like he has answers I don't.*

"We make camp here," I announce, my voice carrying the authority I've always wielded. "Rest while you can."

But as I dismount, as I busy myself with tasks that don't require looking at her, I hear her voice behind me. Soft. Curious. Already drawn to this new piece of the puzzle that is her destiny.

She doesn't look back.

Once, I was the one who walked beside her. Now I'm the ghost she left behind.

Walter drifts closer again, keeping his distance but offering his strange, wordless comfort. This time, I don't push him away. I can't afford to lose what little loyalty I have left.

My shadows settle around me like a cloak, hiding the cracks in my composure. In the growing darkness, I tell myself it doesn't matter. That I've survived worse losses. That she was never really mine to begin with.

But the bond pulses between us, and I know I'm lying.

She was mine. She *is* mine.

And I'm watching her slip away, one new connection at a time.

Chapter 39
TORRIC

It's been three days since the quiet started feeling wrong.

The weight of dry wood presses against my shoulders as I make my way back to camp, my fire rune pulsing warm beneath my shirt. Three days of travel with Callum, three days of watching him weave himself into our group like he's always belonged. Three days of small wrongnesses that stack up like kindling, waiting for a spark.

Which is probably why it takes me a moment to realize one of them *is* a voice.

I freeze, letting the bundle of kindling settle against my back as I strain to listen. There—beyond the cluster of pine trees that marks the edge of our camp. Low, urgent whispers that don't belong to anyone who should be awake at this hour.

"...won't be a problem," the voice continues, and my blood goes cold as I recognize Callum's cultured tones. "Not once we reach the valley."

I step forward, careful to keep my movements silent, but a branch snaps under my boot like a gunshot in the stillness. The whispers cut off instantly.

By the time I round the trees, Callum sits alone beside his pack, calmly adjusting the straps on his travel gear. His movements are unhurried, casual, like he's been sitting there for hours instead of seconds.

"Torric," he says without looking up, his voice carrying just the right note of mild surprise to make me doubt what I heard. "Couldn't sleep either?"

I scan the area around him, looking for any sign of who he might have been talking to. Nothing. Just shadows that could hide anything, and the lingering sense that I've missed something crucial.

"Thought I heard voices," I say carefully.

Callum's smile is perfectly calibrated—not too innocent, not too knowing. "Ah, that would be me. I was practicing a long-distance communication spell. Old Guardian trick for coordinating with advance scouts." He taps his temple. "Easier to practice the verbal components aloud, though I suppose it must sound strange to anyone overhearing."

The explanation is reasonable. Plausible. The kind of thing a competent tactician would do to keep his skills sharp.

So why does every instinct I have scream that he's lying?

"Right," I manage, hefting the wood higher on my shoulder. "Communication spell."

"The acoustics in these mountains play tricks on the ear," Callum continues, his tone conversational as he stands and brushes dirt from his pants. "Sound carries strangely, echoes in unexpected ways. Easy to imagine conversations where there are none."

The words feel like a warning wrapped in casual observation. I force myself to nod and walk back toward the dying embers of our fire, but I can feel his eyes tracking my movement until I'm out of sight.

The next morning—the fourth since Callum joined us—brings no relief from the wrongness that's settled in my bones. If anything, it gets worse as I watch how naturally he's inserted himself into our routines. Kaia actually asks his opinion about the terrain ahead. Kieran defers to his route suggestions without question.

On the second day, he'd ridden near Malrik, and I'd caught fragments of their conversation that made my jaw clench even then.

"You've done well to hold her loyalty this long," Callum says, his tone carrying just enough admiration to mask what feels like a probe. "I imagine it's not easy with a mind like hers—always looking for the next move, the next advantage."

Malrik's shoulders tighten almost imperceptibly, but his voice remains level. "Kaia's loyalty isn't something that needs to be held. It's earned."

"Of course," Callum agrees smoothly. "Though I've found that even the most genuine loyalties can shift when circumstances change. When new information comes to light." He pauses, then adds with what sounds like casual wisdom, "Power without control is chaos, after all."

The phrase hits me like a half-remembered dream, familiar in a way that makes my skin crawl. I can't place where I've heard it before, but something about those exact words, spoken in that exact tone, sets every nerve on edge.

The comment hangs in the air like smoke, and I watch Malrik's hands tighten on his reins. Whatever game Callum's playing, he's trying to plant seeds of doubt. Make Malrik question Kaia's commitment, or maybe his own position within our group.

The realization sits like lead in my stomach. This isn't casual conversation. It's reconnaissance.

I guide my horse closer, close enough to catch Malrik's eye. When he looks at me, I see my own suspicion reflected there, controlled, but present. He knows something's off too.

That should be reassuring. Instead, it makes me more nervous. If both of us are picking up on Callum's manipulations, why isn't anyone else? Why does Kieran still defer to his tactical expertise? Why does Kaia listen to his route suggestions like they're gospel?

By the third day, Patricia's formations have broken rhythm entirely. Instead of her usual methodical note-taking, she's scribbling furiously, symbols appearing and disappearing in her wake like smoke. Her patterns don't match anything I've seen before—erratic, desperate, like she's trying to document something that keeps slipping away.

I edge closer, trying to get a better look at what she's writing, but the moment I approach, the symbols evaporate entirely. Patricia jerks back into formation like she's just surfaced from deep water, her movements guilty and sharp.

Even Bob pauses beside me as the last of Patricia's symbols dissolve, his form stiffening like he's noticed something too, but he says nothing (obviously). Just hovers there, radiating the same unease that's been eating at me all day.

"Patricia," I say quietly. "Everything alright?"

She nods too quickly, then begins documenting the landscape around us with forced normalcy. But I catch the way her attention keeps drifting toward Callum. Not like she's suspicious, but like she's... waiting. Tracking. Her usual precision wavers whenever he's in her line of sight, like she's following something only she can see.

Even Kaia's shadows sense something wrong. They're just not sure what it is.

I've spent these four days watching, cataloging small inconsistencies that individually mean nothing but together paint a picture I don't like. The way Kaia now echoes phrases Callum used the day before. How Finn nods along to suggestions that sound reasonable but feel wrong. The subtle way Callum undermines confidence in any decision that doesn't align with his preferences, always with such perfect logic that arguing seems petty.

By evening, when we make camp in a sheltered valley, I'm certain of two things: Callum is not who he pretends to be, and whatever his real agenda is, it doesn't align with ours.

The question is what to do about it.

As the others settle into their bedrolls and the fire burns down to embers, I volunteer for first watch. Let them think I'm being paranoid. Let them assume I'm seeing threats where none exist. I'd rather be wrong about Callum than right about what his presence might mean for all of us.

But as I sit with my back against a boulder, eyes scanning the darkness beyond our camp, I can't stop glancing back at the sleeping forms of my companions. At Callum's bedroll, positioned just close enough to the center of camp to seem protective while maintaining easy access to the perimeter.

At Patricia's empty shadow, nowhere to be seen among the others clustered around Kaia.

I'm not sure who I'm watching anymore. Only that something is very, very wrong.

And after four days of watching it happen—little shifts, familiar phrases in unfamiliar mouths, trust given too easily—I'm the only one who seems to see it.

Chapter 40
KAIA

I need silence.

Not the comfortable quiet that comes with trusted company, but the kind of silence that doesn't ask questions or offer solutions. The kind that lets you fall apart without witnesses.

Four days of Callum's careful observations and helpful suggestions have left me feeling like I'm being studied under glass. Four days of watching Patricia's formations deteriorate while pretending not to notice. Four days of Kieran's distance and the growing certainty that I'm losing pieces of myself I can't name.

The bonds in my chest hum with tension, a web pulled so taut it might snap if anyone breathes wrong. I need space. I need water. I need to remember what it feels like to be alone with my own thoughts.

The lake spreads before me like black glass, reflecting the last traces of sunset in shades of deep purple and gold. It's perfect—isolated, quiet, mercifully empty. I wade in slowly, letting the cold water shock some clarity back into my system.

My shadows drift nearby, uncertain. They hover at the water's edge like they're afraid to follow, their usual protective instincts confused by my need for solitude. Even Mouse has remained at camp, sensing that this grief is something I need to carry alone.

I sink deeper, letting the water rise to my chest, my throat, until I'm floating in silence broken only by gentle lapping against the shore. For the first time in days, I can breathe without feeling like I'm performing for an invisible audience.

That's when I hear footsteps behind me.

"Whoever you are," I call without turning around, "I need a few more minutes."

The footsteps don't retreat. Don't pause. They continue with deliberate, measured precision until they stop at the water's edge.

I turn, expecting to see Torric's concerned scowl or Finn's worried grin.

Instead, I find Callum standing at the shoreline, his silver eyes taking in my exposed shoulders, the way the water clings to my skin, with an assessment that makes my stomach clench.

"You need to leave," I say, my voice sharper than intended. "Now."

He doesn't move. Doesn't look away. Just studies me with the same calculating attention he's been giving everything else for the past four days.

"You thought hiding in water would protect you?" His voice carries an odd note of amusement, like I've done something predictably foolish.

"I'm not hiding." But even as I say it, I know it's a lie. "I came here to be alone."

"Did you?" He steps closer to the water's edge, close enough that I can't rise without putting myself within his reach. "Or did you come here because the bonds are starting to hurt?"

The question hits like ice water, stealing my breath. How could he possibly know about the ache that's been building in my chest? The way the connections feel strained, wrong, like they're pulling in directions that don't make sense?

"I don't know what you're talking about."

"Of course you do." His smile is gentle, almost kind. It makes my skin crawl. "You feel it every time you look at them. The certainty that something's missing. That someone's missing."

My heart starts to race, water suddenly feeling too cold against my skin. "Get out of here, Callum."

"You think it's all about love," he continues, ignoring my demand. "That they chose you. That you chose them." He pauses, letting the words settle. "But your final bond? That was chosen long before you were born."

The world tilts, reality sliding sideways like I'm looking at it through broken glass. "What?"

"It's Darian."

The name hits like a physical blow, sending shockwaves through the bonds in my chest. The connection I've been trying to ignore, trying to bury beneath the others, flares to life with painful intensity.

"That's not possible," I whisper, but my body betrays me. The bond pulses, recognizing truth in his words even as my mind rejects it.

"He was made for it. Just like you." Callum's voice is matter-of-fact, clinical. "Light and shadow. Control and chaos. Did you really think your connection to him was an accident? A leftover from academy drama?"

I'm shaking now, water around me starting to respond to my agitation with small, dark ripples.

"He's not a scar, Kaia. He's the key."

"The key to what?" The question tears from my throat like a scream.

His smile widens, and for the first time since I've known him, it reaches his eyes. "You're the one who opens the gate. And he's the one who makes sure you do."

The words feel like prophecy, like riddles wrapped in certainty I don't understand. But the bond—god, the bond—it recognizes something in what he's saying. It pulls, sharp and insistent, toward something I can't see but feel in my bones.

"Alekir bound you before either of you could walk," Callum continues, his voice soft with mock sympathy. "You were never supposed to choose him. You were supposed to need him."

The revelation shatters something inside me. Not my heart—something deeper. The foundation I've been building my choices on, the belief that what I feel, what we all feel, is real and chosen and *ours*.

"No." The word comes out broken. "No, that's not—"

"Isn't it?" He tilts his head, studying my reaction. "Every choice you've made, every bond you've formed—did you really choose them? Or did they choose you because they had to? Because something in them recognized what you are?"

I can't breathe. Can't think past the horrible logic of his words, the way they fit too neatly with fears I've been carrying since the bonds first formed.

"You're lying."

"Am I?" He turns to leave, his purpose apparently served. "Ask yourself this, Kaia—if it's all real, if it's all choice, why does the thought of him still make you ache? Why does saying his name feel like coming home to something you never chose to leave?"

And then he's gone, leaving me alone with the wreckage of everything I thought I knew.

I stand frozen in the water, his words echoing in my head like a curse. The bond—the one I've been fighting, denying, trying to bury—pulses with recognition. With need. With the terrible certainty that maybe, just maybe, he's right.

"No." I say it to the water, to the sky, to the silence that offers no answers. "No. No. No."

But my magic responds anyway, shadows exploding from the lake bottom like something buried has finally clawed its way to the surface. The water churns around me, dark and violent, responding to chaos I can't control.

I scream—raw, desperate, furious—and my shadows explode outward like something buried has finally clawed its way to the surface. Ice spreads from where I stand, Aspen's power bleeding through our bond uninvited, turning the lake's surface into a fractured mirror of black water and white frost. My shadows writhe beneath the ice, wild and directionless, feeding off my grief and rage.

The magic rips through me, wild and uncontrolled, until I'm drowning in shadows and ice that shouldn't be mine. Until I sink beneath the surface and wrap my arms around herself and wish I could disappear entirely.

That's how Malrik finds me.

Not running toward the chaos—walking.

Like he felt the exact moment my world ended and came to witness the aftermath. He wades into the water fully clothed, his expensive boots squelching in the mud, his silver eyes never leaving mine.

He doesn't speak. Doesn't ask what happened or try to fix what's broken. He just kneels in the water in front of me, opens his arms, and waits.

"I don't know if I'm meant for any of you," I whisper, the words scraping my throat raw. "But I need you right now."

He breathes my name like a vow—"Kaia"—and reaches for me.

And I let him.

His arms close around me, solid and warm and real in ways that make the bonds sing instead of ache. The water swirls around us, still touched with residual magic, but it feels less chaotic now. Less like drowning, more like being held by something larger than myself.

"I've got you," he murmurs against my hair, and for the first time since Callum spoke, I believe that something might actually be mine to keep.

Even if I never chose it.

Even if it was always meant to be.

Chapter 41
MALRIK

I've never seen her like this.

Wrapped in shadow and grief, water swirling with the remnants of magic that shouldn't exist—ice crystallizing in patterns that mirror her pain while darkness writhes beneath the surface. She's pulled power from our bond without meaning to, Aspen's frost bleeding through her desperation, and the sight of it stops my heart.

She needs anchoring. Not answers.

I don't hesitate. Don't call out or ask what happened. The devastation radiating from her through our connection tells me everything I need to know—someone hurt her, broke something precious, and left her drowning in doubt.

I wade into the lake fully clothed, boots squelching in the mud, expensive fabric soaking through as I drop to my knees in front of her. The water is freezing where her borrowed ice magic touched it, but I don't care. She's curled in on herself like she's the only thing keeping her pieces together.

"I don't know if I'm meant for any of you," she whispers, her voice raw and broken. "But I need you right now."

The words hit me like a blessing and a curse all at once. She needs me. Not because of fate or bonds or ancient magic, but because in this moment, I'm what she's choosing.

"Kaia," I breathe her name like a prayer, like an answer to questions I've been asking my whole life.

I open my arms, and she comes to me.

The relief is staggering. She melts against my chest, trembling not with cold but with aftershock, and I wrap her in every piece of strength I have. My shadows reach for hers instinctively, twining together until I can't tell where mine end and hers begin.

"I'm here," I murmur against her hair, tasting lake water and salt tears. "I'm here because I want to be. Not because of the bond. Not because of duty."

She pulls back just enough to look at me, violet eyes swimming with unshed tears. "How can you be sure?"

I cup her face in my hands, thumbs brushing away the water that clings to her cheeks. "Because when I saw you slip away from camp, something in me knew you needed space. Because when I heard you scream, I didn't hesitate. Because you're not just my fate, Kaia—you're my choice."

Our foreheads touch, breath mingling in the space between us. Her shadows swirl gently around my arms, welcoming rather than defensive, and something in my chest unlocks.

"Malrik," she whispers, and then her mouth is on mine.

This isn't like our other kisses—tentative, testing, careful. This is raw desperation, her lips parting under mine like she's drowning and I'm air. I slide my fingers through her wet hair and kiss her back with all the want I've been holding back.

"I've waited so long for this," I whisper against her mouth, tasting the truth of it. "Don't stop."

"I won't," she breathes, and her hands find the buttons of my soaked shirt.

I watch her fingers work, trembling slightly as she pushes the fabric aside. When her palms press against my chest, skin to skin, the bond flares with something deeper than magic.

Recognition. Completion.

"Kaia," I say, my voice rougher than I intend. "If I touch you like this, I won't stop."

Her eyes meet mine, clear and certain despite the tears. "Then don't."

I strip slowly, every movement deliberate despite the urgency thrumming through my veins. She watches me with an intensity that makes my skin burn, her gaze mapping every scar, every line of muscle, like she's memorizing me.

When I'm finally bare before her, she reaches out to trace the shadow mark that curves along my ribs—the royal brand that marked me as heir to a fallen realm. Her touch is reverent, careful, like she understands what it cost me to let her see it.

"You're beautiful," she whispers, and I have to close my eyes against the force of hearing her say it.

I lift her from the water, carrying her to where the boulder extends above the surface, creating a natural shelf warmed by the day's sun. She shivers as the cool air hits her wet skin, but I'm there to warm her, my mouth finding hers as I lay her back against the smooth stone.

"Let me be yours," I whisper against her collarbone, tasting lake water and something uniquely her. "Just for tonight."

Her fingers thread through my hair, tugging my mouth back to hers. "You already are."

I worship her with my mouth first—the hollow of her throat, the peak of each breast, taking time to lavish attention on the sensitive spots that make her gasp and arch beneath me. When I trail kisses down her stomach, she trembles, her hands fisting in my hair.

"Malrik," she breathes, and the sound of my name makes my chest tight with want.

But it's when my shadows join the exploration that she truly comes apart. They wind around her thighs, cool and weightless, caressing places my hands can't reach while my mouth finds more sensitive territory. The contrast of sensations—warm lips and tongue, cool shadow-touch—has her crying out, her spine arching as pleasure builds.

"I need—" she starts, but the words dissolve into incoherent sounds as my shadows tease and my mouth worships. She's trembling, so close, her magic responding by sending her own shadows to twine with mine in patterns of pure sensation.

When she breaks apart the first time, it's with a cry that echoes across the water, her body clenching around the shadows that have been driving her to madness. I hold her through it, kissing her inner thigh, her hip, working my way back up her body as the aftershocks fade.

"More," she whispers when she can finally speak, her hands reaching for me desperately. "I need more. I need *you*."

The first press of her body accepting mine steals both our voices. She's slick and ready from her first release, but still tight around me, her body stretching to accommodate me inch by inch. I have to still completely, buried halfway inside her, fighting for control.

"You feel incredible," I groan against her neck, my entire body shaking with the effort of not moving. "So perfect around me."

She rolls her hips, taking me deeper, and we both moan at the sensation. "Don't hold back," she whispers, her nails digging into my shoulders. "I want all of you."

We find our rhythm in the gentle current—slow and deep at first, learning the feel of each other. I angle my hips, searching until I find the spot that makes her breath stutter, and I focus there, each thrust deliberately driving her higher.

Water swirls around us as we move together, our shadows dancing beneath the surface like extensions of our pleasure. The bond builds between us with each movement, each kiss, each desperate touch—not overwhelming, but inevitable.

"Touch yourself," I whisper against her ear, my voice rough with need. "I want to feel you come around me."

Her hand slips between us, fingers finding that sensitive bundle of nerves while I continue to move inside her. The sight of her pleasuring herself while I'm buried deep makes my control fracture, my movements becoming more urgent.

"That's it," I breathe, watching her face as she climbs toward release. "Let me feel you."

She comes apart with a cry that cuts through me, her body clamping down on me so tight I follow her over the edge, spilling myself inside her as the bond *locks* with quiet certainty. The sensation overwhelms everything else, not just physical release, but the perfect fit of our connection finally settling into place.

I draw her into my arms like she's always belonged there, our bodies spent and breath still shallow. Her shadows drift around us lazily, no longer chaotic but content, swaying like they're singing lullabies I can't hear.

"Are you all right?" I murmur against her temple.

She nods, pressing a kiss to the hollow of my throat. "Better than all right."

I hold her tighter, memorizing the weight of her in my arms, the way her breath feels against my skin. Whatever hell is coming for us—whatever forces are moving in the dark—I'll carry this moment into the fire.

She chose me. Not fate, not ancient magic, not bonds forged in desperation.

Me.

If this is the only time I ever get to be hers completely, then it's enough. I'll hold this night like a treasure, proof that once, in the space between one heartbeat and the next, I was exactly where I belonged.

And she was mine.

Chapter 42
FINN

The bond snaps into place like a lock turning.

I feel it from across camp, where I've been pretending to check the perimeter while actually avoiding the lake. The sensation is familiar now—I've felt it before when Aspen and Kaia came together, that sudden click of completion, like puzzle pieces finally finding their fit.

This time, it cuts.

My knees hit the ground before I can stop them, chaos magic sparking wild around my fingers as the realization crashes over me. It's Malrik. Of course it's fucking Malrik. I should have seen this coming. Should have prepared for it.

But knowing something's going to hurt doesn't make the blade any less sharp when it finally finds your ribs.

The bond settles between them with a finality that makes my chest hollow out. I can feel it through my connection to Kaia—not the details, thank every god in existence, but the *certainty*. The way her magic has shifted, aligned, found its anchor in someone who isn't me.

"Shit," I breathe, pressing my palms against my eyes. "Shit, shit, shit."

My chaos magic responds to the spike of emotion, painting the air around me in streaks of color that die as quickly as they form. Even my power doesn't know what to do with this particular brand of devastation.

I should stay here. Should give them privacy, space, whatever the hell people need after they've just locked their souls together for eternity.

Instead, I find myself walking toward the lake.

Because I'm an idiot. Because I apparently enjoy pain. Because some masochistic part of me needs to see what I've lost with my own eyes.

The water comes into view through the trees, moonlight turning the surface to liquid silver. At first I don't see them—just the gentle lap of waves against the shore, the soft glow of moss drifting across the water like fallen stars.

Then I spot them.

Kaia curled against Malrik's chest in the shallows, her hair dark with water, shadows drifting peacefully around them like they're singing lullabies. His arms circle her protectively, chin resting on top of her head. Even from here I can see the way she melts into him, boneless and trusting in a way that stops my breath.

She never looked that peaceful with me.

The thought hits like a sucker punch, and I have to grip the nearest tree to stay upright. I turn to leave before I can witness any more of their happiness, but my boot snaps a branch. The sound echoes across the water like a gunshot.

Malrik's head lifts, silver eyes finding mine through the darkness. For a heartbeat we just stare at each other, and I see something flicker across his face—not guilt, exactly, but understanding. He knows what this costs me.

"Didn't mean to crash the celebration," I mutter, forcing my usual grin even though it feels like it might split my face in half.

He doesn't answer. Doesn't need to. We both know I'm the one who walked away.

I stumble back through the trees, chaos magic sparking erratically around me like my power's having its own breakdown. My feet carry me to the far edge of camp, away from everyone, away from the bonds I can feel humming with contentment that isn't mine.

I sink onto a fallen log, pressing my face into my hands.

"Well," I tell the empty air, "that's just fucking perfect."

Bob drifts out of the shadows nearby, hovering at a respectful distance. His usually militant posture has softened into something that looks suspiciously like sympathy. Even Kaia's shadows feel sorry for me now.

"Don't look at me like that," I warn him, but there's no heat in it. "I knew this was coming. We all did."

Bob flickers once—gentle, understanding—then settles into a loose guard position. Not abandoning me, but not crowding either. Somehow that makes it worse.

Because this is what I do, isn't it? Create something beautiful and then run scared when it becomes real.

The memories come in a rush, sharp and merciless:

Standing in Malrik's room back at the academy telling them both exactly how I felt. "I have feelings for both of you. And I'm pretty sure you both feel the same way about me."

Pushing them to stop pretending, to acknowledge what we all knew was happening between us.

"I'm proposing we stop fighting this. All of this."

The way Kaia had pulled me close, kissed me like I was everything she'd been waiting for.

How perfect it felt, the three of us tangled together, like we'd finally found the missing pieces of ourselves.

But what did I do after I built that beautiful thing? Ran scared the moment it became real. Started pulling away after Kaia and Aspen bonded, because watching her connect with someone else—even though I'd pushed for it—felt like swallowing glass.

"I created this," I whisper to the darkness, my voice cracking on the words. "I brought us all together, and then I fucking ran when it mattered."

The chaos magic around me flares brighter, responding to the rawness in my chest.

"I'm the one who made it happen, and now I'm just... watching it happen without me."

A sob breaks free before I can stop it, followed by another. My shoulders shake as months of self-sabotage finally tear free.

"I pushed for all of us, and then I couldn't handle it when they actually chose each other."

The words hang in the air like an accusation. Against her, against them, against myself for being too much of a coward to stay and fight for what I'd helped create.

"You're not sulking, are you?"

I jolt upright, chaos magic scattering like startled birds. Aspen stands at the edge of the clearing, ice-blue eyes taking in my disheveled state with characteristic directness.

"Wouldn't dream of it," I lie, swiping at my face. "Just enjoying some quality alone time. You know, communing with nature and all that philosophical shit."

He doesn't buy it for a second. Just walks over and settles beside me on the log, close enough that I can feel the cool air that perpetually surrounds him.

"You've been avoiding her," he says quietly.

The words hit like a physical blow because they're true. Every single one.

"I don't know what you're talking about."

"Since our bond locked." His voice is matter-of-fact, no judgment in it. "You've been finding excuses to be anywhere she isn't."

I open my mouth to deny it, then close it again. Because he's right, and I hate him for it.

"You want to know why?" The words tear out of me before I can stop them. "Because watching her, feeling her bond with you—with anyone—hurts like hell, even though I'm the one who pushed for all of this."

Aspen is quiet, waiting.

"I brought us all together. Me, her, Malrik. I made it happen because I could see what we all wanted but were too scared to reach for." My voice cracks. "And then the moment it became real, the moment she started bonding with people, I panicked and started pulling away."

"Because you were jealous?"

"Because I was terrified." I drag my hands through my hair. "What if I created something beautiful and then discovered I don't actually belong in it? What if the bond between me and her isn't as strong as what she has with you, or Malrik, or any of the others?"

Aspen considers this. "So instead of finding out, you decided to prove yourself right by disappearing?"

The quiet observation hits harder than any accusation could. "Pretty fucking stupid, right?"

"Understandable," he says instead. "But stupid, yes."

We sit in silence for a moment, the weight of my confession settling between us.

"She's been looking for you, you know," Aspen says finally. "Asking where you are, why you seem different. Her shadows drift toward the places you used to be."

My heart stutters. "They do?"

"Bob's been particularly agitated. Keeps trying to herd people toward wherever you've gone." A small smile tugs at his lips. "Patricia's notes have gotten increasingly frantic too."

Despite everything, I feel my mouth twitch. "Even her shadows are calling me out for being an idiot."

"They know what she needs better than she does sometimes." Aspen stands, brushing dirt from his pants. "The question is whether you're going to keep running from what you helped create, or if you're finally going to show up for it."

And then he's gone, leaving me alone with Bob and the echo of words that feel like absolution and damnation all at once.

Chapter 43
KAIA

I wake to gray light and the weight of my own choices.

Malrik's arm is still draped across my waist, his breathing deep and even against my hair. The lake laps gently at the shore below us, and my shadows drift nearby, quiet but alert—watchful, as if waiting.

But I'm not.

With the magic settled and our bond humming warm and solid in my chest, the guilt hits like a sucker punch to the ribs. Not about Malrik. Never about Malrik. But about what came before. About what's still unresolved.

About Finn.

I dress silently in the pre-dawn darkness, careful not to wake him. My shadows stir at my feet, sensing my tension, but I wave them back. I need space. Need to think without anyone watching, without the weight of their concern crawling under my skin.

I slip from camp before anyone stirs, taking Enif and riding toward the head of our column where the scouts range ahead. The rhythmic beat of her hooves helps quiet the storm in my head, but it doesn't silence Callum's words.

You were never supposed to choose him. You were supposed to need him.

My stomach twists into knots. The bond with Darian that I've been fighting, denying, trying to bury beneath the others—it pulses like an infected wound, demanding attention I don't want to give it.

Ahead, I catch the low murmur of voices. Kieran and Revna, scouting the path forward, their conversation carrying on the morning air.

"—was never about what I wanted," Kieran is saying, his voice quieter than I've ever heard it. "It was about what would keep her alive."

"Even if it meant she'd never forgive you?" Revna's response is gentle but pointed.

A long pause. Then, so quietly I almost miss it: "Especially then."

The words stop me cold. I pull Enif to a halt, hidden behind a cluster of pine trees, and listen to my heart hammer against my ribs.

He never looked proud of the bond he forced. Just resigned. Just tired. And maybe I never saw him clearly—maybe I didn't want to.

I ride in silence after that, Callum's accusations and Kieran's admission tangle like barbed wire in my brain. Is anything real? Are any of my choices actually mine, or am I just following a script written before I was born?

The question sits in my gut like swallowed glass until we stop for the midday meal. I find them gathered in a loose circle near the edge of camp—Aspen, Malrik, Torric, and Finn, passing around travel bread and dried meat. They look up as I approach, and something in their expressions tells me they've been talking about me.

"Everything alright?" Aspen asks, his ice-blue eyes scanning my face with that annoying ability to see through my bullshit.

I settle cross-legged between Finn and Malrik, dragging my shadows close like armor. "I need to tell you what Callum said last night."

The atmosphere shifts immediately, tension crackling between us like static before a storm.

"When did you talk to Callum?" Torric's voice is sharp, already shifting toward protective mode.

"At the lake. While I was..." Heat crawls up my neck. "Bathing."

The reaction is immediate and explosive.

"He *what*?" Torric surges to his feet, flames literally licking around his shoulders. "That piece of shit cornered you while you were—"

"Where the fuck was his patrol supposed to be?" Aspen's voice has gone deadly quiet, which is somehow worse than Torric's shouting. Ice spreads from his feet in sharp, angry patterns.

"Guys—"

"I'm going to rip his fucking throat out," Torric snarls, already halfway to standing before Malrik's shadows whip forward like a leash.

"Get in line," Malrik says, his shadows writhing around him like living weapons.

Even Finn looks murderous, his usual humor nowhere to be found. "What exactly did that bastard say to you?"

I hold up my hands, trying to calm them down before they march off to commit actual murder. "He said Darian was my final bond. That the choice was never mine. That it was decided before I was born."

The words hit like a bomb going off. Aspen stiffens, ice condensing around his hands. Torric's cursing becomes more creative and violent. Malrik watches me carefully, letting the others react first.

But it's Finn who leans forward, his voice unexpectedly gentle despite the fury still burning in his eyes: "That's bullshit, Kaia. Bonds respond to *you*. Not the other way around."

"But what if—"

"No." Malrik's voice cuts through my spiral. "Your magic didn't settle until you made the choice to bond with me. With us. That wasn't fate, that was you."

"Was it?" I say, bitter. "Or was I always going to end up here, no matter what I wanted?"

"Does it matter?" Torric demands, his golden eyes blazing. "You chose. That's what counts."

I want to believe them. Want to trust that the warmth in my chest when I look at each of them is real, not some cosmic manipulation I'm too blind to see.

"I don't want to be told what I'm meant for," I say, the words scraping my throat raw. "I want to choose it. I want to choose *you*."

The words hang in the air like a promise and a threat. Malrik's hand finds mine, steady and warm. Aspen's expression softens. Torric nods once, fierce and certain.

And Finn... Finn looks away.

After the others scatter to prepare for the afternoon's ride, Finn lingers. He sits beside me quietly, pulling at the hem of his shirt like he's trying to find words that won't explode in his face.

"So... uh. You and Malrik," he says finally.

"Yeah." I wait for the rest, for whatever's churning behind his green eyes.

"Right. You and Malrik. Makes sense. I mean, if you're gonna go for emotionally devastating, might as well go all in."

I snort despite myself, the tension breaking just enough for me to breathe. He grins—then sobers, the humor draining from his face like water through a cracked cup.

"I keep trying to figure out when I stopped showing up for you," he says, his voice softer than I'm used to hearing. "You're not hard to love, Kaia. Just easy to lose if you're stupid enough to blink."

My heart does something complicated. He's close to something real, something that matters, and I lean forward despite myself. "Finn—"

But he's already pulling back, slipping into humor before things get too honest. "Anyway. Gotta go make sure Bob hasn't unionized your shadow army again. Carry on with your royal water sex or whatever."

He leaves with a crooked smile, but his bond hums low and wounded in my chest. I watch him walk away, noting the careful distance he maintains, the way he always flinches away from the truth.

He's trying. I know he's trying. But it's not enough.

I stare out over the tree line as the sun begins its descent toward the mountains, painting the sky in shades of gold and crimson. My shadows drift around my feet, restless and pissed off, mirroring the mess in my head.

I thought bonding with Malrik would fix this clusterfuck in my brain. That choosing one of them—choosing any of them—would prove that my heart was mine to give.

But nothing's simple anymore. Not love. Not magic. Not fate.

Especially not the bond that's still waiting for me at the edge of everything I can't forgive.

The incomplete connection throbs like a bruise I can't stop pressing, and I want to scream at it to just fuck off already.

Soon, I'll have to face it. Face him.

But not today. Today I can pretend I'm not completely screwed.

Even if deep down, I'm starting to wonder if the only choice I ever had was how fast to fall.

Chapter 44
KIERAN

I leave before the others finish breaking camp.

Not because anyone asks me to scout ahead. Not because tactical protocol demands it. I leave because standing there, watching Kaia move through the morning routine with Malrik's quiet presence at her shoulder, makes something in my chest pull too tight to ignore.

She's settling. With them. Finding her balance in bonds that grew instead of being forced into place.

And she should.

But every time I see it—the easy way she leans into Aspen's steadying touch, the soft smile that curves her lips when Torric brings her tea without being asked, the comfortable silence she shares with Malrik—I wonder if she would've needed them so desperately if I hadn't broken her first.

The thought tracks me up the mountain, silent and patient. Like it knows I won't shake it this time.

My horse's hoofbeats ring against stone as I put distance between myself and the weight of watching her heal from damage I caused. The morning air carries the familiar wrongness of Absentia—corruption that tastes like metal and old death, thick enough to coat the back of my throat.

This is what I do. Look ahead so I don't have to look too close. Motion as habit. Silence as armor.

It's served me well for centuries.

It's killing me now.

The ridge comes into view an hour before dawn, a natural vantage point that overlooks the main pass through the mountains. I've used it before, back when these routes were mine to guard instead of navigate. Before everything changed. Before I learned that good intentions and ancient power make a poison that can destroy everything you're trying to protect.

I dismount, letting my horse graze while I settle into position among the rocks. The pass stretches below me like a scar through the corrupted landscape, winding between peaks that scrape the belly of gray clouds.

That's when I see them.

Six soldiers. Maybe eight. Moving in tight formation down the far slope, their pace measured and deliberate. Not the loose sprawl of a patrol or the urgency of messengers. Something else.

A cart rolls between them, wheels turning with mechanical precision over the rough ground. Two figures sit in the back, heads down, shoulders curved inward. The posture of defeat. Of resignation.

Prisoners.

I shift position, drawing a collapsing spyglass from my pack. The lens brings them into sharp focus—professional soldiers in unmarked leather, weapons worn but well-maintained. The kind of men who follow orders without asking questions, who transport cargo without caring what's inside.

The wind shifts, catching at loose fabric. One of the hooded figures sways slightly, and for just a moment, her hood slips back.

Violet hair catches the morning light like a banner.

The spyglass doesn't waver in my hands. My breathing doesn't change. Centuries of practice have taught me to observe without reacting, to catalog information before emotion can interfere with judgment.

But I note it. The unusual color. In a world where survival means silence, purple hair is either defiance—or bait.

I don't follow the thought. Not yet. It's not mine to name.

I just watch. Record. Prepare to report what I've seen without the weight of what it might mean pressing against my ribs.

The convoy disappears around a bend in the path, swallowed by twisted trees and morning mist. I remain in position for another quarter hour, making sure they don't double back, that this isn't some elaborate trap or misdirection.

When I'm certain they're gone, I pack my equipment and mount my horse for the ride back to camp.

By the time I crest the final ridge, the others have nearly finished preparing for the day's ride. Horses stomping impatiently. Packs secured with military efficiency. The orderly chaos of a group that's learned to move as one.

Callum stands near the center of it all, gesturing toward his map with confident authority. "The main pass is the obvious route," he's saying to a cluster of warriors. "But obvious means watched. We should take the northern approach, avoid unnecessary contact."

I don't announce myself. Don't interrupt his tactical assessment. I just stop at the edge of the group and wait for him to notice me, the way I've been doing for centuries whenever lesser commanders need to feel important.

When he finally looks up, I keep my voice level. Matter-of-fact.

"There's a convoy on the main pass. Six soldiers. Clean formation. Moving with purpose."

Callum barely glances at his map, his dismissal swift and calculated. "Not worth the engagement. We maintain our route."

"They're transporting prisoners," I add as Kaia and the others approach, drawn by the discussion. "Cart. Bound figures."

"Still irrelevant to our objectives," Callum says, his tone sharpening with authority. "Any deviation would compromise our timeline, regardless of their direction."

Something cold settles in my chest at how smoothly he writes off potential captives. How his logic feels rehearsed, too clean.

"Prisoners should be freed," I say, my voice carrying more weight than before.

Callum's mouth curves, not in amusement, but like a man calculating how much morality he can afford. "Noble sentiment. Poor tactics. We can't rescue everyone we encounter."

I watch his face carefully, noting the calculated nature of his responses. The way he positions himself as the voice of reason while discarding lives with surgical precision.

Something's not right.

But before I can pursue that thought, I add the detail I don't realize will change everything:

"One of them had purple hair."

Kaia freezes.

It's not fear. It's not surprise. It's something older. Something scarred.

The words drop into the clearing like stones into still water. Simple. Factual. Devastating.

Every line of her body goes rigid, shadows stilling around her feet like they've suddenly forgotten how to move. The others—Torric, Aspen, Malrik, Finn—all freeze as well, their faces shifting from confusion to the same stricken understanding that's written across Kaia's features. I watch them all react to something I don't understand, cataloging the signs of shared recognition, shared dread.

"Are you sure?" Her voice is quiet. Controlled. But I hear the fracture underneath, the hairline crack that threatens to split wide if pressed.

"Yes."

The silence that follows is deafening. I watch them all process something I clearly don't understand—some shared knowledge that turns their faces grim and determined.

When Kaia speaks again, her voice carries the weight of absolute certainty. Command that brooks no argument.

"We follow. We intercept at dawn."

The response is immediate. Torric moves toward the horses without question. Aspen begins redistributing supplies with fluid efficiency. Malrik's shadows coil like living weapons as he calculates angles and approaches.

Even Finn drops his usual humor, chaos magic sparking around his fingers as he prepares for whatever's coming.

Callum protests—something about unnecessary risks and mission priorities—but his voice fades into background noise. No one's listening to him anymore. They're all focused on her, on the steel in her spine and the fire in her eyes.

This is what she looks like when she stops asking permission.

This is what she looks like when she remembers she's a Valkyrie.

The camp transforms around her, shifting from travel formation to strike preparation in the space of heartbeats. Orders flow without being spoken. Equipment appears without being requested.

I should be helping. Should be coordinating our approach, planning contingencies, doing what I've done for centuries.

Instead, I find myself standing at the edge of it all, watching her move like the commander she was always meant to be.

She doesn't cry. Doesn't flinch. Doesn't let emotion cloud her judgment or compromise her effectiveness.

But I saw it. Just for a second. That break in her voice when she asked if I was sure. That look in her eyes when the possibility became certainty.

Whatever that hair means to them, it's carved something raw into her—like something that was never allowed to heal.

The thought sits in my chest like a physical weight as I finally move to join the preparations. As I fall into the familiar rhythm of pre-battle planning, checking weapons and reviewing approaches.

But my eyes keep drifting back to her. To the way she holds herself now—taller, sharper, more dangerous than the girl I carried into my sanctuary.

She's becoming exactly what she needs to be.

And I wonder—if she ever forgives me—will I believe I deserve it?

Dawn can't come soon enough.

Chapter 45
TORRIC

We haven't stopped in six hours.

Kaia sets the pace from Enif's back, her winged mount cutting through Absentia's corrupted air like a blade through smoke. The rest of us follow on horseback, pushing our mounts harder than we should, but none of us dare suggest slowing down.

Not when she looks like that.

Her spine is rigid, shoulders set with the kind of determination that doesn't bend until it breaks. She hasn't eaten since Kieran's report, hasn't spoken except to bark course corrections or wave off offers of food. Even her shadows know she's running on empty—Bob drifts beside her with less of his usual military precision, Patricia's frantic note-taking has slowed to occasional, weary scribbles.

But Kaia doesn't see it. Doesn't want to see it.

When Enif finally touches down for the horses to water at a stream, Aspen approaches carefully.

"She's innocent," Kaia says before he can suggest we rest longer. Her voice cuts like conviction, but there's a tremble in it only someone who really knows her would hear. "She doesn't deserve this. If she followed me into this realm because of something I did, something I said..."

She doesn't finish the thought. Doesn't need to. We all hear what she's not saying, that if Seren's capture is her fault, then saving her becomes the only thing that matters. Everything else—rest, food, tactical planning—is just delay.

Aspen falls back without arguing, but I catch the look he shares with Malrik. The same concern that's been eating at me all day, growing heavier with each mile we cover.

No one doubts Kaia's certainty that the purple hair belongs to Seren. But believing it's her and believing we can save her are two different things entirely.

When Callum suggests we slow our pace to account for terrain risks, Kaia's response is sharp enough to draw blood.

"We maintain speed," she snaps, not even turning to look at him. "Every hour we delay gives them more distance."

"But if the horses—"

"The horses are fine." Her shadows flicker with irritation. "We keep moving."

Callum falls silent, but I catch him muttering something about "chasing ghosts" under his breath. The words make my jaw clench, not because he's wrong, but because he might be right.

As the sun begins its descent toward the twisted peaks ahead, Kaia finally calls for camp. Not because she wants to stop, but because even she can't deny that pushing through Absentia's darkness is suicide.

She takes first watch without asking, positioning herself on a rocky outcrop that overlooks our backtrail. Stone-faced. Unmoving. A sentinel carved from guilt and determination.

That's when I know we need to talk.

I catch Aspen's eye first, then Malrik's. A silent conversation passes between us—the kind that comes from months of being together, of reading each other's expressions in the space between heartbeats. Finn notices our wordless exchange and drifts closer, his usual grin notably absent.

Even Kieran, standing apart as always, seems to understand what's happening. He approaches our loose circle without being asked, his ancient eyes scanning the darkness where Kaia keeps her vigil.

Callum starts toward us, but Malrik's shadows shift, not threatening, exactly, but clear enough in their message. This conversation isn't for him.

"She's pushing too hard," I say once we're out of earshot, keeping my voice low. "Not just for Seren. For herself."

"Her magic's slipping," Aspen adds, worry bleeding through his usually controlled tone. "The shadows are lagging. She's running on fumes and doesn't realize it."

Finn runs a hand through his auburn hair, for once not reaching for a joke to lighten the mood. "She thinks saving Seren will redeem something she hasn't forgiven herself for. Like if she can just rescue one person, it'll balance out whatever scales she's been carrying around."

"She needs this to work," Malrik says quietly, his silver eyes distant. "To save someone. To not fail again."

The weight of that settles over us like a shroud. We all know what 'again' refers to—not just Thorne's betrayal or the academy's fall, but something much older. The Valkyries who died so she could live. The entire race that was destroyed while she was hidden away, safe and ignorant. The guilt of being the one who survived when everyone like her didn't. The weight of carrying an entire people's legacy when she never asked for it.

"It's too clean," Kieran speaks for the first time, his voice carrying centuries of tactical experience. "The convoy isn't hiding. They're not taking evasive routes or changing direction. They want to be followed."

"A trap?" Aspen's breath mists in the cold air, ice crystals forming around his fingers.

"Or bait," Kieran confirms. "And she's taking it because she can't afford not to."

The silence that follows is heavy with unspoken truths. We all see it, the way Kaia's driving herself toward whatever's waiting at the end of this chase, consequences be damned. The way she's turned Seren's potential captivity into a personal mission that's bigger than tactics or survival.

"We can't stop her," I say finally, because someone has to voice what we're all thinking.

"We don't want to stop her," Malrik corrects. "But we can keep her grounded."

"How?" Finn asks.

I look at each of them in turn—these men who've become brothers in all the ways that matter, bound together by something deeper than blood or magic. "We don't slow her down," I say. "We remind her why she has to lead, not just charge. We hold her up before she breaks."

Aspen nods, understanding immediately. "I'll stay close on her flank. Make sure she's eating, drinking. The basics she's ignoring."

"I'll manage our rest breaks," Malrik adds. "Under the guise of rechecking formations. Force her to stop without making it about her."

"And I'll make space for her to talk," Finn says, his voice unusually serious. "When she's ready. If she's ready."

"I'll monitor terrain with actual scrutiny," Kieran finishes. "Not just Callum's word. If this is a trap, we'll be prepared."

It's a good plan. Simple. Focused on what we can control rather than what we can't. But as we separate back to our bedrolls, something cold settles in my stomach.

Because I've been watching Kaia all day, studying the rigid set of her shoulders and the desperate edge to her determination. And I think I finally understand what's driving her forward with such relentless purpose.

"She thinks she's chasing Seren," I say quietly, just loud enough for the others to hear. "But I think she's chasing forgiveness."

No one disagrees.

And that terrifies me more than any trap Alekir could possibly set.

Because forgiveness isn't something you can rescue from a convoy or earn through a perfectly executed mission. It's something you have to give yourself.

And Kaia's never been good at that.

Chapter 46
FINN

The fire's down to embers when I finally work up the nerve to approach her.

Kaia sits on the rocky outcrop like a statue carved from guilt and determination, her gaze fixed on the darkness where our enemies might emerge. She hasn't moved in over an hour. Hasn't blinked, as far as I can tell.

I toss a wrapped ration at her feet, the sound sharp in the silence.

"Fuel for the guilt machine," I say, settling onto a boulder a few feet away. Close enough to talk, far enough that she can't pretend this is just another one of our easy conversations.

She glances down at the food but doesn't reach for it. "Thanks, but I'm not—"

"Hungry. Yeah, I figured." I study her profile in the dim light, noting the sharp angles that weren't there a week ago. "When's the last time you actually ate something?"

"I'm fine, Finn."

"Sure you are." I lean back, chaos magic sparking absently around my fingers. "You got a minute, Trouble?"

The nickname hangs between us, weighted with everything we used to be. She finally turns to look at me, and something in my expression must tip her off because her guarded expression shifts to concern.

"What's wrong?"

I almost laugh. Of course she notices something's off now, when I'm about to tear my chest open and show her exactly how wrong everything's been.

"You ever feel like you're losing someone who's sitting right in front of you?"

Her face softens with understanding I don't want. "Finn, I know you're worried about Seren too, but—"

"I'm not talking about Seren."

The words stop her cold. I watch confusion flicker across her features, followed by the dawning realization that this conversation isn't going where she expected.

I stand, pacing to the edge of our small camp because sitting still feels impossible. My magic responds to the agitation, painting the air around me in restless streaks of color that die as quickly as they form.

"I'm talking about you," I say, not looking at her. "And me. And the way you stopped seeing me weeks ago."

"That's not—"

"It is." I turn back to face her, and the protest dies on her lips. "You still smile at me. Still throw barbs back and forth like we're playing some game. Still feel what little bond we have hum in your chest. But I don't think you've looked at me—really looked—in weeks."

She opens her mouth to argue, but I keep going because if I stop now, I'll lose my nerve entirely.

"I watch you carry this weight like you've lost everything that matters. Like this realm, these bonds—everything—have carved pieces out of you

you'll never get back. But the biggest gap? That's me. And I'm still right fucking here."

The silence that follows is deafening. Kaia stares at me like I've grown a second head, and maybe I have. Maybe this version of me, the one that's tired of pretending everything's fine, is someone she's never met before.

"I don't understand," she says finally, her voice smaller than I'm used to hearing.

"I know you don't. That's the problem." I run a hand through my hair, frustrated by my own inability to explain this properly. "You want to know why I've been pulling away? Why I've been giving you space instead of fighting for it?"

She nods, shadows coiling anxiously around her feet.

"Because I thought it would be easier. Letting you go. Stepping back so the others could take up the space you needed." The admission tastes like ash. "I thought if I gave you room to breathe, maybe you'd choose me. Maybe you'd realize what you were missing and reach back."

"Finn—"

"But I think I waited too long. Or maybe you stopped reaching before I let go. I don't even know anymore." The chaos magic around me flares brighter, responding to the raw edge in my voice. "All I know is I miss you. And I'm right here."

The words hang between us like a challenge. Like a plea.

Kaia's face crumples slightly, and she reaches for my hand. "Finn, I never meant—"

I step back before she can touch me. Not cruel, not angry, just done. Done pretending that casual contact will fix what's broken between us. Done settling for scraps when I used to be a full meal.

"You don't need to say anything," I tell her, gentler now. "Just... see me, Kaia. Just once. Before whatever's waiting at the end of this kills one of us."

Her shadows writhe like they want to reach for me but don't know how. Carl flickers toward and starts to fade before Bob snaps him back into formation. Even her magic doesn't know what to do with the space I'm creating.

I turn to go, but something makes me pause. Look back one more time at the girl who used to light up when I walked into a room.

"For what it's worth, Trouble," I say, my voice carrying across the distance I've put between us, "I'd still burn the world for you. But I don't know if I belong in it anymore."

Then I walk away, leaving her sitting alone with her guilt and her shadows and the ration she won't eat.

The fire dies to nothing behind me, and for the first time in months, I don't try to rekindle it.

Chapter 47
KAIA

I wake from dreams that taste like blame.

Finn's words echo in the gray space between sleep and consciousness, each one cutting deeper than the last. *The biggest gap? That's me. And I'm still right fucking here.* My chest aches with the truth of it, with the realization that I've been so focused on holding myself together that I've let pieces of what matters most slip through my fingers.

I rise before dawn breaks, moving quietly through camp to avoid the others. My shadows give me space—unnervingly so. Even Bob maintains his distance, his usual protective hovering replaced by something that feels like cautious observation. Patricia doesn't even pretend to take notes. Mouse, normally draped across my shoulders like a second heartbeat, lingers near my feet instead, his small form twitching with unease. Like they're all waiting to see which version of me emerges from whatever reckoning is coming.

I throw myself into action instead of reflection. Check weapon supplies. Scan the terrain ahead through Kieran's spyglass. Adjust our defensive formation for the third time this morning. Anything to keep my hands busy and my mind from spiraling back to the way Finn looked when he walked away from me.

The way he called me Trouble one last time, like he was saying goodbye.

"You're going to wear a path in that rock if you keep pacing."

Kieran's voice cuts through my spiral. I turn to find him approaching with his usual measured steps, but there's something different in his expression. Not the careful distance he's maintained since the bonds formed, but something that looks almost like... partnership.

"The terrain ahead narrows," he says without preamble, settling beside me on the ridge. "Three choke points in the next five miles. Perfect for ambush."

I study the landscape below us, noting the way the path funnels between rocky outcroppings. "We can handle it."

"Can we?" His golden eyes meet mine, steady and unreadable. "You're doing everything alone, Kaia. Planning, watching, carrying the weight of every decision. That's not leadership—that's martyrdom."

My jaw tightens. "I'm fine."

"You're managing." The correction is gentle but firm. "There's a difference."

The word hits me wrong, making something crack inside my chest. "Manageable," I repeat, and my voice breaks on the syllable like glass under pressure.

Kieran doesn't flinch at the sound. Just continues to watch me with those ancient eyes that see too much. "You're leading like you're trying to prove you should be followed. But no one here is questioning that except you."

The observation stops me cold. I open my mouth to argue, to deflect, to do any of the things I've perfected over months of keeping him at arm's length. Instead, what comes out is the truth.

"If I don't lead them out of this," I whisper, staring at the twisted landscape below, "if I fail Seren too, it'll mean they were all right to doubt me from the start."

"Who?" Kieran's voice is soft, patient. "Who was right to doubt you?"

"Everyone." The word scrapes my throat raw. "The board at the academy. Lady Virath. Every person who looked at me and saw a threat instead of a student. Every voice that said I was too dangerous, too unpredictable, too unstable."

"Maybe they do doubt you," Kieran says quietly. "Maybe they're afraid of what you could become. But fear and doubt aren't the same thing, and neither means you've failed. They don't know the weight you carry. I do. And I'd follow you anyway."

For the first time in days, I take a real breath. The kind that reaches all the way down to the places I've been holding too tight. My shadows respond to the shift, drifting closer with tentative relief.

"How do you know?" I ask.

"Because I've been where you are." His smile is small, sad. "Carrying the weight of everyone's expectations while forgetting that the people who matter most just want you to survive it."

Something loosens in my chest. Not fixed, not healed, but... eased. Like a knot that's been pulled too tight finally finding room to breathe.

That evening, I outline the plan to intercept the convoy. Not from a place of desperate determination, but with the clarity that comes from actually thinking instead of just reacting. I listen when Aspen suggests an alternate approach route. Delegate reconnaissance to Torric and Malrik. Let Kieran's tactical experience guide the timing.

Finn watches from the edge of our circle, silent but present. When our eyes meet across the firelight, I see something shift in his expression. Not forgiveness, that's too much to hope for, but maybe understanding. Maybe the beginning of it.

When Callum starts to object to the plan's timeline, I don't snap or argue. I just look at him with steady eyes and say, "Not tonight."

Even Callum knows better than to argue with that tone. The firelight flickers across faces that, for the first time in days, seem to believe we might actually make it.

The group makes camp in a defensive formation, everyone moving with the practiced efficiency of people who've learned to trust each other's strengths. Torric and Malrik take first watch, their easy coordination a reminder of how well we work when we're not fighting ourselves.

I move toward my usual watch position, but Aspen intercepts me with gentle firmness.

"You'll lead better in the morning if you sleep," he says, ice-blue eyes holding mine.

Every instinct screams against it. Against letting my guard down, against trusting that the world won't fall apart if I'm not vigilantly holding it together. But something in his expression—faith, maybe, or simple stubborn care—makes me hesitate.

Then nod.

I settle into my bedroll on the outskirts of camp, close enough to respond if needed but far enough away that my restless energy won't disturb the others. My shadows drift nearby, their movements finally relaxing into something that resembles peace.

For the first time in days, I let my eyes slip shut without fighting it. The sounds of the night hum around me like a heartbeat just out of rhythm—wind through corrupted trees, the soft murmur of voices on watch, the distant call of something that might once have been an owl.

I don't see the shadow that moves past the edge of camp.

Don't feel the breath on my cheek.

Don't hear the whisper that answers the darkness:

"Hello again, Little Shadow."

THANK YOU

To the readers who followed Kaia's journey through shadows, battles, betrayals, and slow-burn chaos—you made this world real.

Thank you for devouring each chapter, for screaming in DMs, and for falling in love with these morally gray disasters right alongside me.

To the betas, ARC readers, and late-night sprint buddies: I see you. I couldn't have done this without your eyes, your feedback, or your memes. Truly.

And to the quiet voice in the back of my mind that kept whispering, *"She's not done yet"*—thank you for being right.

Oh... almost forgot:

Survival Tip #10: Bring snacks, emotional support wine, and (at least) one morally gray boyfriend.

About the Author

Zora Stone writes romantasy with teeth: fierce heroines, protective men who'd burn the world for them, and enough emotional wreckage to keep things interesting. When she's not plotting betrayals or steamy chaos, she's drinking iced coffee, dodging laundry, or daydreaming about enchanted forests.

You can find her online at:

Website: ZoraStone.com

TikTok | Instagram: @ZoraStoneAuthor

And on Amazon and Goodreads.

Want behind-the-scenes chaos and sneak peeks? ZoraStone.com/Influencers

ALSO BY ZORA STONE

The Ether Chronicles

Crown of the Mist
Into the Ether
Ashen Oath
Veil of Echoes
Shattering the Void
To the Final End

Arcanum Academy

Shadows of Change
Shadows Rising
Shadows Found
Shadows Revealed

Author's Note

Shadows Rising was the book where everything cracked open—for Kaia, and for me.

It pushed boundaries, deepened bonds, and dragged us all into darker territory.

If you finished this book breathless, a little heartbroken, and ready to burn the world... same.

Book Three is going to ruin us—in the best way.